This Is

Graceanne's
Book

Also by P. L. Whitney

The Alligator's Farewell, Writing as Hialeah Jackson

For a Reading Group Guide to use with *This Is Graceanne's Book*,
click on "Reading Group Guides" on our website
www.stmartins.com

This Is
Graceanne's
Book

P. L. Whitney

THOMAS DUNNE BOOKS
St. Martin's Press
New York

THOMAS DUNNE BOOKS.
An imprint of St. Martin's Press.

An altered version of the first chapter of *This Is Graceanne's Book* appeared in *Ellery Queen Magazine,* July 1998, as a short story titled "Hard Labor Creek."

www.stmartins.com

Design by Nancy Resnick

Library of Congress Cataloging-in-Publication Data
Whitney, P. L.
    This is Graceanne's Book / P. L. Whitney.
        p. cm.
    ISBN 0-312-20597-X (hc)
    ISBN 0-312-27278-2 (pbk)
    I. Title.
  PS3573.H5337T48 1999   99-18059
  813'.54—dc21   CIP

First St. Martin's Griffin Edition: August 2001

10 9 8 7 6 5 4 3 2 1

This novel is for my children,
Jay and Daisy

April 1960

The Astronomers

One

$\mathcal{W}$e were warned and warned to stay away from the river.

But Ugly Blue Man came into our lives anyway, down one of the spiderleg creeks that feed the Mississippi, and I learned how to keep a secret.

The Mississippi went over its banks at Cranepool's Landing three times that spring. By mid April, the water was running so fast and wide that whole acres of freshly turned topsoil were sucked off the shore farms and dragged out into the middle of the river, racing in swirling black half-moons all the way down to the town of Ste. Genevieve before they sank under their own weight.

From the window of the green "Measles Room" (called that because any kind of illness sent us into quarantine in that small olive-drab chamber) at the top of our old brick house on Lewis and Clark Hill, the brawny river seemed to throb with thousands of living pulses under its swollen skin. And the currents were so contrary, so separate from the rest of the river's momentum, so independent, that it often looked like the fastest and straightest water out in the middle was a snake, suddenly rearing its head, swiveling around to look north and then, overwhelmed by its own rolling force, opening its wide jaws to swallow its body and choke on its tail.

We were warned and warned, but we didn't have to descend into the wretched sinfulness of outright disobedience for us to get a kid's full share of this unexpected drama. The Mighty Muddy Cruddy Flood, and the reeking corpses of animals caught in its spate, had already pushed across the bottomlands to become part of us. Without going anywhere near the river, we found ourselves standing in its wash and surrounded by its heavy strength.

In the town of Cranepool's Landing, the old river valley farming rhythms still wrote our calendars, but that April the brutal rush of the river over its banks muscled us out of familiar patterns, delayed the planting, closed businesses, and reshaped the land, giving us new reference points and ways to log who we were and where we came from and where we might be going.

Because the water was so cold and full of grisly, squishy things, we played what we called "Noah's Softball" in our red rubber boots on the old Jefferson Barracks Parade Ground, with a set of crudely negotiated but ironclad new flood rules. We had banned the use of gloves because the object was not golden-glove fielding but rather hurting and humiliating each other.

Only the real power hitters ever got on base, because (1) any ball hit into the shallow new lake covering the field sank and was ruled dead, and (2) the count on the batter was frozen while the ball was found and squeezed out. The rare base runner was automatically out if he touched the floating base first with his foot because headfirst sliding was mandatory. Indeed, it would have been strangely lax of our ringleaders to waste such an opportunity for exploiting the gift of the river, those twelve blessed inches of stinking water standing on the parade ground at the bottom of Lewis and Clark Hill.

The flood wash was so full of rotting things on their way

to heaven or hell, and was such a powerful new strategic element in our games, that the army engineers from Jefferson Barracks Fort sometimes came out to watch us play ball in it. The headfirst-sliding rule made some batters, including the occasional soldier who took a turn, think twice about putting the wood on the ball, and deliberate strikeouts became so plentiful that our pitchers got good workouts for their bean-balls. And there was no such thing as a foul ball. Anything hit in the air was fair, and the fielder was allowed to call if he thought he could control the soggy incoming ball with a maximum of one drop. "Whale shit," the fielder would call as he stood under the ball, holding out his hands and waiting for the splat.

Outfielders, bending over and groping in the water during the inevitable lull while the cowardly end of the order was up to bat, could sling drowned squirrels and rabbits at the infield, but the corpse of a muskrat scored an automatic earned run for the defense and the game was halted so we could slit the soft skin under the tail and extract the greasy musk glands. These were understood to be the exclusive property of the power hitters, who wrapped them in waxed paper with the purpose of preserving them for private experimental use the next day at school.

The floods produced field architecture changes in our other games, too. The dead-kids rope had to be moved closer to the shore of the swimming hole at French's Limestone Quarry. The dead kids (those of us who did not know how to swim) lined up in the icy water up to our necks and held onto the rope for safety while we watched the swimmers play Jump-or-Dive Murder from the peeling sycamore trees jutting out over the limestone quarry rocks. The cobweb vault of mottled white branches, just coming into bud, hung heavily over the crystal water. The swimmers, their flesh scratched and stung by the trees, would climb out onto the highest limbs, squeezing water and bugs from the sopping dark patches of bark as they put their hands down on the shaggy boughs.

The dead kids—our teeth chattering, our skinny pelts blue, our fingers twisted around the rope—watched the swimmers launch themselves one at a time off the branches, cascades of bark water and tree scales traveling with them into the air. The airborne swimmer attempted to suspend gravity in mid-air—to listen for that moment when the dead kids would holler either "jump" or "dive"—and then twist headfirst or cannonball into the water, depending on what we dead kids decided. We would delay to the last stupefying moment of reaction time before yelling out the word, the object being to engineer as many painful bellywhoppers as possible. We never maimed anyone during this game: The object was only painful mortification, and the dead kids were almost invincible that spring with the water so high and the soaked branches so low.

And school was on half days. The basement of Our Lady of Lourdes Academy was full of water and the electricity was shot, so the grades got split up. The dead kids used the sunny upstairs classroom in the mornings, and the older kids had to clean up after us when they came in to study in the afternoon.

We didn't get beat up as much when the broken schoolday put the power hitters on a different schedule from us, but the real bonus for the dead kids that spring was getting an early taste of freedom as we were turned loose, without the usual leashes and restraints of mothers and nuns and older siblings, with fierce and reiterated warnings to stay away from the river.

For me, along with this spectacular burst of freedom, there came a peculiar loneliness. Although we all took on a ducklike, uneven gait—a sort of universal lameness—as we slogged through the glutinous mud, I was actually lame, and the brace and corrective shoe I wore then under my red boots, com-

pounded by the miracle of black sludge that had buried the
streets and sidewalks of Cranepool's Landing, put me consid-
erably behind the pack of kids trailing across the gooey land-
scape of the town like cold knives through chocolate frosting.
After they had passed me, the other kids would turn around
and shout, "Hey, Taxi!"

I had lived much of my nine years in the shadow of two
muscular sisters whose arsenal of pinching fingers and loaded
vocabularies was a measure of their deep resentment at having
to babysit a clubfoot younger brother sixteen hours a day. To
me, being left behind and magically alone was the biggest and
most mysterious of the Mighty Muddy Crud's contributions
to the town of Cranepool's Landing.

Being alone for even an hour a day was a heady experience.
I had always been surrounded by children and included in
every game and activity. My sisters, both power hitters in
every sense of the term, would have beaten the daylights out
of anyone who tried to bar me from softball games, because
my mother Edie's unchallengeable rule was that if I couldn't
play, the Farrand girls—Kentucky Athena and Graceanne
Regina—couldn't play.

Softball wasn't the only game in which I had a role pred-
icated on the babysitting duties of my ferocious sisters, but
my mother was kept in the dark about most of the others. I
became the indispensable key to the dead kids' string of vic-
tories in Jump-or-Dive Murder (because of my sense of tim-
ing, keenly developed as a lame boy dodging his sisters' expert
punches). And I was necessarily "it" in hide-and-seek: I
couldn't run fast enough to hide from the other kids, so our
brand of the game evolved into a superior exercise in tactics
and guile. With my unmoving and monopolistic vantage point
on the secret landscapes, I became an expert on all the good
hiding places. And that was probably the reason I was the
one, even with a clubfoot, who would find Ugly Blue Man

and keep from bragging about the secret.

To make the hiding game more sporting that April, they handicapped my talents by creating an enormous and popular incentive for the winner. They tied me to "home," my torso thrust through a rotted but very high tire swing behind Tyler Rodgers's house on Lewis and Clark Hill, so I couldn't escape and slink away out of boredom or frustration or fear, and made me guess where everyone was. They took turns being "Jezebel," the runner appointed to seek out the hiding places at my instruction. The last person we caught won the game and the honor of untying me and rolling me down spongy Lewis and Clark Hill to the parade ground, past all the other "turn-of-the-century-tall" houses that faced the river.

The trick for me was to outthink them, sending the Jezebel out with hideous selectivity in an effort to guess the least violent kid's hiding place last; and, to counter my growing wisdom, it was their sworn duty to make the hiding places increasingly more devious. In those measureless days, hiding in Cranepool's Landing reached new heights of invention, because rolling me to the parade ground was a loud, messy spectacle, and watching me clean sludge out of my nose and mouth was a badge of passage for the select, clever few. We called it Rolling Pin, and it was a version of hide-and-seek that even a dead kid could win, because brawn was of no use in eluding me.

My central role as a dead kid in the spring games did not make me popular, but it did make me unavoidable—except for those trips through the mud when suddenly I was alone for an hour. After I made it home alive two days in a row with only dubious supervision, my mother suddenly, and for all time to come, revised the iron rule that had bound both of my sisters to me.

On that third day, Kentucky and Graceanne didn't get out

of bed to get me to school. My mother made me oatmeal and let me out of the house herself. She said goodbye from the foot of the highly waxed hardwood stairs leading up to the bedrooms from our front parlor. Our stairs were probably the only shiny ones on the Hill that spring. Every other woman in the town had given way before the tide of dirt pouring in through every door with every child. But not Edie Farrand.

"Charlemagne Farrand," she said, a subtle elation in her pale blue eyes and her freckled hands squeezing my shoulders, "when you came along, I made a decision. I decided I would like this child, because you were so good and so quiet. Well, today I've made another decision. Today you are a man." She walked me to the door and closed it firmly behind me, and I wished she would just call me "Thumper," the way everyone else did.

Two of my mother's firmest beliefs had apparently collapsed under the prospect of entertaining me until the floods subsided:

A: Some bully would beat me to a pulp.
B: I would take off my brace and ruin my progress in turning the clubfoot.

These fundamental beliefs rested on two equally fundamental miscalculations on her part.

A: The two worst bullies in Cranepool's Landing were *already* exercising their license as family members to beat me silly—"whale on you, young man"—on a regular basis, leaving all other potential assailants the status of respectful, but backward, admirers of my sisters' originality and prowess.

B: I wanted to be *normal,* and my brace was the palpable, dependable, objective evidence that someday I would reach that exalted plateau.

So I knew, despite the fact that I was evidently being given blank check authority in Cranepool's Landing to come and go without an escort, that I was nowhere near being a man. I was just a dead kid.

Even after I found Ugly Blue Man that same day.

As I stepped across the sopping porch—concrete, too, was swelling with moisture that spring—I heard piggy snorts issuing from the open bathroom window upstairs. Graceanne was hanging out the window, her glasses slipping down her small nose, one of her loose blond braids dangling across her open mouth.

"That's what she said to me when I got my period, you little freak," she screamed like a hyena. " 'Graceanne, today you are a woman.' " She banged her head on the window, but she kept on yelling. "Hey! I'm a twelve-year-old WO-MAN. I'm gonna be the youngest person in the state of Missouri to vote and buy liquor. But I'll be damned if I'll get married and have brats until I'm at least thirteen." She started tossing tampons out the window. "Charlie's got his period, Charlie's got his period, Charlie's got his period." One of her projectiles, aimed with the strong arm and killer eye of our best shortstop, struck the side of my head. "Stick that where the frog sings, Thumper."

I knew better than to respond, because if I yelled back, my mother would know something was going on; she'd punish Graceanne, and then Graceanne would punish me. Punishments were diluted in intensity on their way down the pecking order, but their creative management increased inversely when Graceanne was involved. So I started to walk away, limping toward the little crowd already headed for the parade ground in their red boots.

"Pick up those plugs," Graceanne squeaked, emitting a thin, penetrating hiss like a steam radiator in her scream-whisper. "Are you trying to get me in more trouble, you little skunk?"

I crawled around the porch and the steps, listening for Edie and shoving damp tampons into my pockets. The passing troop of dead kids coming by our house on the Hill watched my operations curiously. Graceanne had explained tampons to me under her bed one night the previous winter, so I knew enough to be embarrassed, assuming that her graphic crayon drawings on a paper bag represented actual physiology and not a devious and cruel mind at work.

"Don't tell about them plugs," she screeched and pulled the bathroom window down.

I followed some other dead kids down from the top of the Hill, and I tested the thickness of the mud by listening to the sucking and plopping sounds of my mismatched rubber boots—I had to wear two different sizes to accommodate my brace and my normal foot.

The wild surface of the river was running in silver-brown crashes and bumps, as though great boulders impeded its path, but there were no boulders this far south in the Mississippi. Whole trees were riding the water, their giant roots spinning at the center of raging eddies until they were towed down by the savage undercurrents, but even the trees couldn't tear the skin of the river that stayed whole and strong. I saw a white-tailed deer shoot past a whirling elm, over near the Illinois side. The deer's soft brown mouth was wide open, its antlers broken, its hooves pawing the rapids.

When I got to the parade ground, it was only dead kids fooling around in the water before school. Since that would have been a good time to get our own muskrat glands, we were all bent over with our hands in the water. A goat came floating by on its side, all chewed up by its ride down the river.

And I found a leg, over about by third base. It wasn't any goat leg. It was a man's leg and the rest of the man was with it.

I found his shirt collar and started yanking at him. I got his head out of the water and dropped him with a quick splash because his face was all blue, and his tongue was almost bitten off, half of it hanging out of his mouth, and he was so ugly I almost threw up. And on his forehead there was a bright and big reddish purple triangle mark, a wide indentation so deep that it looked like the river had let loose and walloped him with all its force with a piece of stout oak.

Dead kids didn't know much, but we all knew better than to get caught with an ugly blue man, so I shouted at the other kids. We all pulled together and Ugly Blue Man came unstuck from the mud with a noise like my boots and floated on the skin of the water.

I didn't know any bottomless water except French's Limestone Quarry. We got the hide-and-seek rope from when I'd get tied to the tire swing at Tyler Rodgers's house, and we fastened the man's feet together and dragged him as hard as we could, all the way across the parade ground and through the mud at Our Lady of Lourdes Academy and over the lip of the playground where we could look down at the quarry. We got behind Ugly Blue Man and pushed him hard. He slid fast down the mud, down the slick slope of limestone, into the quarry lake, feet-first with hardly any splash.

But he came up again. And then he just floated around on his back, his ugly blue face like the hub of an old bicycle wheel and his arms the broken, spiny spokes.

Since it was just us dead kids, we couldn't go out to him on our own. We all took off our boots and left them on the rocks, all except my right boot, which I couldn't get off. We untied the safety rope at one end but kept the other end knotted tight around the sycamore tree where the swimmers had made it fast. We lined up along the rope, and I got to go first.

When I was in up to my chest, leading the dead kids, and I was turning blue from the fierce grip of the stinging cold water, the other kids behind me handed over a long branch that had bugs squeezing themselves out of the bark. And the way they passed that stick made me think of the fire brigade we'd watched one night when Geronimo Pinnell's house burned to the ground.

I almost went under trying to hook Ugly Blue Man. My hands were shaking from the bitterness and the reaching and the fear that I couldn't get him.

But I snagged his ankles where we'd tied him and we dragged him and ourselves back to the white edge of the quarry lake. We were all too cold to stop moving, so we quickly scrambled around for rocks, stuffing them in Ugly Blue Man's pants and his pockets and his shirt, and when he looked like a blue overstuffed scarecrow, we let him loose in the water.

He sank slowly, spinning gently until all we could see was his blue face and the purple and red triangle mark gouged on his head. And then his head went in.

We stood there shivering, watching the wobbling water where that vivid, lively triangle had disappeared, but he didn't come back up.

I suppose I must have looked like some kind of half-squashed insect as I went back home, with the shivering and the jerking and my limp. And I thought I was still blue.

When I got home, instead of going upstairs to change my wet clothes, I went into the sunroom because my father was sitting in his uniform with the starch smell and the shiny medals on his pocket. He was reading the St. Louis newspaper.

He reached out and gave me a hard smack against my right ear. "You little pest, Thumper," he said. "I'll whale you good for tracking all that crud into Edie's house. And why the hell aren't you to school?"

I did glance down at the floor, out of a sort of habitual routine to see what I'd brought in with my limp onto Edie's floors, but I didn't care about crud or getting whacked on the head or about school. On the front page of my father's newspaper was a photograph of a deer, perched on his skinny stick-legs on a loose rock in the middle of the foaming, tearing waters of the Mississippi just above Cranepool's Landing. Behind the deer was a pack of white water after him. And I knew he'd never make it to shore. And the deer knew it. I could see it in his eyes.

"Daddy," I said, "what's going to happen to that deer when he dies?"

I could smell the old and musty combat soldiers on my father's breath—combat soldiers were the empty brown Pabst bottles we sneaked out of the basement and filled with mud so we could see who could throw a combat soldier the farthest.

"Thumper," he said, laying down the paper open on his lap so I couldn't look at any picture of a terrified creature in the angry river, "in a place called Animal Heaven it's always nice, and that's where all the deer will go."

I knew my father didn't believe in religion, but I stood up straighter because I loved him for telling me a nice lie, even with the combat soldier on his breath when he told it.

I could see then more pictures inside the newspaper on my father's lap. There was a pregnant woman sitting all by herself on the roof of a house, her stomach as big as an August watermelon under her wet dress. Her eyes looked like the deer's. And her house was up to the eaves inside flooded Hard Labor Creek that was bearing down on its way to the Mississippi.

Lower on the page there was a story about prisoners escaping when the flood waters took off the gates and shut down the electricity at the state penitentiary just south of Hannibal.

That didn't seem as worrisome as the woman on the house. I looked at the picture of her more carefully. She was clutching a long-handled shovel to her. I didn't know what kind of shovel that was, only that its business end was a triangle and that she was hanging on to her shovel like it was an extra baby.

I thought maybe the pregnant woman was looking back at me from out of the picture resting on my father's legs.

Dead kids can't swim, but they have a lot of time for figuring about things after they've been told a thousand times to keep their stupid mouths shut. So I didn't tell anyone about the newspaper, about the woman on the roof and her shovel and the way its triangle looked like the one I'd seen slip into the quarry lake.

That was the first time I ever knew something important by myself, without anyone threatening to whale on me if I told.

Two

*T*hat was an unusually uncomfortable time for me, because of Ugly Blue Man and the secret of him, and because I had to take off my brace and change my clothes for school and re-hide the soaked tampons in my blue corduroy slacks, and Edie might catch me at any minute, and because Graceanne was upstairs in the green Measles Room. She wouldn't be going to school in the afternoon because she was "poorly." And we all knew why.

The older kids had decided they were tired of Rolling Pin and that we'd have to move on when a Champion for Eternity was finally crowned. Of course, my twelve-year-old sister Graceanne—braving the hellfire that my mother would shower on her when she was found—never heard the word "champion" without her ears standing out from her head. She had kept us all out looking for her past ten o'clock at night earlier in the week, until, scared out of our wits, we gave up.

I was untied from the tire swing and everyone trickled home, looking over their shoulders and up into the trees, wondering where Graceanne would spring from, wondering if she had been swept into the river, wondering if she had been kidnapped (or recruited) by tramps swarming the flooded river bottom around Cranepool's Landing and scavenging the household treasures and animals floating down from farms and towns upriver. Edie called the sheriff and the army engineers and the Flood Relief Committee and stayed up all night praying. Graceanne didn't come in for two days, and we learned that she had been holed up in the flooded basement of the school the whole time. She did not report home until she had rolled me through the thickest and blackest sludge on Lewis and Clark Hill, and I was caked in cold packed mud. Only then did she go home to face Edie.

We could all hear Graceanne screaming from the green Measles Room. The sounds forced us to retreat down the Hill, but we could still hear her from a block away. We knew by the sounds that it was a coat hanger whistling across the back of her legs. Graceanne was a problem kind of hero because, to our notions, a hero should not wail like a siren when she took what was coming to her. Still, by some unanimous and mysterious consensus, the big flooded classroom downstairs at the school was for many years called the Graceanne Farrand Memorial Pool, in respectful acknowledgment of her achievement—long after the water was finally pumped out by the army engineers.

The day she came home victorious, and I did not yet have the feel of Ugly Blue Man on my hands, I sneaked into Graceanne's room, which was "off-limits" (military terms like *reveille* and *inspections* and *KP* and *order of the day* abounded in the red brick house on the top of the Hill, the highest of the river homes that had deteriorated into housing for the families of enlisted men). A puddle of yellow light oozed from under the bed. I got down on the hardwood floor on my belly and shoved myself under the bed, sliding over the polished boards on my wet shirt, my lumpy teddy bear "Sergeant Useless" squeezed in the bend of my elbow. Graceanne was lying on her stomach, her head down on a set of three thick spiral notebooks she had tied together with red yarn, and her flash-light was wedged into the bedsprings. She was thin as a broomstick and only about as tall as a decent chest of drawers, so there was plenty of room under the narrow army bed.

"What are you doing?" I whispered. "You're supposed to be in the green Measles Room."

"What the hell does it look like I'm doing?" she hissed. "Get out of here, Thumper."

She did not turn her head toward me. Her voice did not carry any of the sounds of crying, except for a husky scraping that seemed to come from the back of her throat.

"Have you been crying?" I asked.

"No."

"Why not?"

"It's a **technique**. If you scream loud enough, it keeps you from crying like a little baby later."

I put my cheek on the floor and thought about that. Grace-anne was certainly expert enough to make pronouncements on this subject. It was too dark under the bed for me to see her legs clearly, but I could tell that her flannel nightgown was hiked up over her hips.

"What are you doing?" I repeated.

Graceanne had her right arm wound around the pile of notebooks. She had started out as a lefty, and she still batted left, but the combined forces of Eden Farrand and Our Lady of Lourdes Academy, in rectifying nature's mistake, had given Graceanne a monkeylike appearance when she was writing. Her forearm curled around in a crescent over the paper, and she gripped her pen overhand. The resulting script was a mess, but at least she was now using her right hand like a Christian.

"I'm writing a book."

"What's it about?"

"It's **private**."

"Can I see it?"

"It's private property."

Her left arm slinked up and covered her head. For such a power hitter, Graceanne was shockingly skinny. The muscles in her arms looked like clothesline ropes. Edie had taken her to Dr. Lodenson about her weight, and he had prescribed malt supplements. Edie was always stirring spoonfuls of what looked like sawdust into Graceanne's food.

"Can I see your book?"

"Why would I show it to a moron like you?"

"There ain't nobody else under the bed."

She rolled over onto her side, keeping her skinny arms over the open notebook on top, and stared at me through her tortoiseshell glasses. Her nightgown was covered with tufted, puffy holes, places where she had ripped off ribbons and bows Edie had sewn on. "You'll tell."

"No I won't."

"Yes you will."

"No I won't. I can keep even a big secret."

"Like anybody would tell you a big secret!"

"I won't tell, Graceanne."

"Will you die first?"

"Yes."

"Well, just this one page." She lifted herself on her elbows, keeping her head down. Her thin shoulders brushed the bedsprings. "It's a poem."

I looked. The whole page was covered with Graceanne's messy scrawl. It said:

EDEN FARRAND, R.A.*

> I hate her.
> I hate her.
> I hate her.

I hate her.
I hate her.
I hate her.
I hate her.
I hate her.
I hate her.
I hate her.
I hate her.
I hate her.
I hate her.
I hate her.

*Road Apple

"Are you sure it's a poem?" I asked, giving the lines a critical glance.

"Of course I'm sure. It rhymes perfectly."

"Is that all you've got in your book? Just poems?"

"I told you. One page, that's all you get."

"Tell me what it's about."

Graceanne sighed and put her arms back over the stack of notebooks. She put her face on her arms and rubbed her cheekbone over the spiral center so her glasses would fall off. Without her glasses, Graceanne's hazel eyes looked small in the dark, like a canary's. She cleared her raspy throat. Whenever she used a vocabulary word, her voice went up an octave in artful and shamelessly accurate imitation of Sister Mary Clothilda and Graceanne's head dipped the way Sister's did, so that instead of sounding more learned, she sounded younger, and a little stupid.

"It's got a lot of things, like poems and lists, but the **plot** is about this girl who finds a nine-channel radio in her basement. There are nine knobs on the front of this radio, each one colored and shaped **proportionally** like one of the planets—

you know, red for little Mars, grey with the giant red spot for Jupiter, blue for the gas giants Uranus and Neptune. The knobs for the big outer planets are big. And the girl can just choose a knob and listen to programs from any of the planets. I write down what they say on the programs."

"Is there a knob for Earth?"

"Of course. For the Cardinals games."

"What kind of programs come from Mars?"

"Scientific programs. Astronomy is like religion there, and they have preachers who come on and talk about how you should send in money for more research, because when they finally know everything, then everyone will be happy."

While I was thinking about that, I heard a door slam downstairs somewhere. Graceanne jerked the flashlight out of the springs and shut it off. The yelling lasted about ten minutes, and a door slammed again. And then it was quiet.

"Get to your room. Don't you dare get caught," Graceanne whispered. As I scooted out from under the bed, she grabbed the collar of my pajamas in her fist and twisted it. "You tell about my book, you even *hint* about my book, and I'll whale you good, Thumper."

I nodded and got to my knees.

She poked her head out. "I'll whale you within an inch of your life, young man. And that goes for Sergeant Useless, too."

"Are you gonna play Rolling Pin tomorrow?" I whispered.

"What for? Nobody will play that game again for a long time, Thumper. It's been won. Besides, the only thing I'll be fit for is standing in the water with you dead kids."

"If Mama lets you out."

"I gotta go to school, at least."

"Graceanne, what's a road apple?"

"You sure ask enough questions. It's what a horse leaves behind to sign his name. Now get out of my room and don't let Mama see your shadow." She grabbed her glasses and stared at me through the lenses she was holding about a foot from her face.

"What the hell got into you to get all nosy, anyway, Thumper?"

"Nothing," I said.

"You're a liar."

"So?"

She put her glasses all the way on and slipped back under the bed. I bent down and lifted the blanket so I could look at her.

"Graceanne, were you ever a dead kid?"

She snorted. "Better than you."

Three

$\mathcal{I}$t had never entered my mind that I was better at anything than Graceanne, not even being a dead kid, but it didn't seem fair that, after I knew about her secret book and about a secret that even she didn't know, I'd get another dose of tampons. But when I finally left again for school, she popped up at the bathroom window and slung a big heave like she'd throw someone out at the plate. This time she struck my eye and made it tear. "Thumper, stick that the only place where you can sing baritone."

I thought knowing Graceanne's secret would make her stop treating me like the top of the order on the Parade Ground. I was thinking things didn't change just because you had a secret. I walked away, limping toward the little crowd headed for Our Lady of Lourdes Academy, all of them in fresh dry clothes too and as late as I was.

"Don't tell about my poem," Graceanne scream-whispered and pulled the bathroom window down.

I followed the other dead kids to school, down from the top of the Hill and onto the basin of Cranepool's Landing, again measuring the might and slime of the muddy crud by listening to the sucking and plopping sounds of my awkward rubber boots. I thought about astronomy on Mars, wondering about the connection between knowing everything and being happy.

After our delayed morning mass—a steamy and stinking ceremony that consisted of rote responses in Church Latin and spontaneous mud-flicking—the fourth grade splashed across the parking lot, into our upstairs classroom, and saluted the flag.

Sister Mary Clothilda was wearing rubber boots, too, but she was too fat to bend over and take hers off, so we all got to wear our boots in the classroom, including whatever wild-life we had gathered in them—inadvertently or craftily—from the sloppy new lake covering the town. This was another piece of unusually kind fate for me, because I could not take the boot off my braced foot unassisted.

The school day always started with a vocabulary quiz. Since all of us dead kids had worked hard because of Ugly Blue Man and we were more or less fasting—except for hunks of tooth-paste, which we swallowed before school in large quantities on our understanding that toothpaste was exempt from the rules regarding Holy Communion—we were hungry, and the Mothers Club brought in strawberry jelly doughnuts with white ic-ing rings while we took the quiz. We were allowed to eat while we worked, but none of us mistook this practice for special magnanimity on Sister's part. She always had a doughnut, too, and the presence of the mothers kept us from cheating.

"*Ramate,*" Sister intoned, and those of us who were able to spelled and defined the word.

"*Ocular.*"

I shifted in my seat, taking the weight off my right hip. The brace and corrective shoe, sunk into six inches of mud and water in my larger boot, produced a powerful drag on my trousers. One of the tampons popped out on the floor.

"*Disaster.*"

I glanced around, but the mothers had returned to the front

of the room by the blackboard and were packing up their paper bags and napkins.

"Extreme."

I stuck my larger boot out into the aisle with a heavy thump and a squish, but I couldn't reach the tampon.

"Ritual."

Since that was five words, we wrote our names on our papers and passed them, shoulder over shoulder, toward the front, along with our nickels for the doughnuts. The mothers collected them, put the vocabulary papers on the corner of Sister's desk, and departed. The tampon was swelling on the wet floor.

"I have the results of the Stanford-Binet Batteries, and all the other tests we gave you last fall," Sister announced as we started getting out our math books with as much collective noise as possible without drawing attention to any individual. "Let's have some quiet in here." Sister frowned at us over her glasses. "Your IQ is a very important number, because it tells us how intelligent you are. IQ: It means Intelligence Quotient. I must say, some of these scores are very surprising." She wrinkled her fat forehead, the folds of flesh pushing up the beige stain on her wimple. "Very surprising."

There was a general squirming in desks, accompanied by squishing boots and slopping water. I leaned over, ostensibly to drain some of the water out of the boot on my clubfoot, but surreptitiously reaching into the aisle with my hand, and another tampon popped out of my pocket and onto the floor. The thin wet paper wrapping quickly absorbed dark brown water and lay there next to the first one, the two together looking like a couple of exotic turds on the linoleum. Bobby Stochmal was sitting across the aisle from me, and he poked the girl in front of him and pointed to the floor. She looked down, and pretty soon the word was passed around the classroom on a silent wave of nudges and glances.

"Now, while it's true that the grades you earn in your subjects are very important," Sister was saying, as the dead kids were ducking and looking under their desks, "your IQ is also very meaningful, because it tells us how high your grades *should* be. That helps us know if you are doing your very best. Pay attention."

Sister began to lumber around the room, gesturing with a ruler and holding a clipboard. Even though the tampons were soaked from the quarry lake, the brown water on the floor was causing the second tampon's cardboard applicator to expand, and the fibers inside were ballooning the whole thing out as the paper wrapper seemed to dissolve on the floor. "Charlie Farrand did very well. His IQ of 148 means that he's a very gifted student, and he should be making straight A's. Which he is."

I heard my name and dragged my eyes away from the tampon.

"Charlie, congratulations. You are almost a genius." She turned to Bobby Stochmal. "Bobby, you're almost as smart as Charlie. Your IQ is 139. We have some smart children in Our Lady of Lourdes." She continued her waddling stroll, turning her back to me as she went down the list of IQs. I ducked down and leaned way out of my desk again, fishing for the swelling tampons, and two more popped out of my pockets. Bobby laughed—on purpose—and Sister slewed around, her black veil swinging across a couple of desks.

"Bobby, how dare you laugh?" She had just read Tony Knolke's score of ninety-two. "God has blessed you with a very high IQ, but it's not very smart to laugh at those whom God has chosen to endow with different gifts. Tony's a much more pleasant person than you are."

All the kids burst out laughing.

"I wasn't laughing at Tony, Sister Clothilda," Bobby said righteously.

"I hope that's the truth. A smart boy won't get into heaven on his brains. He's got a thing or two to learn from the nice boy." She gestured with the clipboard. "Now, the children in the upper grades were tested, too. And we were very surprised to learn that the highest IQ in the school belongs to none other than Graceanne Farrand, of all people. Her score of 165 tells us that she is a very bright girl who should settle down and bring those grades up." She smiled, her lips spreading apart and showing the gap between her bottom front teeth.

She was now at the head of the aisle where the tampons were bulging on the muddy linoleum like a cluster of mushrooms. She paced slowly down the aisle, her long black habit trailing on the soupy floor and her shoes rubbing inside her boots with long, fruity gasps of squashed air.

"What is that?" she demanded suddenly, pointing the clipboard at the tampons.

"Charlie's got his period," Bobby said, his face a perfect mask of innocent willingness to share information. "I heard Graceanne saying so this morning, Sister."

A rosy flush blossomed up over her jiggling face, starting from her white collar and speeding up to her greasy wimple. I knew her horror was genuine. Graceanne had told me that the nuns were all virgins and prohibited from tampering (thus the term *tampon*) with God's design for the river of the menses, condemned once a month to drip on the floor or the ground, which explained Sister's peculiar odor. She turned on me.

"Did you bring those things in here, *Charlie Farrand?*" Her voice had gone up an octave and her head dipped, in the same odd tic she displayed with vocabulary words. "You wouldn't think of such a crude thing yourself, so I'm afraid you've been led into a *near occasion* of sin if you brought them in here. Did you?"

Before I could even nod my head, she must have seen the truth in my eyes, and the little dance I was doing with my boot had overbalanced me in my desk and I slipped off the edge. That caught me by surprise, and I fell out all the way. I landed in the other aisle, slid across the watery linoleum on my side, and banged against the wrought-iron grillwork of Tony (IQ 92) Knolke's desk. I shook my head involuntarily, surprised that my eyes were watering.

"Get up, Charlie Farrand, before you take cold from that nasty water," she said, waving the clipboard backward toward the door of the classroom without watching where she was waving it. Bobby (139) ducked. "You better take these things in the aisle and report to *Father Weiss*."

I crawled under my desk into the aisle with the tampons, clutched them in my fist, and stood. I limped through the ghastly silence toward the door.

"And," Sister said, air hissing through her bottom teeth, "I'm calling your mother at *recess*. She'd better see to your sister's sense of humor."

I walked out of the classroom, my right boot dragging, and into the hall. I dropped the tampons into a garbage can and looked around at the tiled walls. They were Graceanne's tampons all right and she was going to get it again and I guess she had led me into a near occasion of sin, but she was already in trouble with Edie and wouldn't care much about any stupid sin she could just confess away later.

I went to the stairs at the end of the corridor and sat on the top step. I practiced whistling for a while, and counted the tiles on the south side of the stairwell. I could see the dirty water covering the bottom half of the flight leading down into the Graceanne Farrand Memorial Pool. On my seat, I went down a few stairs quietly until I could see how high the water was under the ceiling. Graceanne must have been hanging from the pipes when she became Champion for

Eternity, because the water was at least five feet deep down there. I started thinking again about the astronomers on Mars, about knowing everything and about being happy and about how long it would take the astronomers to get finished.

I went back up the stairs and out the door. The sun was shining on the shimmering black world of Cranepool's Landing.

I started limping home, alone, thinking about the astronomers, wondering what our flooded town looked like from 49 million miles away.

Four

$\mathcal{W}$hen I got to the top of Lewis and Clark Hill, my sister Kentucky was sitting out on the front porch, her hair in brush curlers with pink plastic picks to hold them in place. The picks in the top curlers were making red dents in her forehead. She was barefoot, and her knees were red and shiny.

"What are you doing?" I asked, sitting down beside her and kicking the heels of my boots against the concrete to pull them off.

"Don't do that, you little pest. You'll scrape holes in your boots."

I sat quietly for a while. There was a new red barn riding downstream on the silver skin of the Mississippi, and I thought it was probably empty, because it was too early for hay. If there was anything alive in the barn, I couldn't hear it over the pounding of the water.

Kentucky's hair looked damp around the curlers.

"Aren't you going to school?" I asked.

"If you must know," she said, pinching my nose, "Graceanne is still feeling poorly. I'm staying home to look after her."

The only resemblance between Kentucky and Graceanne

showed on the parade ground when they got up to bat. Grace-anne always hit third, with Kentucky coming up behind her. Nobody—not even the big boys—hit harder than Kentucky. The way it usually worked, Graceanne would hit a double or triple—sliding into the bases headfirst through the water that April—and Kentucky would get up and belt her home on the first pitch. Kentucky's arms were massively developed, and she could hit the ball past the parade ground and through the gates of Jefferson Barracks Fort itself. The post guards in their white belts and helmets and fatigues and combat boots used to field Kentucky's hits for us, because if we had to chase down her stuff ourselves, the games would never end before dark.

At almost sixteen, Kentucky was what Edie called "the beauty of the family." She had dark red hair that Edie dyed, and big fierce blue eyes, and long fingernails that never broke or chipped, and a sweet voice. She wasn't flat like Graceanne, or beady-eyed like Graceanne, or as loud as Graceanne. And now I knew she also wasn't as smart as Graceanne.

"Graceanne's smarter than you," I said.

"That's a lie."

"No, it's not. Sister Clothilda told us."

"What'd she say?"

"She said that Graceanne has the highest IQ in the school. And nuns don't lie."

"That's what you think, Charlie." Kentucky grabbed my right leg and hauled my boot onto her lap. "IQ isn't every-thing. There's other kinds of smart." With one vicious tug and a turn of her powerful wrist, she yanked the boot off and dropped it on the steps. "You track mud into this house and I'll whale you good, young man. I liquid-waxed the stairs this morning." That was why her knees were shiny and red. "Gimme your other foot."

It felt like she had wrenched my leg out of its socket.

"I'll do it myself," I said.

"Gimme that foot."

I stood up, resisting, wobbling on my left foot, the clubfoot still on her lap. Her hand was around my ankle, curved through the metal brace.

"You make me break a nail, and I'll make you sorrier than sorry." Kentucky's voice was sweet, always sweet like a song, but I did not make the mistake of disregarding the threat in her words. I sat back down, and she pulled off my other boot. "You go around back and wash those out, Charlie."

"Where's Graceanne?"

"The green Measles Room."

"Has she been there all day?" I asked, not looking Kentucky in the eye.

"I told you. She's poorly."

"Why's your hair in curlers?"

"Because we're dressing for dinner tonight. Mama put it up for me."

"Why?"

"Because Grandma and Grandpa are coming."

"Is Daddy coming home?"

"Mind your business and go wash those things out."

"Is Graceanne coming down for dinner?"

"I said mind your business."

I picked up my boots and limped around the side of the house toward the south yard. I turned the hose on my boots, rinsed them inside and out, and carried them dripping clean water around to the back sunporch.

Edie was trying to get an early tan, lying on an army blanket on the faded picnic table. She was asleep. Her right hand was tucked inside one of her medical books. Edie took courses at Saint Audrain's Hospital over in Prathersville, studying to become a medical technologist. She was always practicing on us, sticking our fingers with needles and typing our blood.

"You have extremely rare blood, Charlemagne," she had told me. "Type AB negative."

"Is that good?" I asked.

"It means you're the universal recipient. If you ever need blood, anybody can donate it."

"What's Graceanne?"

"She's AB negative."

"Is that good?"

"She's the universal recipient, like you."

"What's Kentucky?"

"AB negative."

"What's so rare about it if we all got it?"

"You're probably the only children in Cranepool's Landing with AB negative. If you ever need blood, you can give to each other."

"Graceanne said she could kill me with her blood."

"How? Has she been threatening you?"

"She said her blood was poison."

"I don't know what I ever did to deserve such a devil as Graceanne for a child."

Now I looked at the picnic table and saw the medical book rising and falling on Edie's stomach. I went quietly up the painted green stairs onto the porch and put my boots under the card table where we kept canned goods stacked in pyramids. I took off my shoes and brace and socks and put them beside the boots. I slipped inside the screen door. I could smell cooked onions and green peppers and fried margarine in the kitchen. There was a box of rice and two cans of tomatoes on the table, and a big can of paprika. Edie was making Spanish rice.

I went into the dining room. The table was set with our good dishes. I counted the places. Seven plates, and seven milk glasses, and seven folded paper napkins, and seven rubber placemats. The dining room curtains were pulled, and the room was dark.

I went up the slick stairs in my bare feet, holding on to the banister and trying to figure out a way to keep my weight on my left foot, because I was getting close to *normal* and I didn't want to turn my foot back. The stairs curved near the top, into a spiral of three wide and shiny triangles. I went down the bedroom hall past the bathroom and started up the stairs to the green Measles Room. I could hear voices, so I got down on my knees and crawled up.

"And the big skillet and the little cast-iron pot, for beans and fried eggs," Graceanne's hoarse voice announced.

"We take both pots, and Mama's gonna tan our hides." That was Kentucky's voice.

"Don't be so stupid, Tucka. If we run away, how's she gonna tan our hides?"

I crawled around the corner of the stairs to the edge of the door to the green Measles Room. Graceanne was sitting on the bed on a pillow, her back against the olive green wall, her knees propped up, a tablet of lined paper lying on the bed beside her. She had a pencil in her hand. Her nightgown was wrinkled, and her legs were covered with a sheet.

"We'll also need potholders and towels," Graceanne said in a businesslike voice, picking up the tablet, balancing it on her knees, and writing in her overhand way, her head down so she could see under her fist. "And soap, and a dishpan."

Kentucky was sitting in the window seat with her back to Graceanne, staring out at the river. "You mean to be as clean when we run away as we are in this pus-bucket of a pretend hospital? Mama's got a hand sitting in formaldehyde down on the sunporch in a jar. I never saw such an ugly thing. It's from the Saint Audrain's morgue, and she's studying the veins and things for a test she's got to take for the certificate."

"You're right." Graceanne scratched the pencil noisily over what she had written. "No soap, no towels, no dishpan. No **sterile** procedures."

"Think we should take Charlie?"

"No. He'd just slow us down if we have to run for it, you know, if she sends the sheriff after us, and, besides, Edie never whales on him. He should stay here, get his foot corrected, and go to college. Bread, butter, and sugar. For carbohydrates, lubrication, and energy."

"Lubrication? Butter is for lubrication? What the hell does that mean?"

"It helps you with your movements."

"I never knew that," Graceanne said, after a thoughtful pause. "I wonder if you can give a person an overdose of butter?"

"I tried it on Charlie when he was a baby, but nothing different happened. Maybe I didn't give him enough."

"How much did you give him?"

"About a pound."

"Didn't he make a fuss?"

"He liked it."

Graceanne shook her head and her braids made a dry, swishing noise over the tablet. "What happens when we **exhaust** our supplies?"

"I'll get a job singing," Kentucky said. "And you can write your book."

So Kentucky knew about the book. The disappointment leaping in my chest almost made me choke. The sense of inclusion, of sharing, of hidden wisdom that I had carried with me to school and back was gone. Kentucky knew about the astronomers, too.

"Think anyone will hire you to sing? Who hires people to sing?"

Bars and taverns," Kentucky said, nodding her head sagely.

"Bars and taverns and nightclubs. I'll be a torch singer. Write down to pack my red dress."

Graceanne bowed her head over her knees and scribbled with the pencil.

Kentucky was a true and pure coloratura soprano. She was the keystone of Our Lady of Lourdes choir, and she always had the solo part in "O Holy Night" at Midnight Mass on Christmas Eve with her name in the program. She spent the greater part of the year brawling and bullying and belting home runs, and making Edie say "I don't know what I did to deserve such a hell terror," but one night a year Kentucky was a descendant of the angels, with nobody asking what they did to deserve her. The rest of the choir dressed in black robes over their heavy sweaters, but Kentucky wore a sparkling white drape Edie had made. The drape left one shoulder bare, and Edie threaded a silver ribbon through Kentucky's long red hair.

We would turn around and gaze up at the singers in the choir loft when they started lighting their candles in the dark church, passing the flame along to each other during the Epistle. We were breathless before we heard the first notes of the song, the tenors singing melody, the altos singing harmony:

O holy night, the stars are brightly shining.
It is the night of our dear Savior's birth.

The flames of the white candles they held flickered before their faces. Then the second sopranos would join in, swelling the melody:

Long lay the earth, in sin and error pining
Till He appeared and the soul felt its worth.

Then the first sopranos would bring in the high notes of the second harmony:

> A thrill of hope, the weary world rejoices
> For yonder breaks, a new and glorious morn.

Then a hush would fall. And the gooseflesh would start on us even before Kentucky stepped up to the rail of the loft for her solo in the highest, sweetest, most silvery notes a human voice has ever sung. When she sang it out, I didn't think she *was* human:

> Faaaaall on your knees. O *hear* the angels' *voi*-ces.
> O ni-ight, di-i-vine, O-oh night, when Christ was
>   born.

Then the whole chorus would lift its voices with hers to sing the final words:

> O night divine, O night, O night divine.

But Kentucky's ringing voice separated itself from the others and seemed to float out over the church. The lights would go on and old Father Weiss would read the Gospel about Jesus being born, but Kentucky's eighteen solo words were all we really heard for the remainder of the mass. People wept during her solo and after her solo—even people who only went to church once a year, even people who, later in the parking lot, would say they only went to church as a seasonal thing, or just to hear the solo, not because they believed any of that "outdated claptrap."

I was weeping now outside the green Measles Room. They were going to run away and leave me in the house on Lewis and Clark Hill. And Kentucky knew about the astronomers.

"What's that leaking noise?" Kentucky said. She came out into the hall and grabbed me by the ear. "You little sneak. I ought to throw you down the stairs and break both your legs."

"I want to go, too," I wailed.

Kentucky clapped her big hand over my mouth and squeezed my lips until they were folded back over my gums.

"What baseboard did he crawl out of?" Graceanne demanded from the bed.

Kentucky gave my lips another twist and fixed her blue eyes on me. "You gonna squeal again if I let you go?" Her long thumbnail was digging into my nostril.

I shook my head, still attached to her fist. Her arm waved back and forth.

She released me, and my lips slowly unfolded, like flower petals. My mouth felt dry and I passed my tongue over my teeth.

"Get in here, Thumper," Graceanne snapped.

I hobbled into the green Measles Room on my knees.

"Where's your brace?" she asked.

"Downstairs on the porch with my boots. I didn't see the formaldehyde hand." My words were strangely hollow-sounding, the consonants malformed. I licked my lips.

"Never mind hands. Don't you want your clubfoot to turn? Stand up: you're not crippled. Just look at your foot. It's almost **standard**." She cackled. "Charlie doesn't have feet— he has *stand*ards."

I stood up. My ear and my lips were hot. "I want to go, too."

"We're not going anywhere, Thumper."

"But I heard you and Tucka."

"You heard nothing. Just because people say they're running away doesn't mean they're running away. It's just making **conversation**."

Kentucky walked up behind me, giving my ear another Chinese Massage, and picked up an empty milk glass from the table by the bed. She looked at Graceanne. "You fix Charlie.

I gotta get downstairs and brown the hamburger meat. I'm on KP."

When she was gone, I sat down on the edge of the bed.

"Get off there," Graceanne said, flicking my face with the end of her pencil.

I went to the window seat and stared at her. Her hair was pulled into two braids so tight they stretched her eyes toward her ears. Edie must have done her hair. When Graceanne did the braids they were loose and softer. She was quiet for a few moments, working her pencil overhand on the tablet.

"What are you doing?" I asked.

"Why ain't you in school?"

"I got thrown out for the plugs."

"What?! You *showed* them?"

"They fell out of my pocket."

"Oh, God." She put her head down on the tablet. "Is Sister gonna tell Mama?"

"She said she was."

"Oh, God. I'm dead. Oh, God. I'm dead. This is a **disaster**. Now I'll have to run away." She pulled the sheet away and started to get up.

"Mercy," I said, but now my mouth was completely dry and the word was a cottony croak. Her legs were lumpy and swollen, the backs purple and grey with long, thin black scabs. Her mouth was hanging open, the shape of the letter *O*, and I remembered the white-tailed deer in the river.

She held her weight up on the palms of her hands clenched on the bedframe, her body swinging from her shoulders. The ropy muscles in her arms stuck out as though trickles of concrete had been poured through her veins. She hovered there, the *O* of her mouth frozen. Slowly, she lowered herself back to the mattress. Her forehead was covered with sweat, and her nightgown was clinging to her ribs. She turned and lay on her back, drawing her knees up into the air. "No. I'm safe." Tears rolled from her eyes and into the hair pulled tight at her temples. "Mama couldn't hit me now."

I edged over to the bed and stood looking down at her. "Why are you crying, Graceanne?"

She squeezed her eyes shut. She took a deep, shuddering breath. "I'm not crying. This is leftover from the **technique**."

"Are your scabs poisonous?"

"**Fatal** and getting worse. From now on, anybody touches me and my blood gets on them, they die."

"Can I do anything, Graceanne?"

She rolled her head from side to side.

"You won't run away, will you, Graceanne?"

She rolled her head again.

"You want me to fetch you your book?"

Her eyes flew open. "Don't you dare! Mama'd see it."

"I'm sorry."

"Thumper?"

"What?"

"You want to do something for me?"

"What?"

"I want you to go write something in my book."

"What?"

"I want you to go down and write, 'The Martian astronomers are making **frantic** appeals for more money today.' Can you spell all those words?"

"Sure. I'm almost a genius."

She narrowed her eyes and studied my face. "What makes you say that?"

"Sister said so."

"She did not."

"She did too. The Stanford-Binet test scores came back to the school and she read off everyone's IQs."

"She *did*?" Graceanne closed her eyes. "That's the meanest thing I ever heard her do. I wonder why she did it. Sister is just a roly-poly squeeze ball without a mean bone in her body. I like her as much as some of the kids." She opened her eyes. "She say anything about my IQ?"

I hesitated. I was afraid to tell Graceanne that she was 165, because, if she knew how smart she already was, maybe she'd stop thinking it was important for the astronomers to learn everything so everyone would be happy, and she wouldn't write any more of the story under her bed. But somebody would tell her. "She said yours was 165, the highest in the school."

"Well, howdy doody. God, I'm so **inspired**." She frowned so hard she looked like an old lady. "Thumper, if I'm so smart, how come I'm the one lying here in bed when everyone else is walking around outside in their right color skins?"

I thought about that for a while. I thought it was smart to win the game from me and find a place to hide so good you'd be Champion for all time, but I guess it wasn't. Graceanne knew a lot of things I didn't, so her 165 didn't surprise me much.

"Graceanne, what's it called that Tucka did to my mouth just now with her hand squeezing on it?"

"That was a French Lemon."

Five

$\mathcal{E}$die came into the dining room while I was putting on clean socks. She was wearing a towel around her swimming suit, and my brace was swinging from her freckled hand.

"Charlemagne. Oh, I see you're taking care of your feet yourself. Keeping them warm and dry. Let me help you with the brace."

"His shoes are still out on the porch," Kentucky hollered from the kitchen, where she was on patrol.

I wanted to get the shoes myself so I could see the hand, but Edie retreated from the dark dining room. I sat there in the dark, thinking about the astronomers talking on Grace-anne's radio. I had written what she told me in the book under her bed, but I had added a sentence of my own. After "The Martian astronomers are making frantic appeals for more money today," I wrote, "Today Thumper found Ugly Blue Man."

My brown shoes were clean when Edie brought them into the dining room. She handed me the right shoe, and, while I was tying it, she said, "You're home early today. Did the school close?"

"No. Sister threw me out."

"You? Why would she throw you out?"

"I stole some of Graceanne's plugs and took them to school."

"You stole what?"

"Her plugs."

Edie looked around helplessly. "Charlie, what are you saying? What's a plug?"

"You know, a plug. For your period."

Edie turned as red as hamburger meat. "Did Graceanne put you up to this?"

"Graceanne? She'd probably kill me if she knew what I did."

"Has your sister been threatening you again?"

Edie wasn't listening to my lie, and I wished I could take it back so I wouldn't have to report it later in Confession because it seemed I'd never get rid of the tampons the way I was going and I couldn't turn the blame around. It was going right back on Graceanne. "You don't understand. Graceanne doesn't know anything about this. Sister even said nice things about her today. She said she has the highest IQ in the school."

"Well, I'm not surprised. Brains run in the family. You come of very good stock, Charlie. But if Graceanne's so smart, why can't she be a good girl?"

That summation was close to Graceanne's own assessment of her situation in the green Measles Room, but, while I could not put my finger on the exact spot where their conclusions differed, I knew that there was something about Graceanne's version that made more sense than Edie's. Since I was so smart, though, it seemed to follow that I should be able to get in trouble more successfully than I was.

"Did Sister say what your IQ is?" Edie asked.

"It's not near as high as Graceanne's."

"Never mind about Graceanne. Tell me about your score."

"It's 110," I lied. If Edie was making connections between brains and goodness, I didn't want her thinking I was an IQ angel.

"Are you sure that's what she said? That can't be right." Edie put her thumb on one end of her mouth and her ring finger on the other end. She pulled them slowly together in the middle. "You get straight A's."

I thought about what I had written in Graceanne's book and about having my own secrets and about turning the blame around from other people. "That's because I cheat like a sumbitch."

Edie laughed. "Where'd you hear a word like that?"

"Aren't you mad that I cheat?"

She laughed again. "Who would you cheat off? You're the smartest boy in the school. If you were cheating, you'd have lower grades, not straight A's." She put her freckled hand on my shoulder. "Charlie, why are you trying to get in trouble?"

"Because then maybe you'd forget about Graceanne and she wouldn't be in trouble and up in the green Measles Room," I blurted out, immediately aware that I had made a bad mistake.

Edie stood up. She looked stiff. "Graceanne's not in trouble. She's feeling poorly."

Kentucky was standing in the dining room doorway, a big ball of raw hamburger meat in her hands. She glared at me and slowly lowered her eyes to her right hand, twisting it into the meat the way she had twisted my lips. She looked back at me.

"Oh," I said. "Graceanne's sick?"

"Yes," Edie said. "Graceanne had a fall, and she's feeling very sick."

"You gonna take her to the doctor?" I saw Kentucky's hand sink into the meat, her nails coming out the other side. "But, she's probably not that sick."

"No," Edie said. "She's not that sick. You just finish up putting your brace on and find something to do. I don't want you playing outside, because we're dressing for dinner tonight and the house is clean."

Edie went toward the stairs, brushing my hair with her fingers. I put on my other shoe and went into the kitchen. Kentucky was crumbling the meat into a skillet on the gas range.

"What are you doing?" I asked.

"See what I mean about there being other kinds of smart than just IQ smart?" she said. "You wouldn't catch me telling Mama to take Graceanne to the doctor." She wiped her hands on a tea towel. "I've heard that the smartest people often go insane."

"Graceanne's smart, and she's not insane."

"Oh no? You think it was sane to hide out in the school and not come home? It's the craziest thing she ever did. She was asking for it."

"Graceanne wanted to win the game, is all."

"Anybody who wants to win that bad is insane."

I sat in the one-armed rocking chair by the old range, swinging my legs. This was turning out to be the most intellectual day of my life. I made a list in my mind:

    A. I was almost a genius.
    B. I couldn't be a cheat, because I had no one to cheat off.
    C. My older sister Kentucky, the heaviest of the heavy hitters, was conversing with me about being smart.
    D. Intelligence could lead to insanity.
    E. Graceanne was smarter than me.
    F. Graceanne had permitted me to write in her book.

I wondered how far this new conversation would go. I decided to try some more on Kentucky. "Do you think Richard Nixon's insane?"

"What the hell are you talking about?"

"Well, he's smart, right?"

"I guess."

"And he wants to beat John Kennedy the way Graceanne always wants to win everything."

"So?"

"So, is he insane?"

"Get the hell out of this kitchen before I whale you good."

I cleared out, wandering around the dining room. I counted the places again. There were still seven, so maybe Graceanne was coming down to eat dinner. I looked out the window toward the river. Some dead kids in their red boots were throwing sticks and junk into the water. They weren't supposed to be out that close to the river. And until now the warnings had been obeyed. I wondered what their target was.

I took off for the stairs. My braced shoe thumped on the shiny steps. When I got up to the green Measles Room, the door was closed.

I opened it and put my head inside. Graceanne was reading her history textbook.

"What are you doing?" I asked.

"What do you want, Thumper?" she said, not looking up from the page.

"I want to look out the window."

"Can't you find some other window to look out?" She raised her eyes from the page. "This house only has about a hundred and eighty windows."

"This is the highest window. I want to look at the river."

"Why? You've seen the river a million times."

"The dead kids are throwing sticks into the water."

"Get over there, quick," she said, throwing back the sheet.

I knelt on the window seat. There was a kid in the water. "There's a kid in the water," I said. I heard Graceanne gasp behind me, but I did not take my eyes off the river. I felt her hand on my shoulder.

The dead kids were running along the bank, trying to keep alongside the child racing on the current, picking up sticks and boxes to throw to him.

"Thumper, get Tucka. *Quick*."

"I'll never get her in time."

"Quick, I'll show you how." She grabbed the sheet off the bed, and I could tell that she almost couldn't bear the pain on her legs from standing. "Sit on this and go down the stairs on your butt. Hurry up!"

I snatched the sheet and ran clumsily out of the green Measles Room. I sat on the sheet, clutched the fabric, and pushed off. I flew down the stairs, the banister poles flashing by too fast to see. In the bedroom hall, I tripped on the sheet, but I got my footing and headed for the main staircase. Again I plopped down on the sheet and pushed off. I sailed down those freshly waxed hardwood steps, my butt bouncing on each step with a jarring crash that didn't seem to last because each crash launched me into the air. At the bottom of the stairs, I dropped the sheet and stumbled into the dining room.

"Graceanne?" Kentucky had come running into the dark dining room. "I thought I heard Graceanne."

"There's a dead kid in the river," I shouted, catching my breath in ragged gasps.

She took off without a word, through the kitchen, out the back door, and down Lewis and Clark Hill at a speed I'd never imagined. She never had to run fast because she always hit home runs. I followed as fast as I could. She was way out in front, but I saw her run along the banks and go flying into the river headfirst. Then I couldn't see her anymore, just flashes through the bushes of silver-brown water and broken trees rushing by.

I sat down in the mud and tried to breathe. I had a stitch in my side. I looked back up at the house. I could see Grace-anne in the window of the green Measles Room.

I waited there in the mud. After about ten minutes, I saw Kentucky coming out of the bushes downstream with a bunch of the dead kids in their red boots. She was carrying a body in a mustard-colored jacket. She dumped him on the wet ground with a splash. I could tell she was yelling at him. Then she reached down and punched his head.

She came striding back along the bank, swinging her arms and talking to herself. At the bottom of Lewis and Clark Hill, she started taking the curlers out of her hair and throwing them on the ground, pulling out mud as she went.

"Is he all right?" I asked.

"Probably. He's too stupid to feel a good punch upside the head."

"He woulda died in the river, Tucka." I stood and walked beside her up the hill.

"I hope his parents ground him for ten years. You kids were told to stay away from the river."

"Who was it?"

"Bobby Stochmal. I never saw such an ugly jacket."

"He got me in trouble today."

She looked down at me strangely. "Yeah? Well, Graceanne and I'll give you the musk glands we've got laid up in waxed paper. You can fix him good tomorrow. I'll show you how. But if you bring any of that mud into the house I'll whale you good, young man."

Kentucky cleaned herself off with the hose and got a towel from the back porch and went inside. I went up on the porch and looked under the card table. In a big jar behind some cans of tomatoes and chicken soup there was a hand floating on its wrist and I wondered if there was any blood left in the veins and if the blood was AB negative or poison and how you took a test on somebody's hand and where the rest of the person was.

Six

Kentucky brought Graceanne piggyback down the shiny stairs. The rest of us were dressed for dinner, but Graceanne had to wear her old blue overalls with her Christmas blouse.

Graceanne didn't get up from the table when Grandma and Grandpa Morgan got there.

"What the matter with that child?" Grandma asked.

"She's poorly," Edie said. She fussed with the ruffles on the sleeves of her good black dress.

"Seems like there's always something ailing that child. Why, just look how skinny she is." She took her glasses out of her apron and put them on her nose so she could stare at Graceanne. "All skin and bones. She eating all right? Plenty of red meat?"

"She eats okay. The doctor's got her on malt supplements."

Grandma and Grandpa had come in their pickup truck all the way from Chillicothe, and it was our house, but Grandma had on her regular starched white apron over her dark blue dress. Edie made her sit across from me and Graceanne. Kentucky had to squeeze between the old people, their shoulders lined up like a fence. Edie sat at the foot of the table: The chair at the head of the table was empty.

Grandpa had on his black suit and his Shriner's hat, and
Edie gave him a look. He took off the hat and put it beside
his plate. There was a long silence while Edie folded her
freckled hands and studied us, deciding who was going to ask
the blessing. Grandma and Grandpa weren't Catholics.

"Charlemagne, you can ask the blessing."

I made the sign of the cross and bowed my head over my
hands. "Bless us, Oh Lord, and these thy gifts, which we are
about to receive from thy bounty, through Christ our Lord.
Amen."

Grandpa reached around the candles and lifted the heavy
platter of Spanish rice. He spooned some onto his plate and
passed the platter to Kentucky. Edie passed the stack of sliced
bread to Grandpa. There was a pickle plate in the middle of
the table, and I pulled it toward me.

"Charlie, why don't you start the conversation?" Edie said.
"Don't take the black olives."

There were five rules regarding dinner table conversation
in the red brick house on the top of Lewis and Clark Hill:

1. It couldn't be about politics.
2. It couldn't be about religion.
3. It couldn't be about sex.
4. It had to be of general interest.
5. Anyone who "made it a business" to complain
   about the food had to do the dishes.

John Kennedy was out because of one and two. I didn't know
much about three. Until this April day when I had talked to
Kentucky about insanity, nobody had ever been interested in
anything I had to say, so I was confused about four. That left
five, because it seemed to be the only item with a loophole.

I tasted the Spanish rice. Kentucky must've dumped more

than the regular three teaspoons of paprika in with the hamburger meat, because it burned my mouth without having any hamburger or rice taste. I thought about five.

"This tastes like road apples," I said. "But it's very good," I added immediately, certain that I had met all the stipulations and conditions for dinnertable talk.

"You gonna wash his mouth out with soap?" Graceanne asked, turning her head to look at Edie, but not before I saw the light in her hazel eyes behind her glasses.

"Charlie doesn't know the meaning of what he just said," Edie said. "Your brother's going through a stage where he's picking up the bad language you and Kentucky bring home. You girls watch your mouths. A lady is only permitted an occasional 'damn,' and then she must mutter it under her breath."

Graceanne whipped her head around at me. Her braids flew out over her plate. "Charlie, I apologize all over myself for teaching you something as bad as road apples. Just wait'll I get my hands on the horse that taught me."

"That'll be enough of that, Graceanne," Edie said. "I'll start the conversation. I understand there was quite a rescue today. Mrs. Stochmal called me to say she's sending over some nut brownies." She bent her head around Grandpa and fixed her eyes on Kentucky. "Tell Grandma and Grandpa about what a hero you are."

"I just pulled the little snake out of the river," Kentucky said. Her red hair was combed back from her face and pulled into a knot at the back of her head, and the collar of her plaid dress dug into her neck. She didn't look like a girl who could dive into the insane, flooded, swollen Mississippi and come back out alive to eat her dinner, much less give Bobby Stochmal bruises where she'd signed her name on his head. "The little kids have been warned and warned about going near the river."

"How did you happen to be by the river?" Edie asked. "What were you doing there?" I could see Edie didn't like that part, and that she'd been chewing it over.

I could see Kentucky thinking. She took a bite of her Spanish rice and looked across at me and Graceanne. "Graceanne saw him from the green Measles Room and sent Charlie down to get me. I was in the kitchen making these road . . . rice."

We all ate for a while. Then Edie started up again.

"How did Charlie come get you fast enough if he was all the way up to the third floor? It takes him a long time with his brace."

The collar of Kentucky's dress was working as she swallowed. I turned to the side so I could look at Graceanne.

"Pass me a *damn* olive," she said, under her breath.

"Kentucky, go get your sister's malt," Edie said.

Kentucky left the table and went into the kitchen. Under the table I could see Graceanne's left hand turning over on the knee of her overalls, back and forth, back and forth. "I don't want no malt."

"*Any* malt. You don't want *any* malt. The doctor says you have to gain ten pounds."

"I can gain ten pounds tomorrow when the nut brownies get here. I have a sore throat."

"Graceanne, you don't have a sore throat. Don't be untruthful."

Grandma was watching across the table over the top of her glasses. "What ails you, Graceanne?" She had the Spanish rice platter. "Pass me that child's plate, and I'll warm up her Gallon of Goodies."

"That's Spanish rice," Edie said.

"I call it Gallon of Goodies."

"Gallon of Goodies is leftovers," Edie said. "This is fresh made."

"Why is it called Spanish rice?" I asked.

"Because," Edie said, lifting her little finger where she was holding her milk glass, "the onions and green peppers are *sautéed*."

Graceanne snorted like a hog and waved the tip of her braid the way Edie had done with her little finger. "*Sauté* is French. It must be French rice."

"Don't correct me, little miss. That's unbecoming behavior in a young lady aspiring to polite society."

"I've got a sore throat," Graceanne said. She drew her left hand out from under the table and raised it over her head. "Can I be excused?"

"*May* I be excused," Edie said.

"May I be excused?"

"Not until you eat."

"I can't swallow."

"Try," Edie said. "You're just not trying, Graceanne."

Grandma stood up and walked around the table. She came to stand behind Graceanne and reached into the front of her starched white apron. When she brought her hand back out, she was wearing a china thimble with tiny pink flowers on her middle finger.

Kentucky came back in from the kitchen with the jar of malt and Edie spooned it out onto Graceanne's plate.

"Now, you eat, child," Grandma said from behind Graceanne. "Got to put some flesh on those bones."

"I can't. I've got a mean sore throat."

Grandma tapped her on the head with the thimble.

"I can't."

Grandma tapped her again.

"I can't."

Grandma tapped her again.

"I think Graceanne's really hot, Mama," Kentucky said. "You want me to get the thermometer?"

"Graceanne's just being disrespectful and stubborn." Edie

put her thumb on one corner of her mouth and her ring finger on the other, and pulled them together toward the middle, fixing her eyes on Graceanne and breathing through her nose. "Graceanne, the rule in this house is you have to eat what's put before you. When you have your own house, you can make your own rules. But as long as you're living in my house, you will respect my rules. You came to live with me— I didn't come to live with you."

From the way Graceanne's jaw was moving, I could tell she was grinding her teeth. She always did that when she got up to bat. She'd turn her shoulder to the mound, kick the plate a couple of times with her right foot, move her hips slowly back and forth, and grind her teeth. Kentucky tried to get her to chew bubblegum, but Graceanne said gum gave her a headache.

I looked across the table at Kentucky. She was staring down at her plate. I looked at Grandpa. He was eating. I looked at Grandma. She was standing behind Graceanne and holding her thimble up to her nose like she was smelling it. I looked at Edie. She was looking at Graceanne.

In a quiet little voice, Graceanne said, "I didn't come to live with you of my own choice and free will, Mama. I woulda gone somewhere else if I had the say. God sent me to you."

Edie drew a sharp breath, and Grandma's thimble came down with a whack.

"Don't do that!" Edie snapped at Grandma. "I can discipline my own child."

Suddenly Grandpa laughed. "You women are just like a pack of stray cats in Nigger Town, fighting over who gets to get the fattest leg of the skinny mouse. Leave the child be."

"You shouldn't talk like that in front of the children, Father," Edie said. "It puts prejudice in their minds." But the hardness in the faces around the table was gone, and Grandma went back to sit down. "I've been telling the girls not to say nigger."

"Nigger, nigger, nigger," Graceanne said, the words coming out in a tumble. "What difference does it make? It's just a word. Nigger Spanish rice. Nigger malt. Nigger dinner. Nigger conversation. Nigger, nigger, nigger."

Edie put her thumb on one corner of her mouth and her ring finger on the other corner and started pulling them together toward the middle, just like she'd done before, but now I could see that what she was wiping off her lips was a smile. The shock made me jump and I dropped my fork on the floor.

"Graceanne, you excuse yourself from the table and say goodnight to your Grandma and Grandpa," Edie said, her fingers still on her mouth.

Kentucky was watching Graceanne grind her teeth. "I'll take her up, Mama, since she's been poorly."

"I'll take my child upstairs," Edie said. "You all go on and eat your dinner without me." She tried to lift Graceanne out of the chair, but I saw Graceanne go limp on her, putting all the dead weight she could into it. "Put your arms around me, Graceanne Regina."

"Let me take her up, Mama," Kentucky said, rising from her chair. "I know how to carry her."

Edie slowly released Graceanne. There was a white mark on Graceanne's cheek where Edie had pressed her face.

Kentucky backed up in a crouch to Graceanne's chair and let her climb on piggyback.

"Make sure she takes two aspirins," Edie said. "And give her a wet washrag."

Kentucky stood up and carried Graceanne out of the room.

And then there was silence and it made me think, as I looked around the dining room, that I was alone again. Grandpa was still eating. Grandma was tapping her thimble on her rubber placemat. Edie sat back down at the foot of the table and started serving herself a little more Spanish rice. I felt suddenly like I was in a room with some robots covered in human skin, or maybe they were eating with formaldehyde hands. I wasn't even sure if anyone knew I was there.

Nobody said anything. We all just ate the Spanish rice. I was lifting food into my mouth, but I wasn't tasting it or chewing it. I just let it sit there for a while, burning, until it felt dissolved. Then I swallowed.

"Charlie, that's the wrong utensil," Edie said.

I looked at my hand in surprise. I was using the serving spoon.

"Go take it to the kitchen and wash it with soap and hot water so we don't all get your germs."

Kentucky came back into the dining room. I hadn't heard her come down the stairs. "I'll do it," she said. She leaned over the table and took the spoon from me and went into the kitchen. I could hear her running the water.

Then I heard the back screen door slam open against the card table on the sunporch and something crashed and spilled and my father's rich baritone voice was singing: "I am a *combat* soldier, I've got my *combat* boots on." He appeared at the dining room door, his arm around Kentucky's shoulders. He was only about an inch taller than she was, and his head was bald, and he was wearing a uniform. "Father, Son, and Holy Ghost," he shouted out. "Whoever eats the fastest gets the most!"

"Don." Edie pushed her chair away from the table and stood up. "You've been drinking." She laid her napkin on the table.

"You ought to be proud of me. That's the closest I'll ever get to being Catholic. Laugh, Edie, that's funny."

"You need not insult my religion, even though you insist on insulting my home."

"It's my home, too, Dinky. It's my home, too. And these are my children." He glanced around the dining room. "Two of my children. My combat army brats. Where's Graceanne?"

"She's poorly. I tried to tell you last night but you were in a condition."

"Graceanne's as tough as hickory and as smart as a whip. You ought to leave her alone and then the whole world will see what a splendid child an old soldier made."

"I'll thank you not to tell me how to raise the children," Edie said.

Daddy took his arm off Kentucky's shoulders and stepped across to Edie. He took her chin in his hand and shook her head back and forth without getting mad, just like she was a robot in plastic skin. "You want to see if you're as tough as Graceanne?"

"You strike me and I'll call the police."

Daddy released her chin, spun around, and went into the kitchen. I could hear a loud tearing sound. When he came back he had the telephone in his hand. He had ripped the wire out of the wall. He went to the head of the table and sat down. He put the telephone next to his plate. He reached across the table and grabbed the Spanish rice platter. He held it up on its side and the rice fell onto his plate. He put the empty platter down and started eating. All the time, he kept his hazel eyes on Edie.

Edie and Kentucky sat down, like robots.

Daddy picked up the receiver in his left hand, and, still eating, he dialed a number. "Hello," he said into the receiver, his mouth full. "This is Chief Warrant Officer Donald Leslie Farrand. Let me talk to the commander in chief." He reached over, took an olive, and popped it into his mouth, rolling it around in his cheek. "Ike? Dwight David Eisenhower himself? This is Don. I got a question. The Queen of Egypt and I are having a little discussion over dinner, and we want to know who runs the White House, you or Mamie? Uh-huh. Hold on a minute."

He put his hand over the receiver and rolled the olive in his cheek. He looked at Edie. "Ike says it's him."

Daddy uncovered the mouthpiece. "Ike? I got another question. Who runs the Vatican? Uh-huh. Hold on a minute. I gotta say something to the Queen." He put his hand over the receiver again. "He says it's the Pope."

He uncovered the mouthpiece. "Ike? I got one last question. Who runs the universe? Uh-huh. That's what I thought. Well, thanks, I appreciate your time. Thank you, sir. Say hello to Mamie." He put the receiver back on its cradle. "He says it's God." He stared at Edie.

Daddy picked up the receiver, holding it in his hand like a club. "The President, the Pope, and God." He banged the receiver down on the table. The candles jumped and one of them fell over into my plate. Wax dripped into my dinner and the flame burned pieces of onion, sizzling into black curls on the bed of red rice. He banged the receiver again. The flame went out.

"That's three men, Edie, running the country, your church, and the whole goddamn world." He banged the receiver again and again on the table, rattling the dishes and sending the jar of malt crashing onto the floor where it shattered into hundreds of pieces, all covered with powdery ash. Specks of malt floated through the air. He held the receiver up over the table, his hand as steady as a rock. "I'm the president of this family"—bang—"the pope of this family"—bang—"and the god of this family!" He hurled the receiver at the foot of the table, but it caught in midair on the end of its cord and snapped back like a boomerang, smacking into the empty Spanish rice platter. "I'm the Father, Son, and Holy Ghost!"

He stood. His face and bald head were red. He glared at

Edie. He walked down to the foot of the table and bent his head over her where she sat with her freckled hands clenched on the sides of her plate. She sat there like a stone, staring straight in front of her. He opened his mouth and the olive dropped onto her lap.

"Happy anniversary," he said.

He turned and went out through the kitchen.

July 1960

Fort McBain

Seven

*T*hat summer was dry and hot in Cranepool's Landing. Day after day of temperatures in the nineties dried up the residue of the floods, and the earth's cracking and splitting was so loud and mournful we could hear it. Crops had gone in late and, after they withered and died, they were short, stunted, and oddly youthful in their dry, crackling death throes. The tiny, ridged ears of young corn were harvested quickly for feed before they could shrivel up, but even that desperate grasping at the meager product of the land only underscored how devastating the weather was—as bad as the spring floods. Weather prophets along the Mighty Muddy Cruddy, now sunk below its banks and flowing turgidly past Cranepool's Landing, said that the silence in the air, the absence of birds and insects, presaged a dry autumn and a thin apple crop.

Graceanne's sore throat, which none of us had taken seriously, had turned into honest-to-goodness tonsilitis. She had stayed upstairs in the green Measles Room without complaining, reading her books, until one night her throat was so swollen that Edie panicked and rushed her to Saint Audrain's Emergency Room.

The result was that Graceanne went, as she put it, "under

the knife," and her tonsils came out. There were advantages accruing to me from her operation:

1. I was allowed to eat ice cream with her on the bed in the green Measles Room.
2. We watched together out the window as spring turned to summer over the river.
3. She taught me how to draw Martian astronomers. They looked like all her stick figures, except that they looked like they had softball bats growing out of their eyes.

Her recovery was long and painful, she missed the end of school and all of her exams, she lost her place on the county softball team, and she had to attend the "Summer Enrichment Program"—summer school. "I don't mind being with the slow kids," she said. "But the **putrid** vocabulary quizzes are killing me."

I used to visit Graceanne at lunch at Our Lady of Lourdes Academy when the heat set in. My brace had come off at the end of May, and, although I still had to wear the heavy brown corrective shoes, my limp was gone. "You ain't normal, yet, Thumper," Graceanne said. "Just less **peculiar**."

I walked from Lewis and Clark Hill, through the town, and usually stopped to catch crawdads in the drying puddles of the creek at Sulphur Springs Park. Edie was finishing up her medical technology certificate at Saint Audrain's. I guessed she passed the test about the hand, because it had disappeared from the porch, and she was taking other tests. My freedom and loneliness were almost complete. The only obligation I felt was Graceanne's plea that I be her lifeline between morning softball practice on the parade ground and "*Maximum* Lourdes Enrichment Penitentiary." When I joined her on the playground for lunch, she grilled me on Kentucky's batting average, on team temper tantrums, on uniform disputes, especially if anyone got number twenty-two, her lucky number.

By July, there was no more talk of her book, or drawings of the Martian astronomers. I thought she had forgotten them, after her long residence in the green Measles Room and her forced and fretting absence from the softball arena and her incarceration in summer school, but I hadn't forgotten.

One hot morning in early July, with everyone out of the house, I went into her room and lay down on her bed, crossing my legs and putting my hands under my head. I looked around. Graceanne didn't have any old dolls or dress-up clothes like Kentucky, or a teddy bear like I had Sergeant Useless. I remembered Peggy the Bride Doll she had gotten the last Christmas, but she had pulled that doll apart and given its legs and arms and brown wig and winking eyeballs to the dead kids as bribes to smuggle things like colored chalk into their classroom and put it on the chalk ledge to make Sister Clothilda twitch when she went to put a math problem on the board. Only white chalk was allowed in school, and it was funny when Sister caught herself writing with colored pieces. The dead kids would have smuggled worse than col-

ored chalk into school for Peggy's eyeballs, which made click-
ing noises when they blinked. Graceanne had begged for that
doll, whining for months until Edie gave in and got it for her.
Now the eyeless, wigless head was sitting on a chest of drawers, looking like a miniature plastic skull, like a part from a
robot factory.

The chest of drawers was next to the door, with Graceanne's softball glove on top next to Peggy's head. There was
a plastic basket with Graceanne's ironing next to the chest.
She had a little vanity dresser with a cloudy mirror next to
the ironing, and on the dresser's tiny shelf was a piggy bank
with a butter knife stuck in the slot, and a diary Grandma
had given her for Christmas, and a bowl full of rubber bands,
and a roll of masking tape that she sometimes used to hang
her clothes with because she'd gone through all her safety
pins mending her school uniforms.

I got off the bed and went to the vanity. I tried to pull the
knife out of the pig, but it was stuck so hard I was afraid I'd
break the bank. I opened the diary, but the pages were blank
and stiff with newness, their gold edges rubbery and thick. I
walked over to Graceanne's closet and opened the door. There
were a few uniform skirts hung up on hangers with tape, a
few white short-sleeved blouses, and her red winter coat. Back
in a corner on the floor was a pile of books. I sat down and
pulled them out. They were from the Cranepool's Landing
Public Library System. She had mostly science fiction and
mysteries, but they were not from the Young Adult Section
where she was supposed to check out books. These were adult
books. I flipped to the back of the first book and saw that it
had been due April 29. I checked all of the books. They were
all overdue. I looked around for a pencil, but, not finding one,
I did the math in my head. At two cents a day, with thirty-
one books, over sixty-four days, I figured Graceanne owed

$39.68. And since Graceanne didn't have any money, I thought, except what was stuck in her piggy bank, it was really Edie or Daddy who owed the library $39.68. I pushed the books back into the dark corner, wondering if Graceanne had read them all and if she knew they were overdue and what she was going to do about them.

I slid under her bed on my back and looked up at her bedsprings. The three notebooks with the red yarn tied through the spirals were shoved up between a couple of metal straps in the springs. I pulled Graceanne's book out and lowered it to my chest. The edges were all curled and dirty and grey. I rolled over and flipped through the notebook on top. I found the two sentences in my handwriting: "The Martian astronomers are making frantic appeals for more money today. Today Thumper found Ugly Blue Man." Now I thought it looked funny, as if the Martian astronomers were frantic *because* of Ugly Blue Man. I wanted to erase the sentence about Thumper, but there was no pencil.

There was more after that. I kept seeing a question and answer that was written all over, sometimes in the margins.

   3. What is the score?
     8 to 0

The score stayed the same, but the question and answer were written many times.

   3. What is the score?
     8 to 0

There were drawings of her tonsils and of a stick-figure doctor with big hands. There was a poem about springtime.

SPRINGTIME
by Gloria

River, river, flowing by
Dropped some muskrats with a sigh.
She wished she'd kept them in her bed
When kids did not respect the dead.

I didn't know who Gloria was, but I knew those muskrats. After the poem, the story of the astronomers from Mars started.

They have discovered a new pink substance that they use to patch all the holes in the night sky on Mars. Their telescopes are clean and ready. While the sky is under repairs, the astronomers wait and make notes.

I opened the volume to the front of the spiral notebook on the bottom. If Graceanne had added notebooks to the top as she went along, the bottom one would have the earliest entries. It seemed like starting a book somewhere in the middle. On the first page, in her rough script, it said:

I am Graceanne Regina Farrand. This is my book. This is private property. I live at 27 Lewis and Clark Hill in a brick house. I go to Our Lady of Lourdes Academy and I am in the sixth grade. My favorite things are

There was a blank, as if Graceanne couldn't think of any favorite things. She had started the book last year, because she was finishing the seventh grade this summer. So far the book was fairly legible, but when the story began, in the next line, the penciled lines became jagged, badly spaced, and darker, much darker. The writing was ugly.

> Once upon a time, there was a girl named Gloria Rosina Festitootitoo. She live in a big brick house that had a fabulous basement where she found an old radio like they had in the 1930s that you see in books about Hitler. The radio had nine knobs on the front, and each knob was shaped and colored like one of the planets known then. The radio was all dusty and was just thrown away until she found it.

The story seemed to suggest that other planets had been discovered since the radio had been thrown away, or since Hitler, and I wondered what they were called, and what color, and if they were populated, and if it was the astronomers on Mars who had discovered them. The story was interrupted at this point for a simple stick drawing of Adolf Hitler.

> Gloria Festitootitoo did not tell anyone about the radio because it was private property. She turned the knobs to listen to news from the other planets and even listened to the news from Earth but that was baseball scores that everyone knew. But the

Mars station was always scientists who told about the dreadful need for money for research. They were all astronomers on Mars, and they said that when they had learned everything in the universe, then everyone would be happy.

The story was halted there, and scraps of poems followed, as well as numbered lists. One poem said,

Roses are red
Violets are blue
Hitler is dead
Boo, hoo, hoo.

Some of the lists were an assorted and radical departure from our Lewis and Clark Hill legal code. One, under the heading "Hammurabi's Dinnertable Conversation," said,

1. Complain about the food.
2. Complain about religion.
3. Complain about politics.
4. If you say anything about sex, it better be something nice or you'll have to screw the cook.

The Catholic catechism, too, had undergone revision according to Graceanne:

MACKEREL CATECHISM

1. Who made you?
   God.
2. Why did God make you?
   To respect, respect, respect my mother in this world, and play softball in the next.

> 3. What is the score?
>   4 to 0

I lay under the bed and thought about the score. Between who and who? Which side was Graceanne on? Four what? Why Mackerel? And when had the score gone up?

It was hot under the bed and sweat dripped off my forehead onto the pages. I fanned the pages with my thumb, producing a wave of hot dusty air. I closed the bottom notebook and flipped open the middle one. There were more drawings and more lists and more of the story.

> Gloria turned the knob for Saturn and she heard
> the music of the circles. The circles turned and
> turned and squeaked against each other.

None of the planets received the same depth or repetition of attention that Graceanne gave Mars. The astronomers appeared again and again, always asking for more money— money for knowledge, knowledge so people could be happy. And frequently, catechism question number three showed up, but the score kept changing, going up.

> 3. What is the score?
>   7 to 0

I fanned the pages.

> 3. What is the score?
>   8 to 0

On the last page of the middle notebook, there was a drawing of a fish:

This is a MACKEREL.

A mackerel has prison bars on its back.

At the bottom of the page, it said, "When the astronomers learn everything, then everyone will be happy, even mackerels."

Eight

I put Graceanne's book back in the bedsprings and slid out into the room. I stood, thinking maybe I should start returning her books to the library, to keep the fine from going higher, but I worried about interfering in a design that had Graceanne's fingerprints on it. For all I knew, she was keeping the books out on purpose. I heard muffled noises out in the yard, and I went to the window. The glass panels were cranked open but not a breath of air was stirring, and the river looked yellow-brown and lazy, with the bad currents hidden under the skin, and Illinois seemed to have gotten closer. Two colored men were carrying furniture out of our house and down the front steps. I stared at them for a moment.

Then I grabbed Graceanne's lumpy feather pillow and ran out of her room. I jumped on the pillow and tried to use it to sail down the main staircase, but the pillow did not have the magic properties of the sheet, and I fell off, sliding down the stairs on my shorts and crashing into the wall and bannister poles on my way down. Before with the sheet, I could get a grip and hold on, pulling like I had a rudder, not having to think about it. Without the sheet, I was at the mercy of the wax and the hardwood. I crash landed on my stomach and shoulders in the front hall and skidded all the way to the front door.

The door was standing open. I saw the colored men carrying our old brown sofa across the lawn toward the back. Now that I was on the ground floor, I did not know where I was going so fast. Edie was at Saint Audrain's. Kentucky was across town on Leonard Wood Field at league practice for a special game with the Pike County team. That left Graceanne. I got up and raced out the door and headed for Maximum Lourdes Enrichment Penitentiary.

The town of Cranepool's Landing was dead silent, except for the dried mud I could hear cracking and whining as my heavy corrective shoes pounded over its parched surface. There wasn't anybody moving, not even behind windows and screen doors, and I was alone, and my house was being robbed by colored men, and I had a stitch in my side, and the air was so heavy with heat I seemed to be running through invisible molasses. I took the shortcut across Sulphur Springs Park. I stopped to drink from the thin, fast-running trickle of the creek that leapt around the small puddles in the stream bed. It tasted like a match when it's first lit.

By the time I got to the quiet school parking lot, my tongue felt like it was stuck to the roof of my mouth, the way it did when Kentucky gave me a French Lemon on my lips, but I started yelling "Graceanne, Graceanne," and she must have heard me or seen me through the windows because when I got to the tiled corridor she was standing in the door of the classroom in her uniform looking out.

"What ails you, Thumper?"

"You gotta come. There's colored men robbing our house."

She stepped back into the classroom. I bent over, clutching my knees, catching my breath and easing the stitch in my side, but I could see her talking to Sister, whose round face was beet red and shiny in the heat. Her black habit and veil must have weighed a ton and they were made out of wool. I knew that from the smell of the material when it got rained on.

Graceanne came out with her Penitentiary books and we walked outside the school together.

"Thumper, I guess you *are* almost a genius. The way you came flying up over the knoll and into the parking lot was **particularly** believable. You really got Sister going."

"Graceanne, it's true."

"I take it back. You are a full-fledged, 100 percent, all-American genius. You sprung me from the cooler, which I don't know why it's called that because it's like hell in there. Wait till I tell Tucka. Even with your IQ, I never thought you had any brains."

"Graceanne. Listen. There's two buck niggers carrying our parlor sofa across the lawn. They're both real big and they look mean as hell."

"You're shining the moon."

"No I'm not."

She smacked my ear with the side of her hand. "What the hell's the matter with you, Thumper, standing there telling lies like that?"

"I'm not lying." The heat shimmered between us. "You hit me again and I'll hit you back."

She put her books down on the steps. She gave me a long look and stepped back. She put some spit in her palms and rubbed it around. "You sure about that, Thumper?"

"I'm sure." I did the way she did with the spit.

She grabbed my shirt collar and marched me around the side of the church. It was cool over there because it was the north side and shady all day in the summer.

"You can still back out, Thumper, before I lay you out good."

"I'm not backing out."

"You want mercy, now's the time to ask for it."

"I don't want mercy."

We'd never had a formal fight before, with palm-spitting and the offer of Indian Mercy. She took off her glasses and put them on the low stone ledge of one of the stained-glass windows, which from the outside made Jesus and the women look grey and brown like mourning doves, their bright real colors invisible in the gloom behind the church. Graceanne always claimed she could see as well without her glasses as she could with them, but when she took them off, her left eye wandered, and that gave her face a weak look that made her look like she was surprised.

"You go first," I said, licking my lips. "You're the girl."

"You're damn right," she said, and she was all over me like a rash. She had me on the ground in about one second. Graceanne had a lot of places to grab, with her braids and her skinny arms and her loose clothes, and all I could do was hold on while she rolled me around the ground and whaled the daylights out of me.

I don't know what made me think I could take her, or even get a lick in. Maybe it was the heat. Hardly anybody ever messed with Graceanne, and, in Cranepool's Landing, kids who didn't get messed with had already proved something major. I knew that a big kid named Frank Handt had pulled a light pole out of the ground with his bare hands, and nobody messed with him, and I wondered what Graceanne had done to earn her reputation for nerves of steel and fists of iron and heart of fire, and if it had been a light pole, or maybe a grizzly bear.

I ended up on my back with her sitting on my shoulders, which were wedged against a rock, and I realized they hurt from my crash landing at the foot of the stairs. She was squeezing my head with her knees and her sharp shins stuck into my shoulders. And I turned my head and bit her leg.

She gasped. She stared down at me, her eyes bugging out, the left eye looking at something in the distance. "That's dirty!" she yelled. She reared back with her little fist and I could see her grinding her teeth and I knew she'd just been playing with me up to that point, and I wondered what the grizzly bear looked like. I closed my eyes and she landed her first real punch on my chin. My teeth jammed together and I thought my head would go shooting across the ground, and I knew she'd been going easy on me for nine years.

She got up off me and got her glasses. She came and stood over me. "Thumper, you *never* bite. That's dirty fighting. You don't use your mouth and you don't put anything in your hand. I'm ashamed of you."

I started bawling, more from shame than hurt. I'd never been in a formal fight before, but the rules had been drummed into us dead kids so we wouldn't fall into shame any more than we'd fall into the river.

"Stop your crying. It's undignified. You're not a little baby."

I couldn't make myself stop crying.

"I didn't hit you hard enough to make you cry. Something hurts you—you holler, boy. What a sissy."

I tried holding my breath to stop crying.

"Get up."

I rolled onto my knees and one of my teeth fell out onto the dry, rocky soil.

"You better pick that up. It's worth a dime."

I put the tooth in my pocket and stood.

"Stop that crying. You're makin' me puke."

I walked around the side of the church and headed for Lewis and Clark Hill, tears falling down my face and into the new gap in my teeth. Graceanne caught up with me after she picked up her Penitentiary books from the school steps.

"You gonna take it back about the niggers?"

"No. There's two niggers robbing our house."

"Real niggers?"

"No. They're plastic robot niggers from a plastic robot nigger factory down in St. Louis."

"You don't have to be **sarcastic**."

We walked on in silence across the cracking earth.

"Thumper?"

I didn't answer. I was sucking the space where my tooth was gone, tortured by a fear that I looked like Sister Clothilda now and awestruck by the sudden suspicion that Sister's missing tooth was also Graceanne's work.

"Thumper? Where'd you learn to be *sarcastic?*"

"At sarcasm school."

"Seems to me you've been learning *something somewhere.* You never tried to hit me back before."

"And I'm not ever going to try again."

"Nobody tries it on me more than once." She smiled like she regretted it.

"How come, Graceanne? You're not that big."

"Fighting has nothing to do with size. Fighting is willingness—and I could tell you didn't like it, Thumper."

"I'm sorry I bit you."

"You want to get a bad reputation in this town, Thumper, you'll bite somebody who ain't related to you."

We kept walking.

"Graceanne, what'd you ever do so nobody tries it on you much?"

"What're you talking about?"

"I mean, did you do something to make everyone think you're too tough to fight? Like Frank Handt and the light pole on the base?"

"Well, I ate three worms once, but that was just stupid."

"Oh."

"But there was the time all the kids sneaked out after midnight and went to French's Quarry to the swimming hole. I stayed under water for ten minutes, and I guess that did it."

"Ten minutes? Nobody can do that, can they?"

"Not if they don't find the little shelf I found under the water where there's a little cave and an air pocket. You tell anybody about this, I'll knock the rest of your teeth out."

I could see the heat waves rising from the ground. It was like looking at Cranepool's Landing through a pair of silk stockings hanging on a clothesline. It was so hot my nose was running and I could tell by the shiny look of Graceanne's nostrils that hers was running, too.

"Graceanne? Don't you care that our house is getting robbed?"

"Not much. There ain't nothing in there but Edie's blood kit and her needles and the rest of her play hospital crud. It's probably worth about a dollar ninety-five."

"What about all those overdue library books you've got in your closet? If the niggers take those, you'll owe sixty-two cents a day for the rest of your life."

"What the hell have you been doing in my room? Wait! Jesus, Mary, and Joseph," she hollered. "If they steal those, I'm home free. Edie'll never know they were overdue. Glory be, I'll go play sidewalk-superintendent for the colored men, and make sure they get 'em." She took off running across the broken, cracking earth, through the mist of the throbbing heat. She was faster even than Kentucky. I didn't think Edie would be any happier about paying for stolen books than she would be about paying for overdue books.

I took my time, stopping to rest and look in the window of the Crown Drugstore and Parks Department Store. In Parks there were tennis shoes that I thought would be a lot cooler than my corrective shoes. My feet were sweating like ice on a tar roof. When I got to the top of Lewis and Clark Hill, Graceanne was sitting on the picnic table eating a baloney sandwich and drinking a glass of milk. There was furniture all over the yard.

"What are you doing?" I asked.

"The order of the day is Keep Your Mouth Shut You Won't Catch Any Houseflies. The general-of-all-the-armies herself passed the command down to the troops."

"Mama's here?"

"Big as life and twice as nasty."

"What's she doing? Why's the furniture outside?"

"We're moving."

"Why?"

"Because the general's getting a divorce."

"Why?"

"Mental cruelty is what she said."

"What's that?"

"Making fun of Catholics and not coming home and tearing the phone out of the wall and being in a condition and striking her. That's what Edie said. She's being real nice to me today, but she said to eat and stay out of the way. Anyway, Thumper, since she's getting a divorce, and Daddy's G.I., we have to move."

"Why?"

"Because this house is G.I., and we're not."

"Why?"

"I don't know why, Thumper. That's just the way things are."

"What's G.I.?"

"Government Issue. Things the government owns."

"Where we moving?"

"That's the part where you do without the housefly supplements."

Edie came out the back door with Graceanne's ironing. Her piggy bank and her diary were on the top. "Graceanne Regina, come and fold your ironing. The men can't pack it like this. Charlemagne Victor, you go up to your room and pack anything you'll need for one night."

Graceanne hopped off the table and went to meet Edie.

I stared at the ironing basket. "Is Graceanne's bed G.I.?" I asked. Graceanne didn't wait for Edie's answer. She took off running for the house and I knew she was going after her book.

"Yes," Edie said. "Go pack up your things. Don't take more than you can carry yourself in your own two hands. What happened to your tooth, Charlie?" She put her freckled hands in her hair and pulled. "You children would try the patience of a saint. A broken tooth is all I need today. I don't know what I ever did to deserve demon children like you."

"I fell down the stairs."

That was nothing but the truth, I thought, and I hurried into the house and grabbed a stack of sliced baloney from the kitchen table. I rolled it so it would look like a hot dog and went up the stairs. Over the banister I could see the front parlor was empty except for Daddy's chair and the liquor cabinet and the TV and all the books on the wall shelves. I went to my room and put Sergeant Useless in my suitcase. There was hardly any room left, but I stuck in two pairs of socks and some underwear and I went to the bathroom for my toothbrush. When I came back, I looked around the room. There were only two things in that room that I had any feelings for: Sergeant Useless—that Graceanne had named and that she had used Kentucky's red nail varnish on to make mismatched boots—and my brace.

I took out the bear and closed my suitcase. Sergeant Useless and I took the brace up to the green Measles Room. We passed Graceanne in the hall and she said, "Where you going with that brace?"

"Mind your own business, Graceanne Regina."

"Well, hoity toy. I guess you think you're pretty smart."

The green Measles Room was empty, except for the bed and the cushion on the window seat. I put my brace down on the middle of the shiny floor, because it was G.I., and I put Sergeant Useless on the window seat because soldiers were G.I., and I made him lean against the screen so he could look out and watch for dead kids in the river.

Nine

When the house was all packed up, Edie made us wait on the curb with our suitcases and she went back to stand and look up at 27 Lewis and Clark Hill with her hands on her hips. Then she walked up the porch stairs and locked the door and took the key with her.

We set off walking down the Hill, going north toward the town, away from Jefferson Barracks. Graceanne was wearing her softball glove on her head to keep off the sun and she was carrying a big brown suitcase with both her hands gripped around the handle.

When we got to the Crown Drugstore, Edie put her night case down on the sidewalk and told us to stop.

"I want you children to hold your heads up high just as if we were going on a trip down the Nile on a fancy barge. Anybody stares at you, just put your little noses in the air. You can tell a lot about the quality of people just by the way they carry themselves, and you come of good quality."

"Where we going?" I asked.

"It's an adventure," Edie said. "We're going to the Lewis and Clark Hotel and we'll be treated like visiting royalty."

"Are we rich now, Mama?"

"No, Charlie. But we're just as good as anybody else and a fair sight better than some I could name."

Graceanne was staring off down the street. "What's Tucka gonna do about clothes tonight? She's too big to share with me."

"She packed her suitcase this morning and dropped it at the hotel on her way to practice."

"You told Tucka and you didn't tell us?" Graceanne threw one of her skinny legs over her suitcase and sat down. "That's not fair."

"Well, if you expect fairness from this world, Graceanne, you're going to be mighty disappointed. Kentucky is becoming more like a sister to me than a daughter, now that she's getting older, and I share all my secrets with her."

I could see Graceanne was looking sick. "Tucka know about this sister business?"

Edie grabbed Graceanne's glove off her head and gave her a look. "Are you being smart?"

"No, ma'am. Not very smart."

"Get up off that suitcase and stop acting like a boy."

"What's like a boy about the way I'm sitting?"

"A lady doesn't spread her legs apart like that. It's not nice. You never saw Queen Elizabeth sit like that."

"I never saw Queen Elizabeth do anything. Besides, I think it looks a lot grosser when boys do it."

"Have you been peeking at boys?"

"No, ma'am. Just Charlie."

"Well, see that you don't. I won't have you getting a reputation, Graceanne Farrand."

Edie put Graceanne's glove back on her head and picked up her night case and we followed her past Parks Department Store and around the corner to the Lewis and Clark Hotel. It was three stories high, made out of red brick, with dark green shutters and dirty windows. Every building in Cranepool's Landing had dirty windows then, because the dust from the cracking earth breathed off the land all day and settled down all night.

Inside there were red rugs on the polished wood floor and brass pots and a big desk I couldn't see over. Graceanne's glasses came up just over the top of the desk. She pinched my arm and made me get up on her suitcase so I could see.

"Get down from there, Charlemagne," Edie said. "Mind your manners and don't twist your foot."

I got down and stood there, leaning against the desk and watching Graceanne's glasses. She was running them along the top of the desk in the shadow made by her softball glove and walking along so her face would keep up with them. Edie reached out and grabbed her by the arm and the glove fell on the floor. I could see the nails on her freckled hand digging into Graceanne's skinny arm.

I saw Graceanne's eyes close behind her glasses and she jerked her head. The glasses went flying onto the floor and the left lens cracked. "Look at what you did!" Graceanne said in a loud voice. "You broke my glasses. Now how'm I gonna go back to the Penitentiary?"

"Hush," Edie said, looking around, her hand still around Graceanne's arm. "Don't make such a scene."

"You started it!"

"How dare you!" Edie squeezed Graceanne's arm tighter. "Just who do you think you are, addressing me in that tone?" Edie gave it a shake but didn't let go of her. "Pick up your glasses."

"I can't till you let go of me."

Edie let her go and Graceanne stooped and picked up her glasses and put them on. The crack was right in front of her eye. She stood up and put her forehead against the desk. There were little half-moon red marks on her arm.

Collier Rodgers came out of an office and walked behind

the desk. He was Tyler Rodgers's older brother, and he was the one who had hung up the hide-and-seek tire swing for us a couple years back. He was home from Notre Dame for the summer, clerking in the hotel where a lot of military families stayed when they came to visit their men at the Barracks.

"Can I help you, Mrs. Farrand?"

"Good afternoon, Collier. How's your mother?"

"She's fine."

"She doing much baking in this weather?"

"No, ma'am, but she's putting up her pickles. She had to buy the cucumbers from Knowell's Market, because her vines dried up like everything else in Cranepool's Landing."

"Well, that's a shame, Collier. They won't be as good if they're store bought." Edie took a deep breath like she didn't want to say what she came for. "I need a single room for the night."

"A single?"

"That's right. A single."

"Well, I've got plenty of singles, but are the kids staying, too?"

"Of course. Where I go, they go. Whether I like it or not, ha ha."

Collier looked at Edie. "Do you want me to send up a cot or anything?"

"Is it extra?"

"Two dollars."

"We won't need a cot. Just a regular single."

Collier and Edie traded some papers back and forth and then she paid cash for one night.

"Need help with your bags? I can call a bellboy."

"No thank you, Collier. The children are my little bellboys. Ready children?"

Graceanne had her forehead pressed against the desk. "I'm not your bellboy. I'm your slave and your property."

Edie's hand shot out and she grabbed Graceanne's arm again. "You want me to take you outside and shake some sense into you, Graceanne?"

"No, ma'am."

We followed Collier to the elevator and stood around until the door opened. It was so hot inside the elevator Graceanne said it felt like sticking her hand inside an oven. Collier stood by the button panel and didn't look at us.

"Collier," Graceanne said, "do bellboys get paid?"

"They just get tips."

"What's a tip?"

"Money folks give you for helping them with their suitcases and all."

We got out on the third floor, which was almost as hot as the elevator. Collier opened the door right across from the firestairs and went in to open the windows.

"I'm sorry it's so hot, Mrs. Farrand. We have to keep the windows closed on account of the dust."

Edie stepped into the room. "Do you think we could have a fan, Collier?"

"I'll see what I can do. I'll bring it up myself so it won't cost you extra."

She put her hand on Collier's arm like he was family. "Thank you. You're good people, Collier."

"Thank you, Collier," Graceanne said, after Edie said it. "You're good people."

He turned red and left.

Graceanne dragged her suitcase into the room and looked around. "Who's sleeping on the bed?"

"Never mind that now. Let me look at those glasses." She took Graceanne's glasses from her face and sat on the bed. She turned them over in her hand. "The scratch didn't go all the way through." She handed the glasses back to Graceanne. "Put your things over against that wall so they won't be underfoot and take your brother for a walk."

"It's hot outside."

"It's hot everywhere."

"Can we go to Tucka's Pike County game?"

"*May* we go to Kentucky's game. Put your glasses on."

Graceanne put them on. "*May* we go to Kentucky's game?"

"I reckon that's all right, but you have to have some sensible limitations first. As long as your glasses are broken, you better not run. I'll give you seventy-five cents, but you have to split it even between you. No candy. There'll be a lot of colored people around Leonard Wood Field and you better not talk to them. There's nothing wrong with colored people; it's just not polite to go up and talk to them. They take it as a liberty."

"You can't split seventy-five cents even," I said.

Edie stared at me. "Don't you be a know-it-all, Charlemagne Farrand."

"Is that all?" Graceanne asked.

"Be back by six o'clock."

"How'm I supposed to know what time it is?"

"Ask somebody, Graceanne."

"But not a nigger, right? Even if they've got the only watch?"

"Don't say that word."

"What are you gonna do while we're gone?"

"I'm going to take an aspirin and have a Quiet Hour." Back on Lewis and Clark Hill, Edie's Quiet Hours meant no talking, not even in whispers, no going outside, no baths, no flushing toilets.

Edie gave Graceanne three quarters and we left. We played around in the elevator for a while, but it was so hot we started smelling each other. When Graceanne said I was ripe, we went into the hotel lobby and Graceanne got Collier to get his car and drive us to Leonard Wood Field. When we got out, she said, "Thank you, Collier. You're good people." She tried to give him one of our quarters but he wouldn't take it so she patted his arm like Edie had done.

Graceanne gave me all the money and went to catch for the pitcher loosening up on the side of the field. The bleachers were mostly empty, what with the heat and Pike County being a long drive and whatever team Kentucky was on always won anyway and it was boring. I sat under the bleachers in the shade and started worrying about Edie looking in Graceanne's suitcase and finding her book. Then I worried about where we were moving to. Then I worried about Graceanne's glasses. Then I thought about clean fighting. Edie hadn't bitten Graceanne in the hotel lobby, and she didn't put anything into her hand that I could see when she latched on to Graceanne's arm, and nobody ever said you couldn't fight if you were bigger than the other person. But I did know one rule the dead kids had been told over and over: You couldn't go after a person who wore glasses without falling into shame.

Ten

*K*entucky explained mental cruelty when we walked back to the Lewis and Clark Hotel from Leonard Wood Field. Like many things I heard her say in her sweet, whispery, silvery voice, mental cruelty reminded me of a church song, a Christmas carol, a story about the baby Jesus. No matter what she really meant, her words made me think of blossoms in the snow and about no room at the inn and about the herald angels.

"Mental cruelty's like spooking a person. They get so they never know what you're gonna do next and their head hurts and they have to take Quiet Hours."

"Then Mama ought to divorce me," Graceanne said, happy like she'd just discovered the recipe for white paint. Her voice wasn't anything but a solid Missouri twang like the rest of the river kids, without any snow blossoms. "I never knew it had that name, but I've been giving her mental cruelty for all my life. She says I'm a born nuisance and a terror from hell."

"You can't get mental cruelty from your own child," Kentucky said. "You can only get it from *a man*."

"Is Daddy fixing to live on Lewis and Clark Hill by himself?"

"I expect he'll live on the base, and the army will give our house to some other family. It's family housing."

"You think they'll have kids?"

"Wouldn't be a family without kids, Graceanne. Don't be so stupid."

"Think they'll go down the stairs on their butts and eat bread, butter, and sugar sandwiches and puke in the green Measles Room?"

"Not if they've got any sense."

"They sound like a passel of sissies."

"You think everybody's a sissy, Graceanne."

"Not everybody. Just the sissies." She was holding her braids in her hands and jerking her head back and forth. "Are we poor now?"

"We've always been poor."

"Well, are we really poor?"

"Mama says poor as church mice."

"Well, well. Poor as church mice. Well, well." She kept jerking her head with her braids. "I guess we'll be gnawing the collection basket with our sharp little teeth come winter."

"Maybe. We sure as hell ain't gonna be putting anything in it. Mama said that tithing has her worried silly."

Graceanne took off walking faster and it was too hot to try catching her, so I just walked along with Kentucky, carrying her bat and swinging it at dust vents. It was almost six o'clock, when the day started cooling down and the dust puffs came out of the ground in little grunts.

"Tucka?"

"What?"

"Does Mama tell her secrets to you?"

"What secrets?"

"*Her* secrets."

"Mama don't even know what her own secrets are, her head's so full of grandeur and the great ladies of history that never sweated, or wore their shirts tucked out, or had children as bad as we are. How's she gonna tell me any secrets? Mama's crazy."

"You mean it?"

"Don't you go telling her I said that. I'll say you made it up and I'll whale you within an inch of your life."

"Young man," I said.

"What?"

"You didn't say *young man*. You're supposed to say, 'I'll whale you within an inch of your life, *young man*.' "

She pulled my hair, but not hard. "Well, look who's getting smarty pants."

I couldn't see Graceanne ahead of us anymore. "Tucka, what's Mama's IQ?"

"She doesn't have an IQ. They only give those to kids. But she's real smart. You can tell by the way she studies those medical books and remembers all about hemoglobin and pro-thrombin time and glucose tolerance." Blossoms in the snow, glucose tolerance, I thought, they were all the same when Kentucky said them like an angel.

We were at the corner and I could see the big sign for the Lewis and Clark Hotel already lit up even though it lacked a couple hours to dark-thirty, which was the year-round name for sunset time in Cranepool's Landing. There was Graceanne hauling a big suitcase up the steps into the hotel with her two hands and talking a mile a minute to a man walking beside her. They went in through the door. We went into the hotel and there they were, standing by the elevator, Graceanne still beating her gums. When the door opened, they got inside and I was going to follow, but Kentucky grabbed me by the collar.

We waited until the elevator came back down and Graceanne stepped off.

"What are you doing?" I asked.

"Painting the picket fence. What does it look like I'm doing, Thumper? Sometimes I wonder if you're right in your head." She went back outside and stood on the stairs. Kentucky and I took the elevator up to the third floor.

"Where's your sister?" Edie said when we got to the room. Her hair was all shiny like she'd had a bath and the room smelled like Prell shampoo and there was steam coming out of the bathroom.

"She's downstairs in the lobby playing Hotel," Kentucky said. "Want me to go fetch her?"

"No. Leave the child be. We'll get her when we go down to dinner. You two go wash the stink off."

I tried to go into the bathroom but Kentucky pushed me aside and went in and closed the door. I sat on the bed and watched Edie brush her hair. Edie saw me looking at her in the mirror and said, "You're the quiet one of the family, Charlemagne. You'll probably grow up to be a judge, or a scientist. Still waters run deep."

"Tucka's the beauty, isn't she, Mama?"

"That's right."

"What's she gonna be when she grows up?"

"Oh, she'll be a singer, maybe at Carnegie Hall. Coloratura sopranos don't grow on every tree."

"What about Graceanne?"

Edie looked at herself in the mirror. "Graceanne? She'll surprise us all, that one. Graceanne could be anything she wanted to be if she'd just straighten up and fly right. Charlie, Graceanne has more brains in her little finger than most folks have in their heads. She'll never be a beauty, but God gave her brains to make up for that. The Good Lord always gives for what he takes away." Edie let her eyes slide over the mirror. "You might not think it to look at me now, but I used to be quite pretty. Your father says I look just like Merle Oberon." She turned on the lamp on the dresser and it lit up her face.

"Yes, Mama." I didn't know who Merle Oberon was, but I took a look at Edie to see what her face was like. It was round and she had a small nose and blue eyes and thin eyebrows and her jaw was kind of square like Graceanne's. Next to Edie's face I could see my face in the mirror beside the lamp. My eyes were dark and my face was long and my skin wasn't freckled like hers.

"Who do I look like, Mama?"

"You look like Don's father. He was a handsome man, Charlie. Looks run in the family."

"Like brains?"

"Brains and looks. If we had money, we'd be perfect, wouldn't we, Charlie?" She laughed.

"I like the way Graceanne looks."

"Well, we'll see what we'll see."

Kentucky came out of the bathroom and I scooted in.

Edie took us to the Crown Drugstore for hamburgers and milk. That was the first time I ever ate in a restaurant. There were a couple of men eating with their hats on, and Edie gave them a frown. We sat at the counter on stools under a big fan. Graceanne and I couldn't reach the floor with our feet, so we swung around while we ate but Edie didn't say anything for us to stop it. It was hot in the Crown, and Graceanne asked to be excused so she could go back to the hotel.

"But I'm going to buy us all lime sherbet in cones so we can eat it going back, Graceanne. That'll cool us off."

"I want to go back now. I'm full."

Edie let her go, and when Graceanne jumped off the stool I heard her jingle when she hit the floor. I knew she had money in her pocket and I wondered where she got it.

We went for a walk and ate lime sherbet in sugar cones and it was getting on about dark-thirty when we got to the hotel. The lobby was quiet and there was no sign of Graceanne. We went up in the elevator and Edie opened the door. Graceanne was sitting on the bed and she had a fan going on the floor by the window.

"Get off the bed, Graceanne," Edie said. "Your shoes are dirty. Oh, look, Collier brought up the fan. Bless his kind heart."

"Bless Collier's kind heart," Graceanne said and she rolled off the bed and stood on the other side. "Who's sleeping where, Mama?"

"You and Charlie can sleep on the rugs. Your sister and I will share the bed." She went into the bathroom and shut the door. Graceanne sat on the floor and looked like she was thinking it over. Kentucky just stood by the dresser.

Finally, Kentucky whispered in her sweet voice, "This ain't fair. Graceanne, you sleep with her."

"I'm sleeping on this rug." She pulled the little throw rug to her and gave it a hug.

"Charlie can sleep with her."

Graceanne made a few low pig noises. "Charlie's a boy. He can't sleep with Mama."

"Then I'll sleep on the floor, too."

"There's only two throw rugs."

"I don't need a rug."

"Mama won't let you sleep on the bare floor like a Red Indian."

"Kiss my ass."

"Kiss your own ass."

"I ought to wallop you upside the head and draw your blood good."

I could see Graceanne's teeth start grinding.

"Graceanne's blood is poisonous," I whispered.

"I'm AB negative poisonous, all right." Graceanne got up quietly and started dancing around on the floor, dust from the rug flying out of her braids, her fingers wiggling over her head. She kept her voice down for once, but she was making that jingling noise. "I'm AB negative poisonous. I'm AB negative poisonous."

The bathroom door opened and we settled down quick and acted like we hadn't been carrying on. "Well, you all look good and tired," Edie said. "Get washed up and Kentucky can sing to us. That'll put us in a mind to sleep."

"It'll put me in a mind to puke," Graceanne said. "Dibs on the bathroom." She ran in and shut the door.

Edie bent over the bed and tossed the pillows off to Kentucky. "The younger children can have the pillows since you and I get to get the bed. You fix it for them."

"I ain't." Kentucky stood there not moving.

Edie straightened up. "What did you say?"

"I ain't."

"What kind of talk is that?"

"It's English."

"It's not proper English. What do you mean you *ain't*?" I looked at Edie's freckled hand dangling over the bed and it was all tight but it wasn't in a fist. She took a step around the bed and reached to slap Kentucky's face with the back of her hand, but Kentucky's fist shot out and she had Edie's wrist so hard Edie's freckled hand started turning purple where Kentucky's red fingernails had her. "What do you mean grabbing me like that, young lady?"

"I'm too old for you to hit me, Mama."

Kentucky's voice sounded sweet like when she was in the choir loft and sang "Fall on your knees" on Christmas Eve and for the first time I noticed that she was taller than Edie and had more flesh, but if it came to choosing which one to fight I'd still want Kentucky because her eyes didn't look wild and mean.

Suddenly the bathroom door came flying open and Grace-anne jumped out. "Look what I found," she screamed. "Silverfish!"

Edie whirled around and Kentucky dropped her hand. Graceanne had four long shiny bugs in her palm and she was holding them out to Edie.

"Where'd you get those filthy things?"

"I found 'em in the tub under the drain sucker. At first I thought they were coins when I didn't have my glasses on. They're good luck, Mama."

"Throw them out the window."

"That'll kill 'em," Graceanne said, backing away and closing her fist around the silverfish. "And kill all the luck."

"I said to get rid of those creatures."

Graceanne went and leaned her head and both arms out over the window sill. Dust was blowing around her in hot breaths. She held her fist out over the street. She drew her arm back like she was going to make a play at the plate, flicked her arm, and let go.

"Now that's enough shenanigans for one night," Edie said. "It's like being trapped in a closet with a tribe of Red Indians in here. Everybody get in bed."

When Edie turned her back, Graceanne stuck out her tongue at her.

I scooted into the bathroom. When I came out, Edie was lying down and Kentucky was next to her, turned over on her side. Graceanne was on the floor. I got down on my rug and put my head on the pillow and took my tooth from my pocket and slid it between the rug and the pillow.

"Mama?" Graceanne said. "Where we moving to?"

"Turn off that lamp."

Graceanne got up and turned off the lamp.

"Mama?"

"What?"

"Do I have to go to Summer Enrichment tomorrow?"

"No. I can't spare you."

"Mama?"

"What now?"

"Why are we staying in this hotel?"

"Because we can't get in to our new house until tomorrow, but the colored men had to come to Lewis and Clark Hill today. It's a two-day job, and they won't work on the holiday."

It got quiet for a while, but Graceanne was rooting around on her rug like a little pig, and Edie told her she had to hush so the rest of us could get some sleep.

"I thought Kentucky was gonna sing to us," Graceanne said.

"Be quiet."

"A song sure would be nice. Might help Charlie sleep."

Kentucky sat up and hollered at Graceanne. "You said it would make you puke if I sang."

"Puking helps *me* sleep."

"Be quiet," Edie said. "It's too hot for songs."

"It's not too hot for puking," Graceanne said.

"*Be quiet.*"

I was lying there on the rug smelling the dust when something dropped on my forehead. I rubbed my hand on it and it crawled down my head. I opened my eyes. Graceanne had her hand over my face and the silverfish were shining in the dark and about to slide off of her fingers.

"I thought you threw them out," I whispered.

"Imagine wasting good silverfish like that. They bring you luck, Charlie. Close your eyes and I'll drop 'em on your head again."

I closed my eyes and Graceanne dropped the other bugs on me.

"You should save one for yourself," I whispered.

"Don't forget to put your tooth under your pillow."

Eleven

*W*hen I woke up I put my hand under my pillow. There was a quarter and a little note on Lewis and Clark Hotel paper from the dresser drawer. It said, "Payment in full for one tooth. TF." It was Graceanne's handwriting. The silverfish were gone, crawled away into the woodwork, I guessed.

Graceanne was still asleep. I looked at her bony little face for a while. She had the smoothest skin I ever saw, except for a tiny scar on her cheek that looked like a puckered little white spider. I reached over with my finger and touched her cheek. I never touched anything so soft.

"What're you touching me for, Thumper? Think I want your goddamn cooties?"

"Let's have some quiet down there," Edie said. "You could wake the dead with that noise."

The sun was up and it was getting hot and Graceanne and I were lying there trying not to make noise. I could hear Edie moving on the sheets.

"Can I get up and use the toilet, Mama?" Graceanne said.

"Just use it and don't ask. You act like you're in jail."

Graceanne was gone a long time. When she came back her head was all wet and she had soap in her braids.

"Turn your head, Thumper." I did and I could hear her open her suitcase. After a while she said, "Okay."

"It's like Grand Central Station in here," Edie said. She got up and went into the bathroom.

Kentucky sat up in the bed. "Mama kicks like a mule when she sleeps. Next time it's your turn, Graceanne."

"I can't sleep with nobody on account of my poison blood."

"You oughta stop making up lies about your blood. People are gonna think you're some kind of monster."

"I am a monster." Graceanne looked happy and she went over to the window and sat on the ledge. She had on blue shorts and a clean white blouse that looked like she'd ironed it herself and blue socks and her tennis shoes. Her hair was wet and sleeked down on her head, the way it was when she'd washed it without taking the braids out. She smelled like shampoo.

Edie came out of the bathroom. She had the bottle of Prell in her hand. "Graceanne, did you take a bath in this shampoo?"

"Yes, ma'am. There's no soap in there."

"It's in my night case. God give me courage, girl, how can I afford you? Get off that window before you fall out."

"I thought you'd be happy I was respectable and clean. Just when I was thinking what a nice day it was, come to find out you can't afford me. You gonna take me back where I came from like a new dress you don't like after all?" Graceanne gave Edie a long look. "Or maybe you'd like it if I went and fell out the window." She leaned back a little and held her arms out at her sides and stuck her chin out like she was asking Edie to hit her through the open window.

Edie took a breath through her nose and went back into the bathroom.

Graceanne jumped off the windowsill. "I'll be downstairs.

When the Empress of all the Russias thinks up another nasty thing to say, tell her I fell out the window and there's gonna be a memorial parade out in front of the hotel. Tell her everybody's talking about it and offering a prize for the best float."

Kentucky threw herself back on the bed and pulled the sheet all the way up over her head. When the bathroom door opened, I jumped up.

"Oh, no you don't, Charlie," Kentucky said. "I'm going first."

"I'm about to burst."

"Go ahead and see if I care."

"Let Charlie go first," Edie said. "It's a well-known fact that women can control their urine better. You can help me shake the wrinkles out of my good black dress."

When we got downstairs with all the luggage, Edie wearing her good black dress and her little black suedes, Graceanne was standing outside the elevator door with a dark green suitcase and a hatbox.

"What are you doing, Graceanne?" Edie asked. "Where'd you get that suitcase?"

"It belongs to that nice lady at the front desk. I told Collier I'd get it upstairs."

"Charity begins at home, miss, so you can just drop that stuff and help us with these. I never heard of such a thing as bothering Collier with your nonsense."

"But, Mama, I promised."

"Never mind that now. I'm surprised at you, Graceanne."

"No, you're not."

"Don't you be so fresh." Edie gave Graceanne a shake and took her night case and went in to the lobby. Graceanne dragged the green suitcase into the elevator. Kentucky and I got off with our suitcases.

"Wait here," Graceanne said. "I'll be right back. Pretty

soon I'll have enough money in tips to hire us a goddamn
maid."

We waited for Graceanne and then we all went to the lobby
together.

"Can I get you a cab, Mrs. Farrand?" Collier was saying
over the desk.

"No thanks, Collier. It's such a nice day, I believe we'll
walk. Come, children."

The sun was burning over our heads and the dust was lying
on the air like fog and the silence was so thick and gritty it
hurt my ears. All I could hear was our footsteps on the
cracked ground and our suitcases dragging. The dust was
turning Edie's good black dress brown. We walked and
dragged until we got to Sulphur Springs Park where we
waited for the McBain Avenue bus. We rode into the north
part of town on Leonard Wood Road that separated Maple
Heights on one side from the Developments on the other. We
got off the bus at McBain Avenue and turned toward the
river.

"This is Nigger Town," Graceanne said.

"Don't use that word," Edie snapped. "It's unkind and
it'll get you in trouble in this neck of the woods."

"That's what everybody calls it."

"You never heard me call it that. And you never will. It's
the Developments, and many people as white as us live here."

"Look at all the spooks staring at us."

Dark faces in the windows of the Developments watched
us as we walked down McBain Avenue. There were new pink
and yellow and blue blocks of stucco set down on gravel lots,
but they were mixed in with tiny old houses, white little
things with green shutters that looked like they were ready to
fall down. But the tiny houses all had real yards with grass
and trees. The colored men with our furniture were waiting
for us in a truck in front of a house that looked like a blue

Saltines box. It was standing in a gravel lot that threw off the heat like a skillet fire.

"Is this our new house?" Graceanne said. She took off her glasses and looked at the crack in them and put them back on. "It's the most **depressing** thing I ever saw."

"Just the top half on the left is ours," Edie said. "That's all I can afford. There's four apartments in all. You'll like this, you'll see. I just wish it wasn't blue, but it's all ours and we don't have to answer to anyone as long as I pay the rent."

Edie went up the tall concrete stairs and opened the door with a key. The colored men started bringing up our furniture. We just sat on our suitcases on the gravel, looking around. A colored girl was staring at us over a metal fence next to the gravel lot. The yard she was standing in had a real house, a little white box with green shutters like all the old houses and a maple tree. She stared at us, and at the movers, and at the blue development house. Her face was shiny and dark, and her hair stuck out all over her head, and her eyes stayed on us like they were made out of glass.

"What are you staring at?" Graceanne said. "We got horns or something?"

"Friday night's cuttin' time. I'm staring so I can slice out your liver 'thout having to feel your skinny bones with my knife."

"Why don't you slice it out right now? I'm busy Friday night."

Kentucky started to pull Graceanne's hair but she was already up and on her way to the fence.

"What's your name?" Graceanne said.

"Wanda Gladwill."

"Wanda Gladwill, why don't you step down to the sidewalk so I can show you where my liver is?"

"Well, ain't she sweet? White girl gonna show me her liver for free."

"I didn't say for free."

"What's your price, white girl?"

"I'm gonna pull your butt out through your throat."

"Ooooh. I'm scared. White trash gotta bad mouth."

"What I've got is a **substantial** vocabulary, Wanda Gladwill."

Graceanne walked slowly along the fence to the sidewalk, trailing her hand on the metal links.

"You better do something, Tucka," I said, pulling her arm. "She'll kill Graceanne."

"Graceanne wouldn't fight nobody she didn't think she could take. She's as tough as hickory and smart as a whip. Besides, we gotta live here now. Better Graceanne should learn now than later."

"Why?"

"Better to measure out that girl in the broad daylight than wait for night. If it gets bad, I'll go in and slam both their heads together."

Wanda took her time walking down to the sidewalk just like Graceanne had done. Graceanne put some spit in her hands and rubbed it around, keeping her eyes on Wanda.

"Graceanne! Your glasses!" I hollered. "They're already broke."

"You stay outta this, Thumper. I know what I'm doing."

Wanda gave her a look. "What the boy says is so. I cain't fight you with glasses."

"You can't fight me without 'em, 'cause I gotta see what's in your hand."

Wanda held out her hands to Graceanne and showed her they were empty. Kentucky told me to stay put and she went over to the end of the fence.

"If I see anything dirty," she said, "I'll wipe you both on the ground." She held out her hand and Graceanne gave her the glasses.

I never saw anything happen faster. Graceanne leapt for Wanda's head and had her on the ground before I blinked. They punched each other and pulled each other and sat on each other and breathed hard and dripped sweat on each other and never said a word, not even cursing. When I could see Graceanne's face, it looked like she was thinking up what to do next. I got up and went to the fence. Graceanne and Wanda were rolling around slowly on Wanda's rocky yard. I thought something was wrong, they were moving so slow.

"How come they're moving so slow?" I asked.

"They're like fighting their shadows," Kentucky said. "They can't either of them win. It'll be over soon."

After about another minute, Kentucky went and pulled them apart. They lay there on the ground, looking at the hot sky, breathing hard. I saw a tear fall from Graceanne's wandering eye, but it wasn't from crying. It was sweat.

"You all about done?" Kentucky asked. "I wanta go see my new house."

"I'm done," Graceanne said.

"I'm done," Wanda said.

Kentucky was turning to walk away when Graceanne suddenly yelled, "Look out!" I saw Wanda pull a little knife out of her shorts and flick it into the maple. Its thin black handle shivered but the blade held good in the tree.

"What the hell'd you pull a knife for?" Graceanne screamed.

Wanda just lay there and didn't say anything. Kentucky went and pulled the knife out of the tree and looked at it. She closed it up and threw it on it on the ground. Then she looked at Graceanne. "She was showing you she had it, Graceanne."

Graceanne got up off the ground and walked back to our side of the fence. She looked at Wanda like she thought she might disappear in a puff of dust from the ground.

We went and got our suitcases from the gravel.

"Who won?" I asked.

"Nobody," Graceanne said.

"Why not?"

"Like as not, it was the heat."

"You gonna fight her again?"

"Maybe."

We went inside. The furniture was too much for the little apartment. There were only three rooms, lined up in a row, and even without the G.I. pieces we had left on Lewis and Clark Hill, we could hardly find room to walk. Edie was sitting out on the back porch and we went out there. The porch was up on a set of nine wooden steps that you could see under because they weren't finished all the way through. An old brown and white dog was chained to a doghouse and his chain had scraped a smooth pit in the cracked earth and gravel in a perfect circle that ran around his house. Kentucky and I went down to pet him.

"Put out your hands and let him smell you first," Edie said. "A chained up dog can be mean."

He jumped up on us, wagging his shaggy tail and whining. "Look, Mama. He's lonely," Kentucky said. She scratched his ears and made noises at him and he rolled over on his back to scoot his spine over the dirt. I'd never seen such a happy dog.

"Come down here and see this dog, Graceanne," I said.

"I can see him from here."

Kentucky and I sat down on the edge of the dog's pit and let him lick our shoes.

Edie put her fingers on her mouth the way she always did. "Children, it's time and more to let you know what quarter the wind is in. Tomorrow's the holiday, and the day after that I start my job at Saint Audrain's. They're going to pay me three hundred and twenty-seven dollars a month. That's not enough to live on, so on most nights I'll have to take call."

"What's call?" Graceanne said. She was standing behind Edie on the stairs and was sticking her two fingers up behind Edie's hair to make Devil's horns.

"That means I'll have to stay by the telephone and when the hospital calls for an emergency, I'll have to go—day or night."

"We still have to go to school at the Penitentiary?"

"You children are lucky to get a Catholic education. The sisters are giving us a reduced tuition rate because of our trouble, which is an answer to my prayers."

"How are we gonna get to school?"

"You'll take the bus. And you girls will have to come right home after so you can get dinner on the table. There won't be any going down to the parade ground to play. You'll be women grown, tending house."

"Doesn't Charlie have to tend house? He eats, too. He eats like a tiger."

"Charlie'll do his share."

"Oh, yeah? What's he gonna do?"

"You never mind about Charlie's business. Now, you all go in and find your swimming suits. We're going to Hulen's Lake as soon as the colored men are done. It's hot enough to roast a turkey on this side of town."

"Can we go back to Lewis and Clark Hill when they have the raking contest in the fall?"

"We'll see. You all go on in and find your suits."

I didn't want to leave the dog there all by himself. He was whining and dragging his rump over the ground when we started to get up. "Can I give him some water, Mama?"

"Get away from that dog," Edie said all of a sudden. "He's got worms."

"He does not," I said.

"Look at how he's rubbing his hind end on the ground. He's got worms all right. Get away from there."

Kentucky and I backed away and went up the stairs. Graceanne was staring at the dog. Kentucky pinched Graceanne's arm on the way into the apartment. "You're scared of the dog, Graceanne."

"No, I'm not."

"Yes you are."

I looked at Graceanne. She was chewing her lip.

Inside the furniture was stacked up against the walls and all over the floor.

"It looks like the county dump in here," Graceanne said.

Edie gave her a little slap on the arm. Dust rose out of her shirt sleeve.

"We'll soon have it looking like white people live here, you'll see," Edie said. "I swear, Graceanne, you can pick up dirt just by being in the same state with it. When we left the hotel you were clean."

Graceanne rubbed her hands together. "I'm gonna call this place the McBain Sanitation Facility."

"No you ain't," Kentucky said. "I already dibsed it and we're gonna call it Fort McBain, because it sounds like we're still stuck with KP all the time."

Edie sniffed. "When you've done as much kitchen patrol as I have, then you can complain."

We found our things and Edie went into the bathroom to change out of her good black dress. While she was in there, I went through the kitchen boxes and found a cake pan and sneaked out and gave the dog some water. When Edie paid the men we went out onto the gravel and she locked the door. I could see Wanda's dark face, and her glassy eyes were looking at us through the window of her house.

"Hey!" Graceanne shouted. "Hey! Wanda Gladwill!"

"Hush," Edie said. "Don't make that infernal racket. What

will our new neighbors think if you stand there braying like a mule, like you haven't been taught better?"

Wanda came out and stood at the fence and looked at us.

"You want to go swimming?" Graceanne said.

"Where you going?"

"Down to Hulen's Lake."

"Go take a flying leap. That's Whites Only."

Wanda went back to her house and sat down under the maple.

On the bus, Graceanne said, "What's **Whites Only?**"

Edie took a deep breath and looked sad. "It's a terrible thing, Graceanne, but no Negroes are allowed to swim in Hulen's Lake. It's un-Christian and anti-American and really backward. But that's the way it is in Missouri. There's a lot of ignorance and meanness and intolerance. It's prejudice and fear."

"Well, I didn't want to bring all the Negroes," Graceanne said. "Just Wanda."

"I'm proud of you for being above prejudice. That's exactly how I'd expect a daughter of mine to behave. How did you come to know that girl's name already?"

"I asked her."

"Well, good for you, Graceanne. It's important that we get off on the right foot in the Developments."

Twelve

*H*ulen's Lake was crowded, because it was The Day Before The Holiday, which in Cranepool's Landing was almost as important as Independence Day. It wasn't like French's Quarry where the Lewis and Clark Hill kids went swimming. There was a beach and the water was warm and there was a pavilion and a hundred-foot slide that started on a hill and a place to rent paddleboats and a whole arm of the lake blocked off from the rest by a hanging fence of honeysuckle and it cost a quarter apiece to get in.

Edie said she was going to have her Quiet Hour there on the army blanket she was spreading out. Graceanne and Kentucky were looking at the slide like they couldn't wait.

"Graceanne, you can mind your brother. He'll have to stay behind the rope."

I could see Graceanne grinding her teeth. And she scratched her cheek the way she did when she was digging in her toes at shortstop, talking up the batter and pounding her glove and saying, "C'mon babe, c'mon babe, c'mon babe."

Edie got out her book and her lotion and lay down on the army blanket. Kentucky stuck her tongue out at Graceanne and tore away to get in line to climb the ladder to the slide.

Kids were going down the slide into the deep water on rubber rafts and on their stomachs and on inner tubes. The end of the slide curved up some, and when they got to the end, they went flying up in the air before they went down into the water. I could hear them screaming and laughing.

Graceanne put her glasses in Edie's bag and we went into the water at the shallow end. The sand ended on the beach and there was only ooze under our feet. Graceanne took me to the rope and said, "You hold on here, Thumper. I'll be right back." She slipped under the rope and I didn't see her for a while. She came up near shore and waded out and took her place in line. I held onto the rope and watched her as the line moved up the ladder. She got to the top and when it came her turn she let loose and went down on her butt. She went up into the air and her braids were flapping and she came down with her arms around her knees in a cannonball. She swam back to the shore and got in line again. The next time she went down she was on her stomach, face first.

I stood there. There were other dead kids around, but I didn't know them. I walked along the rope in the ooze and kept looking back at the ladder. I saw Kentucky sitting out in the deep end on a blue rubber raft with a boy. They were paddling along with their arms and splashing. I didn't know the boy. I kept walking along the rope, back and forth. I could hear the lifeguard on a platform at the top of the slide when he blew his whistle at the kids who were too rough on the slide and I watched him put his arm between kids so they wouldn't go down two at a time. I held my breath and went under. The water was green and the dead kids' legs looked like white snakes standing up and wiggling around and sneaking their heads into the dead kids' swimming suits.

I came back up for air and looked across the lake to the other side where there was no beach and no people, just a curving line of weeping willow trees hanging their long green tears in the water. I tried to count the trees, but the sun was hot and after a while the trees all blended into each other.

For a while I hung my arms over the rope and lifted my feet off the ooze and held my breath and pretended I could swim. The other dead kids got mad at me and told me to get off. I wished I was back at French's Quarry playing Jump-or-Dive Murder or being tied in the tire swing behind Tyler Rodgers's house. I started a list in my head of things I liked better before we moved:

1. French's Quarry
2. Sergeant Useless
3. dead kids I knew

Graceanne came under the rope and gave me a push.

"What the hell's the matter with you?" she asked.

"I don't have anything to do."

"Why don't you play or something?"

"I haven't got anybody to play with."

"What about the other dead kids?"

"They're mad at me because I got on the rope."

"Bunch of little snots. Why don't you drag some mud up on the sand and make an Indian village?"

"The other kids have pails and shovels."

"Well, use your hands, Thumper. Don't be so **incompetent**."

"I'm too lonely to make a village."

"You better come with me."

She took my hand and dragged me out of the water and up on the sand. We went running along the shore and up to the foot of the slide. She pushed me onto the ladder and told me to start climbing.

"I can't swim."

"Shut up."

"But I can't."

"Shut up. You're holding up the line."

The line moved quickly and I didn't look down until we were almost to the top. I could see Edie on the army blanket and the dead kids behind the rope and I could see over the honeysuckle fence and Kentucky was behind it in the water with the boy on the blue raft.

"Thumper, just sit on your butt and let go. Before you hit the water, take a deep breath and hold your nose and kick like hell. I'll be right behind you."

When I let go, I looked over my shoulder to see Graceanne and she was there, but the lifeguard's big arm was holding her back so she'd wait her turn. There was water running under me and I went down that slide so fast all I could think of was banister poles flashing by and a sheet under me and a dead kid in the river. I went up in the air and remembered to hold my nose and kick like hell and came down to the water with a crash, still kicking. I went under and it was green without any dead kids' white legs. I kept kicking and pretty soon I was back on top and Graceanne was coming down the slide standing on her feet. She went off the slide and into the water in a slick dive without much of a splash, right next to me. I went to grab her when she came up, but she pulled back. "Keep kicking," she said. "I ain't gonna let you pull on me. Hurry up, before the lifeguard gets **suspicious**." I kicked. "Stop grabbing at me and use your arms, Thumper, or I'll hit you a good one." I flapped my arms and reached for Graceanne and kicked my legs and swallowed water that tasted like being rolled down Lewis and Clark Hill and got my breath and held it and Graceanne's left eye was wandering and I heard splashing and Graceanne came beside me and showed me how to use my arms like a dog and said to keep my face out of the water and I was swimming.

"Let's get over to the rope before Mama sees us," Graceanne said.

When we got to the rope, I was going to lift it up to go
under, but Graceanne said, "You're not a dead kid anymore,
Thumper." So I held my breath and swam under the rope.

Graceanne stayed with me a while in the shallow end. She
swam around under water and pinched the dead kids and I
went swimming along the rope.

"We better go tell Mama," Graceanne said. "So she can
change your army regulations. I think you get a promotion
now."

We went up to the blanket and Graceanne dripped on Edie.

"Quiet Hour's over, I guess," Edie said. "You kids having
a good time?"

"Thumper can swim."

"Well. You better show me."

We went and I showed her and she said it was a good start
but I still had to stay behind the rope because the big kids at
Hulen's Lake played rough.

"That's not fair," Graceanne said. "Only the dead kids
have to stay behind the rope at French's Quarry."

"If you expect life to be fair, Graceanne, you're going to
be mighty disappointed."

When it got dark, Edie bought us hot dogs and Kool-Aid
in paper cups and even though it was the day before the
holiday, the fireworks started going off like they always did
in Cranepool's Landing on July 3. The sparks fell over the
lake where people were still swimming and all the colors were
on the face of the lake like a mirror. We sat on the blanket
and watched the sky and the fireworks and gave each other
Indian Burns and Graceanne showed me where Mars was at
the horizon.

"Remember the astronomers, Thumper? Things have been
pretty quiet up there on Mars lately."

A radio was playing loud music and people started dancing on the beach.

"Wouldn't it be nice if they played the music from Saturn?" I asked.

"Yeah. It'd be nice."

Somebody made a fire at the edge of the water and the dancing people twirled across the yellow flames in the dark. People were carrying sparklers and throwing them in the air and waving them around to make patterns in the darkness in front of their faces.

Collier Rodgers came walking up from the beach toward our blanket.

Mama put her arm on Kentucky's shoulders and said, "Why, there's Collier Rodgers. I bet he's going to ask one of us to dance. He probably can't tell us apart we look so much like sisters. I'm only making nonsense, but there was a time when many a handsome boy like Collier would have asked me."

Graceanne was on her knees and elbows on the grass, all hunched over like a beetle. Every time the fireworks would go off, she'd make herself go flying up into the air like a bomb had gone off under her and she'd make whistling noises and act like she'd been exploded.

When she heard Collier's name, she stopped horsing around and sat still.

"I think he's going to ask you, Kentucky," Edie said. "And he's a nice boy."

I looked at Collier. He was barefoot and his legs were long and bony and he had on long black shorts and he was coming toward the blanket.

"He's going to ask Graceanne," I said.

"Don't be silly, Charlemagne," Edie said. "Why would he ask Graceanne? She's not old enough. That boy's eighteen if he's a day. He means to ask the beauty of the family."

Collier kept coming.

"Evening, Mrs. Farrand. Evening, Kentucky." He turned to look at Graceanne on the grass. "You want to come dancing, Grace?"

She looked up at him like he was a slab of bacon she was thinking of buying at Knowell's Supermarket. "You're too tall to dance with and I don't know how."

"You can stand on the picnic bench and I'll teach you."

"Okay."

They went off to the beach and I could see them, two black shadows with the little one standing on the picnic bench and the big one beside her holding her skinny waist in her swimming suit and the red, white, and blue sky was lit up again and again over the lake.

October 1960

The Sacajawea Raking Contest

Thirteen

*T*hat autumn was the softest I've ever known. Everything was just nice and warm. The slow winds blowing across the plain from the west gently touched the beaten-up land, and the colors across the river seemed deep and bright and almost shivering in the sun like they'd had a surprise, and made Illinois look like Oz. The local apple harvest was as grim as everyone had predicted, but apples from Washington State were plentiful at four cents apiece and jugs of dandelion wine were stocked at every roadside stand in place of hard cider, with hickory nuts in baskets on the ground, and fat gourds were being given away hand over fist at farms from La Grange down to Ste. Genevieve. The river was still low and the water too thick to see through when we ladled it into mason jars, but it was full of catfish and bass, and they were biting.

In the few spare hours when Graceanne wasn't in school or at the Lewis and Clark Hotel or dodging KP so she could run her Richard Nixon campaign at Fort McBain, Wanda taught Graceanne and me to fish by putting wadded-up Wonder Bread into hairnets on the end of clothesline ropes. Wanda kept her fish and took them home to cook, but Edie said we shouldn't eat fish from the Big Muddy Crud, and

Graceanne didn't like fish anyway. She said they tasted like bony socks, so we always threw back what we caught.

"How do I know I'm not catching the same fish every time?" I asked.

"Fish only go into the net but one-st," Wanda said. "Then they know better."

Graceanne kept her job as bellboy at the Lewis and Clark Hotel, even after Collier went back to college. I stopped worrying about her library fines now that she was turning over some money, even though Edie made her give half of her earnings to the "household kitty," a jar on the kitchen counter. I never knew how honest Graceanne's accounting procedures were when it came to the kitty, but quarters accumulated in the jar and Edie took them out at the end of each month.

Graceanne's attachment to Wanda, which I think at first was an act of pure social pugnacity, grew. The bond between them was as tough as both girls and made out of the same enduring fiber. They argued, and slapped each other, and traded the bits of wisdom they had gathered about the way the world worked on the different ends of Cranepool's Landing that had formed their experiences. Both Wanda's mother and Edie had things to say about the girls finding "more suitable" friends, but nothing they said about that had any effect on Graceanne and Wanda. They were philosophical twins in their shared belief that the world ought to be fair and one day would be, and they were evenly matched in physical courage, and they certainly shared an approach to problem solving—strike first and strike harder. I think Graceanne found in Wanda a ruthlessness that equaled her own, and an intelligence like hers that worked more on imagination and fiction than on the information in textbooks, although "serious" books got traded back and forth between them at Wanda's insistence: "White trash wanta be ignorant all her life and live in Nigger Town forever?"

Graceanne would answer, "White trash don't want to live in Nigger Town *now*," but she accepted her end of the book trade every time, and that October their favorite was William Shirer's *The Rise and Fall of the Third Reich*. Graceanne chose that one. They knew more about the Luftwaffe and about Joseph Goebbels and about opening the Russian Front than they knew about the American Revolution or the Civil War. I was afraid for a while that this freewheeling policy of trading would spill over into their other pursuits, leading Graceanne to accept the carrying of a knife, but she said that carrying a knife was okay for the Negroes since the whole town of Cranepool's Landing was after *them*, but white people had to stick to the rule of not putting anything in their hands for a fight or they'd fall into shame.

Graceanne and I must have grown like weeds that summer. By autumn Edie was forced to buy us new uniforms, and we noticed that the bigger the size got, the uglier and costlier the uniform. That provoked Graceanne into a long but transparent campaign against the tyrannical, expensive—*Fascist*—policies of Our Lady of Lourdes Academy. She wanted to go to Cranepool Junior High with Wanda.

She also wanted to go to Wanda's church. Graceanne said the Baptists got to roll around in the aisles on Sunday and make wailing noises "to testify," but Edie never let her go, saying that for a child baptized into the Catholic church to attend any other church would be a mortal sin against the first commandment, or, as Graceanne's dawning political awareness would have it, "all that **Fascist** Lord-thy-God stuff."

There was plenty of talk in Fort McBain that autumn about the Catholic church and John Kennedy and his family, and about the young senator's love for his children. Edie was fascinated by the Kennedys, and she clipped news articles and magazines and suddenly said we could talk about them at the dinner table but not about the Nixons because they were "politics pure and simple, and not of good family," and she tried to copy Jackie's wardrobe with a sewing machine, fabric remnants, and imagination.

I shared Edie's fascination. The barrage of pictures of the good-looking family, with their smiles and the warmth in their eyes, fueled in me a love for history, because I knew they weren't like my family, and would be remembered forever, and I borrowed Graceanne's textbook whenever I could to supplement the childish information in my own about the pharaohs and ancient civilizations, and I even peeked at *Rise and Fall*, searching for other recorded examples of such tenderness as the Kennedys seemed to embody. What little personal information I had about tenderness came from occasional bits of practical wisdom bestowed offhandedly by Kentucky in that sweet voice and from Graceanne's spasms of fierce giving. It was very hard for me to understand that such ferociousness as Graceanne's could coexist with a generosity of spirit: She had nearly drowned her only brother at Hulen's Lake to cure his loneliness, had knocked out his tooth to teach him fair fighting, and she was showering affection on her best friend by slapping her around and arguing loudly about Germans. Her friend in turn knocked Graceanne around and told her she was as ignorant about politics and history as a catfish. But I never doubted their affection for each other.

There was a general feeling that moving to Fort McBain had improved our young lives, that living in Nigger Town had different pleasures to offer than Lewis and Clark Hill, that we would be happier as well as poorer. I had all the time alone now that I could want. Edie was away from home working most of the time and when she got home she was too worn out to pay much attention to Graceanne. Plus, the pres-

ence of Wanda next door was, as Graceanne said, "a down-
right **convenience**." And the absence of our father we barely
noticed, since he had never been around much on Lewis and
Clark Hill except late at night to fight with Edie and slam
doors and make fun of Catholics. Edie said a judge had issued
a restraining order to keep Daddy away from Fort McBain,
and after a time my father seemed as remote to me as Martian
astronomers, perhaps more remote. The few times I asked
where he was, Edie said, "Never mind about that," and
Graceanne said, "He died and went to hell," and Kentucky
said, in her soft sweet voice, "He's on the base, Charlie, but
he's drinking bad, and you don't want to worry about what
you can't help. Why don't you help me and Graceanne get
supper on the table instead?"

Graceanne had always heartily resented helping with meals,
but that autumn at Fort McBain her frenzied attempts to get
out of KP were so dynamic that Kentucky finally made a
covert deal with her: "I'll cook and set, but you gotta start
the conversation every night *and* scrape the leftovers into the
Gallon of Goodies tub *and* help me with my math homework.
And don't tell Mama." This deal left Graceanne free to carry
on her new interest in politics before dinner without letting
Edie notice that Graceanne was getting out of her rightful
responsibilities. Graceanne started bringing home Nixon campaign buttons and brochures and stickers from Republican
headquarters downtown, and she left them all over Fort
McBain and Our Lady of Lourdes Academy and Cronin's
Grocery where Edie would stop to buy milk on her way home.

Graceanne and I were sharing the front room facing onto
McBain Avenue, because, as Edie said, "Women grown have
need to be closer to the bathroom, so Kentucky and I will
share the Garden Room." She called the middle room that
because she brought home philodendron plants from the hospital when patients who had received them as gifts passed

them on to the staff rather than carry the depressing things out with them when they left Saint Audrain's. Graceanne said that Edie brought the plants home to finish them off, and, indeed, they all eventually died, but Edie said they gave her room "a gracious touch while they lasted."

Graceanne did not seem to mind our distance from "the facilities," and she was glad that she herself had been spared from sharing with Edie the "Philodendron Morgue," but she complained—once—about the lack of privacy for her "personal property" involved in sharing a room with me.

"Thumper's got no respect for classified documents," she said. "He's always gonna be getting into my private personal property."

Edie gave her a look. "You have anything *that* private, Graceanne, maybe I should conduct an inspection right now."

"I only meant *if* I had private property."

Graceanne shut her mouth about that subject and never brought it up again.

Her letters from Collier were a recurring source of friction between Graceanne and me that autumn when we began to share a room. I could not understand then what a college boy like Collier found so interesting about Graceanne that he would spend money on stamps.

"He's helping me with my Nixon work," she said. "Go mind your business."

Graceanne's Nixon work, in addition to the campaign buttons and brochures and stickers and making speeches at recess, consisted of her launching dinner table conversation directed against Edie's new idol.

"JFK's too young," Graceanne said. "He's got his nerve thinking he can run this country after Dwight David Eisenhower, Supreme Allied Commander."

"John Kennedy is my age," Edie would say. "He has wisdom beyond his years."

"Yeah, and JFK's a Catholic, too," Graceanne said. "The pope'll be the one running this country."

"It'll be a good thing to have a religious man in the White House," Edie would say.

"JFK pretends he's a **liberal**," Graceanne said. "He's worse than Abe Lincoln."

"Graceanne, are you crazy in the head? Lincoln freed the slaves! That ought to mean something to you the way you're practically sitting in Wanda Gladwill's pocket."

Graceanne gave Edie a look through the crack in her glasses. "If Lincoln was so great, how come people still call them niggers and won't let them swim in Hulen's Lake and there's Whites Only? They ain't free."

"Well, it's better than when they were slaves."

"Better for who?"

"Better for them. You certainly don't think it's better for white people, do you?"

Graceanne had a look in her eye. "Mama, do you think it's *worse* for white people?"

"Well, you can't deny that this very neighborhood is dirty and disreputable."

"You think that's the fault of the Negroes?"

"*I* certainly didn't make the mess or give the area a bad reputation. And if you're not careful with this kind of talk, Graceanne Farrand, you'll be getting a reputation yourself."

"As what?"

"As a *nigger lover*."

"Well, so's JFK. When Martin Luther King got sentenced to hard labor in the state of Georgia this month *for a traffic violation*, Kennedy called King's wife. Our vice-president, whose name I dare not mention at this table, didn't."

"Well, that ought to make you like Kennedy."

"He should've done something better than calling Mrs. King. What good is that going to do?" She held an invisible phone up to her head. "Hello, Mrs. King. This is Jack. I hear old Martin Luther's in jail. That's too bad. Jackie and I feel real bad about it. Give him our love, we're going out on our boat now." She put down the invisible phone. "What a horse's ass."

"Go to your room."

Edie never won an argument with Graceanne over anything without the use of force, but the arguments about JFK were different from their usual skirmishes because Graceanne came to the table prepared, with facts and anecdotes that she twisted to make Kennedy look bad because she couldn't talk about Nixon at the table. She was tireless in promoting her Nixon work in this underhanded way and she read every newspaper she could get her hands on to find stories and photos that she could use in the dinner table campaign that didn't dare actually mention Nixon's name.

Collier and Wanda and I knew the truth about the Nixon work. "It's the only way I can make sure Mama votes for JFK," Graceanne said. "I'm **provoking** her. She hasn't got any real politics. She's only got magazine photos to vote by."

Not even the Martian astronomers were exempt from Graceanne's politics that autumn. When she was out campaigning or bellhopping, I'd get under her bed to read the latest installment in the fictional life and times of Gloria Rosina Festitootitoo and the real-life saga of the Collier Rodgers letters. I worried sometimes about this violation of Graceanne's private property, especially since I'd had a taste of her fist, but the colored kids on McBain Avenue wouldn't play with me because I was white and the white kids wouldn't play with me because Graceanne was a nigger lover, and Kentucky was only home long enough to get dinner on the table before she went off to be with boys, and I was alone except for Mike the dog, whose worms made my friendship with him a matter of sneaking food from the table and frequent invented errands that took me outside. I never saw any worms, although I looked all over his pit for a couple of months. He belonged to an old colored man named Mr. Otis Ulysses Brown, who lived downstairs and who was nearly always drunk. I was afraid of Mr. O.U.B. until one day when he opened his mouth to grin at me and I saw he had no teeth. I figured he was a worse sissy than me, since I had only lost one tooth. So Mike the dog and Graceanne's book were my friends at Fort McBain that autumn, and, since they were both Off Limits To All Personnel, by order of two Farrands, my social contacts were by necessity highly undercover activities. I spent so much time with that dog and that book, both borrowed from their real owners, that together they gave me an idea for something I could make to give Graceanne for her birthday, an activity that kept me busy for a while and not so inclined to consider my isolation.

I tried for several days to keep a book of my own, but Graceanne's haunted my thoughts and colored my attempts and I gave it up. The only story I could think of was about a little boy who had a sister who found a radio . . . and so on.

The news from Mars that autumn on Gloria's radio was all about the presidential election on Earth.

> The astronomers are keeping their telescopes cleaned and polished so they can learn more about the universe when the people of America vote. They are quite anxious to know if the voters will choose wisely and make the future better for the children. Once again they are making appeals for money to keep the telescopes in proper working order. They are stressing the importance of knowing everything, because when that happens, everyone can be happy. Just look at the Beer Hall Putsch.

The astronomers always seemed to focus on that one goal: knowing everything in order to be happy. I wondered how much of the information in Graceanne's book was common property among the various cultures represented in its pages. Did the circles on Saturn know about the Martian astronomers? Did the astronomers know about the Mackerel Catechism? The catechism question was still in evidence and the score was not going up. It was always 8 to 0, and it was written all over the margins.

3. What is the score?
8 to 0

Graceanne kept Collier's letters in a cardboard pocket she had taped inside the front cover of her book.

Dear Grace:
Yesterday Kennedy made a speech to the Greater Houston Ministerial Association about his religion. He said he believed in the *absolute* separation of church and state. Don't tell your mother that.

I hope you didn't mean what you said about never kissing me. When I come home for your birthday, I plan to bring you something that will make you kiss me.

Yes, I have kissed a girl before, and she liked it, and I hope you will, too. I hope you won't cut your hair—I like your braids. I think you have the most recognizable silhouette in Cranepool's Landing. Nobody seeing you in the distance could possibly mistake you for anyone else, with your glasses and your braids and your slenderness and the *life* in your step. Please don't change any more than you must.

Love,
Collier.

That was the letter that gave my sneaking under her bed away to Graceanne. I watched her every night when she got ready for bed and took down her braids, and I started asking her questions.

"Graceanne, have you always had braids?"

"Just about. Except Mama says I was born bald. I bet I didn't have braids then. Plus, she said I was an infernal nuisance because I cried all the time until I got glasses and could finally see what was going on. I don't think that's such a stupid reason for a baby to cry, but Mama probably wanted me to be the Baby Jesus or something and pass a miracle so she'd have a nurse to take care of me and the house."

"Well, do you think you'll always have braids?"

"Maybe."

"Well, do you think you'll ever cut them?"

"Goddammit, Thumper. Have you been getting into my private property?"

She rubbed her knuckles on the top of my nose real hard, and we turned off the light and went to bed. I lay there for a while, holding the spine of my nose, wondering if what she had done had a name.

"Graceanne, what's it called that you did to my nose?"

"It's a Mexican Hanky. Go to sleep before I give you worse."

Fourteen

*W*hen I learned that I was going to be able to go to the Sacajawea Raking Contest with Graceanne and Kentucky over on Lewis and Clark Hill, I was immediately sure that my life had a purpose. Even when my sisters had been tending me full time and foisting me off on their friends and including me in their games, I had never been allowed to take part in that special event, by order of Eden Farrand. So I got out my oldest dungarees and my rattiest old sweater, and the only regret I had was that I did not own a pair of tennis shoes or any shoes other than my heavy corrective shoes, which, in a perverted twist of their history, were now too small and hurt my feet. They must have been indestructible, because they still looked almost new. I hadn't told Edie about how bad they were to wear because she was always so worried about money and working sometimes twenty hours a day and I kept thinking I'd get a job. For a few weeks in August I had walked up and down McBain Avenue, looking in garbage cans for pop bottles because I could get two cents apiece for them at Cronin's Grocery, but when Kentucky found out she made me stop. "You'll get the gammagoochy or the yellow yang-yang or Irish croup if you go digging around in trash like that. I catch you in there one more time and I'll whale you good, young man." So, with a grand total of seventy-two cents, I couldn't afford new shoes.

Graceanne, too, was showing an unusual interest in her clothes for the Sacajawea Raking Contest, trying things on and throwing them on her bed. She'd never cared much what she wore, but this year's contest was different because she was taking Wanda. When Kentucky found out about that, she sat Graceanne down and said, "Honey, I know you mean well by Wanda, but I want you to think about what you're doing, exposing her to unkindness and ignorance and all the things those Lewis and Clark Hill kids might try. If they pick on Wanda, she'll be the one to be hurt. She's not like some new baseball cap you can wear to show off with."

"If she's with me, nobody will pick on Wanda." Graceanne didn't listen to Kentucky, instead prancing around and saying, "You sound just like Mama."

"No, I don't, Graceanne. I sound like someone who knows those kids and knows something now about living in Nigger Town. It changes things for us."

"How? You can still outhit and outrun and out*rescue* any of those kids. You haven't changed."

"I have changed, Graceanne. So have you. When we were living on Lewis and Clark Hill, neither one of us would have had any truck with a colored person and you know it. Those kids now are like us a few months back." She sat there staring into space and then she looked at me. "Sometimes I think Charlie is the only one who hasn't changed."

That made me feel worse than not having any friends except Mike the dog and Graceanne's book, and suddenly I didn't want to go to the Sacajawea Raking Contest because I thought everyone would see how I hadn't changed.

We set off late in the afternoon, each of us carrying a cardboard carton from the back of Cronin's Grocery and a stick of margarine. It was the day before Graceanne's birthday, and a Friday, and we came right home from school to get changed out of our uniforms. Edie had said she'd make her own dinner, and she left us a note saying that Bobby Stochmal's mother had invited us for dinner over to their house on Lewis and Clark Hill.

"I guess she feels she still owes me," Kentucky said. "But I would've pulled a cat or a dog out of the river just like I did Bobby." She smiled. "But I wouldn't have punched a cat or a dog on the head."

"Mike the dog doesn't have worms," I said.

"What the hell are you talking about?" Graceanne asked.

"Mike the dog doesn't have worms."

"How do you know and why do you insist on telling us and since when are you a veterinarian?"

"I looked all over the pit he dug with his chain and there are no worms. When Mama caught him scratching his butt on the ground, she said it was because he had worms. But I looked all over the ground and there's no worms. Mike the dog does not have worms."

"You idiot! Mama didn't mean he had worms on the ground. He's got worms *inside* his butt."

"You're lying. That's disgusting."

"It's disgusting all right, but I'm not lying. God, Charlie, sometimes I wonder about you."

Wanda'd been walking along all quiet. She took my hand and said, "I can worm that dog if he's your friend, Charlie. You just stop worriting. Old O.U.B. ought to get hisself knifed some Friday night for keeping that dog the way he does."

Graceanne looked like she'd been struck by lightning. "You know how to worm a dog? You know how to worm a dog? You know how to worm a goddamn dog?" It was like Wanda had said she could fly.

"I can worm any creature that's got the Curse of the Earth. My mama knows all about worming, and all the McBain kids that get it come to her."

I thought Graceanne's eyeballs would pop out. "*Kids* can get worms?"

Wanda gave Graceanne a look like she'd look at Old O.U.B. "You think your body's strengthier than a dog's?"

At first the bus driver wasn't going to let us bring our cardboard cartons onto the bus, but Graceanne started acting like she was crying and telling him they were for the needy at Our Lady of Lourdes Clothing Drive and he let us on. Wanda had to ride in the back, so we went and sat down by her. The bus let us off at Sulphur Springs Park, and we walked from there.

All the kids were standing around with rakes at the top of Lewis and Clark Hill in front of our old house. I looked up at the window of the green Measles Room. I couldn't see Sergeant Useless, and they had new curtains on all the windows and a brass horn on the door with Indian corn and husks.

All the leaves had already been raked into two long golden-red walls that stretched all the way down the hill to the parade ground. Between the walls of leaves, the kids had left a corridor that was supposed to be the overland Northwest Passage. Cardboard boxes were lying all over our old yard. I knew what to do, and I started tearing my box apart at the seams to make my racer sled, but all the other kids were just standing there without moving. I stopped tearing, hoping nobody had been paying any attention to me.

"I guess you brought Nigger Town with you," Bobby Stochmal said.

I could see Graceanne start grinding her teeth and scratching her cheek and digging in her feet. Kentucky stepped to the end of the track between the piles of leaves like she hadn't heard anything. "Let's just have the contest," she said. "If I go first, nobody can complain I won unfairly." I knew she said that because the last kids to go down the Hill had an advantage from the buildup in the grass of the margarine on their cardboard sleds. The idea was to sail down as far and as straight as you could without plowing through one of the walls of leaves. There weren't any do-overs in this game; you only got one chance to make the run. Kentucky started tearing her box, and when she was done, she smeared margarine on the side she'd decided would be the bottom. Still nobody moved.

"We don't want any niggers in our Sacajawea contest," Bobby said.

"You little buttholes all know," Kentucky said, dropping her sled at the start of the track. "Old Lewis and Clark took Sacajawea on the Northwest Passage with them so she could show 'em the way. Sacajawea was a Red Indian and a woman. They would have taken her if she'd been a nigger, because she knew the land. Anybody thinks they're better than Sacajawea can just go home indoors right now or ask me to lay 'em out good before I get mad. And anybody thinks they got a better right than me to talk about Nigger Town, they can just step right up and see if I've lost my touch from living among darkies." She stuck her face at the kids and gave them a look. "If you wanta play fair, you'll let the little kids go last so they have a chance."

Everybody started tearing up their boxes and using their margarine sticks. Graceanne showed Wanda how to do it. Kentucky went down first, on her belly on her piece of cardboard, and she tore up the grass on the way down, and she didn't go through any of the walls until she got down to the last house on the Hill. It wasn't a perfect run because, even though she didn't touch the piles of leaves, she was slow and didn't get her distance. But she'd gone first before the Hill got all slick from the margerine, and if anybody bettered her run, I'd be surprised, and I could feel my heart tight inside I was so proud of her.

Kids started going down, screaming and tearing up the walls and scattering the leaves overhead. When Wanda went down she spun around a couple of times and went through the leaves and started laughing when she fell off her cardboard onto her back and skidded. Other kids laughed, but more like they were nervous. Graceanne went after her, but I could see she was still mad, and she only had a run down to about ten yards from where Kentucky had gone out of the track. I was near the end of the little kids and when it came my turn I sat down at the top of the track on our old yard and thought I wouldn't go down on my belly but on my butt, the way I had done on the stairs when there was a dead kid in the river and I shoved off and held on to the corners of my cardboard and went flying but I thought of Sacajawea and how she knew the Passage and about Kentucky and how she knew the kids and I steered like I was going through a tunnel down the waxed stairs and held my breath and heard the kids screaming and I got to the end of the Hill and slid onto the parade ground and I didn't know what had happened until Kentucky came running and grabbed me around the head and started shouting, "You little son of a gun, you did it!"

I stood up and looked around and saw where I was and the other little kids were coming down on their racers. I waited and watched them all go through the walls. Pretty soon all the kids were down at the bottom of the hill, and we gathered around to put our boxes in a pile. The biggest kids ran to the top of the hill and started pushing and raking the leaves down and carrying them in baskets. We got tired standing there so we sat down and watched the leaves flying and coming down at us until there was a huge pile on the parade ground. When it was all there, Kentucky went and got the soldiers from the guardhouse, and they poured gas on the leaves and the cardboards and started the fire. The red flames shot up into the sky higher than the houses at the bottom of the hill and crackled like gunfire and there was a roar in the center that sounded like a tractor running and the smell of all the margarine frying. We stood around until the fire burned down and the soldiers stood there too. I suddenly noticed it was dark. The daylight had gone while I was staring into the fire. Kentucky reached inside the pocket of her blue jeans.

"This is the Sacred Sacajawea Arrowhead that goes to the winner of the annual race in honor of the Indian woman who showed Lewis and Clark the Northwest Passage." She put it in my hand. "Charlie Farrand, next year you get to give it to the winner and you have to make a speech." I looked at the sharp black thing in my hand and Kentucky said, "This little piece of obsidian that came down to us all the way from history belongs to Charlie for one year. It shows that one little kid who used to have a clubfoot did better than all of us on only his first run down the hill and doesn't have to blow off his mouth but just plays fair and hard. Now, Charlie Saca-jawea Farrand, we're going to paint your face."

They brought out a hose from the last house and wetted down the ashes and everybody put their hands in and came by in a solemn line and put a finger mark on my face.

Fifteen

$\mathcal{W}$e didn't go to the Stochmals' house for dinner because Kentucky said we'd already given the kids enough to swallow without bringing "our personal darky into anyone's precious home." We walked home the most direct way, along the river, and came up to McBain Avenue from the back. We ate dinner at Wanda's house. I was surprised when she put baloney and Wonder Bread and a jar of mayonnaise on the table. I'd heard Wanda call Graceanne "white bread" one day, and from then on I had thought that colored people ate chocolate and hamburger meat well-done and dark bread and a lot of barbecue and that was what made them so dark. But my mistake about Mike the dog's worms made me keep my questions to myself, and I just listened while they got the food on the table and talked. I forgot that my face was painted until Wanda started laughing at me and said, "You better get out of my house, Charlie. You're turning into a Negro."

In Wanda's kitchen there was a dresser with a mirror, and I went to look at my Sacajawea face, but I had to look around the sides of stacks of folded white cloth that were piled up in front of it. Tiny pink flowers, and borders of green leaves, and fruits of all kinds, and tiny black and yellow bees, and little bears, and thousands of colorful birds were worked into the pieces of white cloth with stitches so tiny I could not believe a human hand could hold the needle to make such wonderful pictures.

"Did you make these, Wanda?" I asked.

"I know how, but not that good. That over there's my mama's work," Wanda said. "She embroiders for the folks up in Maple Heights and sells some of it to Parks Department Store. And she does the altar cloths for your church."

"But your mama is a Baptist."

"That don't mean she can't sew."

Kentucky came over and looked at the cloths and then she went and washed her hands so she could touch the bees. "I never saw anything like these bees."

"My mama's got the hands," Wanda said. "You got to have the hands to make those bees."

"The hands?"

"The hands of an artist that only come when God blesses you special."

They decided to go to our house to see if we had any vanilla wafers or cereal for dessert. Edie was sitting on the concrete steps of Fort McBain when we came walking across the gravel and at first I thought she was staring at my Saca-jawea face. She was sure studying us and holding a little white envelope in her hand and snapping it against her knee. Then I realized it was too dark for her to see my warpaint. She was just sitting there, waiting and snapping that little white en-velope with a sound like sheets on the clothesline on a windy day. I could see the envelope in the dark, a little white flag flapping against her leg. She was still wearing her white clothes from the hospital and she had on a green sweater. The closer we got, the worse her face looked.

"Wanda, you better go on home," Graceanne said. "Mama's out to kill a bear for sure."

"If she raises a hand against you, I'll slice her freckles off one by one. Eden is real trash for laying on you like she do."

"Go on home now. We don't need any knife."

"I hear you scream, and I'll come runnin'."

"There ain't gonna be no screaming. Maybe she's not laying for me anyway. I'm not the only one who lives in that blue piece of cow pie. Maybe she's laying for Old O.U.B."

Wanda walked over to her side of the fence and walked along it and watched us go up to the stairs. I could see her eyes that looked like glass in her dark face moving along the top of the fence.

Edie tugged her sweater around her. "Well, I've been waiting for you and called over to the Stochmal house. You didn't take your dinner there and I hear you made some trouble with your colored friend."

Graceanne's shoulders dipped, and I could see she thought we were in trouble about Wanda. "There wasn't trouble, Mama. Tucka offered to comb their feathers for them, and then everybody got along okay and wait til you hear who won."

"Graceanne Farrand, you're a sneak and a liar and a thief and you ought to be ashamed of yourself. I don't know why you think I'd believe anything you say." Edie waved the little envelope and her voice sounded like she'd been eating ice. "This is a fine how-do-you-do I got here in my hand. I got this awful letter at the hospital today. Susannah Alexander at the library writes how she's been mailing letters to McBain Avenue for months and maybe they don't deliver the mail in Nigger Town so she'd better get me at work." Edie stood up. "At work!"

Graceanne just stood there and didn't say anything and I started feeling sick.

"What do you have to say for yourself?" Edie was shouting now, and I could see those glass eyes over the fence moving along. "What do you have to say? Answer me! I demand an answer from you, young lady!"

"I don't have an answer," Graceanne said.

"No! How could you have an answer? How could you do this to me, Graceanne Farrand?"

"I'm sorry."

"I'm gonna make you sorry."

"I'm already sorry."

"Sorry!" Edie was screaming and I could hear a couple of porch swings creaking along the street and doors opening. "Well, sorry's not good enough. Not good enough. You owe fifty-nine dollars and sixteen cents to the library and you're sorry? Sorry? What the hell do you need seventeen books for anyway? You pretending you're in college so you can impress that Collier? You ask me you're putting on airs to be interesting. What else are you doing to impress that college boy? He certainly isn't after you for your looks!"

I started thinking. If the letter was about seventeen books, that meant Graceanne had already returned fourteen and paid their fines plus half her earnings from the Lewis and Clark Hotel to the household kitty but she was behind and wasn't ever going to catch up.

Edie was swinging her arms like she was cold. "I'm not made out of money, Graceanne! Are you sick in the head?"

"I tried to take them back and pay the fine but the more I tried the worse it got and I'm sorry Mama and I'll take my medicine and never do it again."

"Well, you've got a big dose coming. You also stole my mail, and that's a real crime and you're lucky I didn't call the police on you, but I've got a name to protect in this godforsaken town and I won't."

Edie came down and grabbed Graceanne's arm so hard I thought she'd pull it off. She gave it a couple of jerks. Then Edie let go and slammed her whole arm against Graceanne's head and I could hear Graceanne swallow her breath and she bent over from the dizziness. Edie started pulling Graceanne up the steps and she was screaming, "You're nothing but a thief, Graceanne, stealing my hard-earned money. You're a dirty little thief! And I'm going to know the reason why!"

Kentucky jumped like she'd been turned into stone and was suddenly coming out of it and ran to the top of the steps. "Let me take it for her, Mama," she said.

"Take it? Take it for her? *You'll* take it for her? It's not a package to pass around like a hot potato. It's what Graceanne's got coming to her. It's her medicine and she'll take it herself. Move out of the way."

Kentucky stayed where she was. "Mama, you've got a tiger in you—like a fire that's burning you up inside and it's gotta get out but it doesn't have to get out on Graceanne. I'll take it for her. I'm bigger and I can take it better."

Edie let go of Graceanne and laid a clip on the side of Kentucky's head. "See how you like taking it! Don't you interfere between a mother and her child." Then she grabbed Graceanne again and pulled the door open and dragged her inside and locked the door. I could feel my heart beating in my chest and my hands were damp and I couldn't swallow and Kentucky sat down on the steps and put her head down on her lap and I could see the glass eyes over by the fence and I could hear Mike the dog whining behind the house but I couldn't hear Graceanne screaming and that scared me more than anything.

"I can't hear Graceanne," I said.

Kentucky talked into her lap but I could hear her anyway. "You can always hear Graceanne when she's got something to scream about. She's got a technique, Charlie. You'll hear her soon enough. Mama's probably just looking for something to hit her with and it hasn't started yet." I went around the house and sat with Mike the dog and held him still because he was shaking all over he was so glad to see me but I didn't hear any screaming and the glass eyes were now along the back fence. It was so quiet I started imagining I could hear Mike the dog's heart and his worms inside talking to each other and saying how they'd like to get out. I got up and walked over to the fence and the dog started whining for me to come back but I went over and looked at Wanda's face.

"I guess it's all right, Charlie. Wouldn't be so quiet if it was bad wrong."

I didn't say anything. We just stood there and waited for the screaming but it never came. I kept trying to work out the math on Graceanne's library books, but I knew it was hopeless to go collecting bottles again.

"Why didn't she tell your ma about the books earlier?"

"I don't know. But back on July third it was already near forty dollars. Maybe it was when she was sick in bed with her tonsils that she got it started. She forgot and then it got bad. And then she probably was too scared to say."

It was quiet on McBain Avenue like somebody'd put a big wad of cotton down on Nigger Town to sponge up the sound. Even Mike the dog had stopped his whining. I went around front and Kentucky was gone. I thought she went inside so I tried the door but it was still locked. I went back to the fence.

Wanda gave me a look. "You wanta come in my house, Charlie? Go to the john and have a drink of water?"

"I better stay out here."

"Yeah, you better had."

"I better."

"You better stay right where you are."

"I better."

"You scared, Charlie?"

"Some."

"The porch light just went on, Charlie."

I hurried over to the steps. Nobody came out. I waited and

waited and didn't know what to do. I looked over at the fence
at Wanda's eyes. I went up one step by one step and didn't
look at the door. At the top I stood and looked at my corrective shoes. They had charcoal all over them from the line
of kids painting my face at the bottom of Lewis and Clark
Hill because I was Sacajawea.

I opened the door and went in. Graceanne was sitting on
her bed, and she had her history textbook open in front of
her face. I sat on my bed and looked at the spine of her book.

"We didn't hear anything outside."

Graceanne didn't say anything.

"We thought you'd scream or something."

She sat there like she didn't hear me.

"Wanda said she'd let me come in her house and get a
drink, but I stayed outside. We didn't hear anything."

She just held her book. Then I saw her glasses on the chest
of drawers. They looked okay from where I was sitting but I
got up and went over close and saw they still only had the
crack from when Edie grabbed her in the lobby of the Lewis
and Clark Hotel. I felt better when I saw her glasses were
okay.

Then I turned around all of a sudden because Graceanne
couldn't be reading that book without her glasses on.

I went and stood by the bed and looked over the book and
Graceanne had the flat end of a wooden spoon between her
teeth and she had almost chewed through it and the long
skinny end was gone. Her mouth was blue and red and swollen up like a softball and her cheek was grey and her eyes
were full of hate and her hands were steady like rocks and
she didn't have her blue jeans on and I looked at her legs and
they were covered with red streaks and slashes and had a little
blood and she looked like she wasn't breathing but she was.

"Graceanne," I whispered and looked at the closed door

between our room and the Garden Room. "Did she hit you on the face?"

Graceanne didn't move or say anything.

"I've got seventy-six cents if you want it to pay Mama."

She didn't move, but her eyes looked softer.

I went under her bed and got out her book and went and got her glasses and handed them to her and looked around for a pencil and gave it to her and took her history textbook and she just sat there for a minute but she took the pencil and opened the book and found the place and put her book on her knees and started writing in her overhand way. When she was done she gave me the book and I could tell she didn't mind if I read what she'd written:

3. What is the score?
   9 to 0

I heard the wooden spoon snap and the end fell on the bed. She picked it up and threw it at the window. She pulled the rest of the spoon out of her mouth but it took her a long time because her lips were stuck together on the spoon. She got under the covers in her clothes and her glasses.

I turned out the light. I thought awhile. I knew what the Mackerel catechism was now. And I also knew why there hadn't been any screaming, why Graceanne had stuck that spoon in her mouth. Edie must have broken it on her on the first hit and Graceanne'd put it in her mouth because she was afraid Wanda would hear her scream and come over and kill our mother with a knife.

Sixteen

*W*hen I got up the next morning, it was chilled in Fort McBain and Graceanne was still in bed with the covers over her head. I opened the bedroom door and went into the Garden Room so I could use the facilities. Edie was gone and her bed was made and Kentucky's bed was empty, too, but hers was all messed up so she'd been home. Next to the bathroom door there was a piece of paper hanging from a tack and I stood there and read it with my feet getting cold on the linoleum floor of the Garden Room.

NEW REGULATIONS

1. Apparently you children feel you can't bring your problems to me to talk them out. To correct that, I have placed a box on my dresser where you can put letters addressed to me. I will read these letters once a week and deal with them as they deserve.

2. I want all of your library cards in the box by 8 this evening. If you need a book checked out, write down its name and I will check it out on

my card. If you need books from the school library, use them there.

3. There will be ABSOLUTELY no interference when one of you children is punished.

4. This house is not a democracy. I make the rules and you follow the rules.

5. It has become clear to me that the Negro element is having a bad influence in this house. If you can't find children of your own color to play with, play with each other. Wanda Gladwill's house is OFF LIMITS to you, and our house is OFF LIMITS to her. I have spoken with Mrs. Gladwill, and she will make sure this rule is enforced in her house.

6. If you are interested in a person of the opposite sex, you may not accept letters or phone calls from that person until that person comes to the house to meet me formally and get permission.

7. If one of you violates any of these rules, it is the duty of the others to inform me.

8. There will be no more political campaigning. It is unbecoming in children to mock their elders.

9. The dog in the backyard is OFF LIMITS because of his health.

10. These rules are not to be discussed outside our own home. If you don't like the rules, just remember you came to live with me, I didn't come to live with you.

I went into the bathroom and took a shower. When I got out, Graceanne was standing by the door reading the New Rules. Her lips had gone down in the night and her cheek wasn't grey anymore. She kept reading the rules and I went and made myself a bowl of Cheerios and left the used milk in the bowl and went and got dressed and put on my coat because it was getting cold outside. I took the used milk and went out the back door to give it to Mike the dog. He lapped it up and jumped on me and smelled my coat and wagged his tail and made it a business to slobber on my face.

I sat down on the edge of the pit he'd dug with his chain and wondered why old O.U.B. kept him. He was a nice dog but the fur was rubbed off his neck from the collar and because he kept pulling his chain around his house in a circle. When Wanda got him wormed, he wouldn't be OFF LIMITS anymore because his health would be better, but since Wanda was OFF LIMITS I didn't know how she could worm him. Since her house was OFF LIMITS I couldn't go over and ask her how to do it myself.

I didn't care about the library card because Susannah Alexander always made me go into the children's section and I'd already read all those books. I didn't want to write letters to Edie about my problems and put them in a box because Mike the dog's worms were my problem and he was already OFF LIMITS. The New Rules didn't say I could write about Graceanne's problems. I didn't have any friends, not even of the opposite sex, so I couldn't ask anybody to come meet Edie and get permission. I already knew the house was not a democracy. It had never been a democracy. Everybody was a dictator except me and I was their slave when they noticed me at all.

But I had won the Sacajawea Raking Contest and I had the sacred arrowhead and that seemed to put an obligation on me but I didn't know what I could do and I didn't know what to do something about. The New Rules confused me. Each rule was clear, but in a set they seemed to make things worse.

I gave Mike the dog a pat on the head and looked at his brown eyes. His eyes looked like Wanda's over the fence. And

I thought that was a trick of my mind because they were both OFF LIMITS. I went across the pit and crawled into Mike's house and got Graceanne's birthday present out. It was under a ratty old army blanket, and I'd had it finished since the end of September. I carried it into the house and looked around for Graceanne and she was in our room, sitting on the cold floor in front of the mirror that had been in Edie's room on Lewis and Clark Hill. It was a full-length mirror from Woolworth's that you could bend a little, its wood frame was so thin. We'd never got it hung up and it just sat against the wall next to Graceanne's chest of drawers.

She was sitting there Indian-style and she'd had a shower. She looked better. Her legs just had puffy pink streaks and the blood was gone and there were only a few thin cuts, like paper cuts, and I thought Edie could have used a newspaper rolled up around one of the window sticks after the wooden spoon broke. Graceanne's hair was wet the way it was when she washed it without taking down the braids. She didn't have her glasses on and her left eye was wandering like she was looking at two things at once.

"Charlie, do you think I'm ugly? I mean, I know I'm not a beauty like Tucka, but how bad is it?"

"I don't think you're ugly."

"Do you think I'm pretty?"

"No."

"Well, you little snake. What do you think?"

"I wish they had corrective shoes for your eye."

"My eye doesn't wander when I have my glasses on."

"Oh, I thought you meant how you look without."

She put her glasses on. "Now what do you think?"

"I think you've got the best face in Cranepool's Landing."

"You're such a liar."

"It's the truth. Graceanne, you have a nice face." I got on my bed and put her birthday present beside me still wrapped in the blanket and looked over her shoulder into the mirror. "When your lips go down all the way to normal again and stop being blue, I expect you'll be a looker and your knockers are coming in and the boys at school all want to fight you so they can get a feel."

Graceanne looked like I'd bit her. "Charlie Farrand, you little pervert! I didn't know you knew about such things."

"I know all about perverts, too, and I'm not a pervert. I'm a jerk."

She scooted around on the floor and looked me in the face. "Is that what the kids are saying at school?"

"Yeah, but they don't have to say it because I already know. I don't have any friends and I make good grades and I bring my own lunch, which I even make myself. I'm a jerk."

"Well, Charlie, I'll tell you something. I think you're a sweet little boy, *sometimes*, and Sacajawea's rightful heir, and you can just ignore those mean kids. They'll all grow up to be just like Edie and live in Nigger Town. It serves her right to be poor and work all the time and have a bad kid like me."

"You're not a bad kid."

"I'm not a good kid. What you got in that blanket? It smells like the dog."

"It's your birthday present."

Graceanne's eyes looked like she was about to cry. "I didn't think I was going to have a birthday this year, Charlie."

She got up and I could tell it hurt her to stand and she waited for a minute and then she came and sat down on the bed and pulled the blanket off the present. It was a wooden box I'd found behind Cronin's Grocery and I'd painted it radio-brown by mixing my red and green tempera pot paints and there were all the planets made out of colored clay lined up along one side and dried and stuck on with glue. I was hoping Graceanne wouldn't think it was junk, and now that

I looked at it in our room it didn't look as good as it had in September.

Graceanne started crying, and I said, "I'm sorry Grace-anne. It was all I could think of and all I could afford. I just wanted to give you something nice."

She took the radio and went over to the window sill and looked out and then she put it on the sill and looked at the planets. "You made Pluto too big," she said. "But all the rest look just like they do in books." She kept her back turned to me. "You made it with your own two hands, Charlie."

I couldn't think of anything to say. I couldn't tell if she liked it. She went and sat down again in front of the mirror.

"You've helped me make a decision, Charlie." She picked up Edie's sewing scissors from the floor. "I've got to start acting more grown up. Start taking other people into account and stop being so selfish. Charlie, it's all over and behind me now. Mama's going to pay the fines and I've got a fresh start. I'm glad it happened."

She held one of her braids in her hand and pulled it down as tight as it would go and she took the scissors and started cutting a few inches above the rubber band. Her hair was wet and thick and cutting it across made her grip the scissors so I could see her knuckles turn grey. Then she did the same with the other braid. She put the scissors down and stared at herself and put her hands on her head and fluffed out her hair. The lines from the braids made it look like she had curls all over her head and she swung her head around, drying it. The drier it got, the shorter it got, until she had a mess of curls all over her head and she looked different.

"Graceanne, what are you going to do about Wanda?"

"You read the rules, Charlie. I can't see her anymore."

"You're going to obey?"

"I'll be her friend when I grow up and move out of this house. I don't want another night like last night."

"Me either."

I didn't think I'd been asleep all night. There was something like a dream, but I wasn't asleep so I didn't know what it was.

I was looking through a wall of honeysuckle, with green leaves and yellow sunlight spotted all around. I was looking over the edge of a giant, bright green leaf that was shining in the sun and the sweet smell of the flowers was all around and I kept picking off the flowers, one by one, and drinking from them to see if it was true that sometimes the wasps missed a flower and you could drink the nectar that would make you drunk on its sweetness. The sun was all around and warm on my shoulders and all the flowers were dry inside but I kept picking them and drinking. The flowers were yellow and looked like little trumpets, the kind you see on Christmas cards but hanging upside down, and the noise of the wasps was getting louder and louder but I believed that there was one flower on the vine that still had its nectar that the wasps had not found. I could see my hands among the green leaves feeling for the flowers and streaks of sunlight coming through the vine and touching the little hairs on my arms and the whining buzz of the wasps was in my ears. I raised up and looked over the giant green leaf and stuck my nose into a flower and I could see Graceanne in the sparkling green water on the other side of the honeysuckle vine and the air was yellow with sunlight and she was not wearing her glasses and I moved my face to suck the yellow flower and just as the sweet nectar spilled into my mouth at last a fierce orange-and-white tiger leapt at Graceanne, roaring through the air with its yellow trumpet fangs dripping saliva and a scream came into my ears and I started choking and the sun moved in the sky and I was hot all over and I sat up in bed breathing hard.

It looked like there were tiny lights like stars dancing

around the room, and I could see the shape of Graceanne in her bed across the room. There was a chill in the air and I pulled the covers up to my shoulders and listened. I could hear Mike the dog's chain moving in the backyard.

Seventeen

*A*bout noon Collier came to the door. He was wearing a Notre Dame sweater and carrying a box wrapped in pink paper with a pink ribbon and I thought about how ugly the radio was that I had made and how the blanket smelled like the dog.

"Hello, Charlie. Is Grace home?"

"She's home but her face looks bad and her hair is cut."

I heard Graceanne scream, "I'll whale you for that, Charlie."

Collier smiled. "You all got a cat since you moved away from the Hill, Charlie?"

"Collier, how come you like Graceanne and not some other girl like Tucka who's more your age?"

"It's a pretty good puzzle, isn't it, Charlie?" he said, but he was smiling.

Graceanne came to the door wearing her red sweater that buttoned up with white plastic seashells and her blue jeans and her hair was all dry like a cloud of blond curls all over her head and her glasses were on so her eye wasn't wandering. Her mouth looked better to me, but I could tell that Collier didn't like it.

"What happened to you, Grace?"

"I fell down the stairs."

"No, you didn't. Somebody hit you."

And I guessed Sacajawea would have told Lewis and Clark the truth so I said, "Mama hit her."

Collier looked at me and he looked at Graceanne. "Why'd she hit you?"

I could see Graceanne thinking it over. It was quiet for a long time, and she finally said, "I'm selfish and it's lying if a person hides the truth, and I brought it on myself."

And then I said, "Mama has a tiger inside that has to get out and it got out on Graceanne last night."

"Poor little Grace," Collier said. And he bent down and kissed her mouth soft like he was afraid he'd break her lips. His face turned red but hers didn't and I said, "What's in the box?"

Collier looked at it like he'd forgotten it was there, and he said, "I brought this from South Bend. Happy birthday, Grace. Happy thirteenth birthday. You're now as old as Juliet."

"Juliet who?"

"Grace, for a girl that knows all about the Battle of Britain, you sure are ignorant about Literature. *Juliet!* From *Romeo and Juliet* by Shakespeare."

"Oh, her."

"Yes, her."

"Well, I bet she never said anything as **influential** as 'this was their finest hour.' "

"As far as I know, Grace, you're the only person in the world who ever compared Juliet to Winston Churchill. And decided she didn't stack up."

He put the box in her hands, and she looked at the shiny pink paper. The wind was kicking up and brown leaves were blowing onto our gravel from the sidewalk. Graceanne's hair was blowing, too, and she put her hand up like she couldn't figure out what was on her face.

"Your hair looks pretty like that," Collier said. "I hardly miss your braids at all. I guess you were right all along about that. Open the box."

She sat down on the steps and opened it and there inside was a Notre Dame sweater like his. She stuck her hands in and lifted it out of the tissue paper and held it up in the wind. "Is this what they wear to the football games, Collier?"

"You can wear it wherever you like, Grace."

"Well, I'm gonna wear it right now." She got up and took the sweater and the box and wrapping paper and went inside. Collier sat down on the steps where she had been.

"Charlie, does your mother hit Graceanne very often?"

I thought about that. "I guess not. She pulls on her arms mostly. Smacks her around. And tries to shake sense into her."

"That's pretty stupid, isn't it?"

I'd never thought about it like that before, or heard anybody say anything like that, and I looked at Collier's face. It seemed like an ordinary face, not interesting like Graceanne's. His eyes were brown and his hair was brown and he had nice eyebrows.

"How old are you, Collier?"

"Eighteen. How old are you?"

"Going on ten come December."

I sat down next to him and we watched the leaves.

"Charlie, do you think you could shake sense into someone?"

"I guess not."

"No. It's much more likely that you'd shake sense *out* of someone."

"Well, if Mama only shakes one third of Graceanne's brains out, she'll still be smarter than most people."

"Oh, yeah? What makes you say that, Charlie?"

"It's her IQ. She's got the highest in the school."

"That's just a test and a number, Charlie. It doesn't mean that your sister can spare any part of her brain, no matter how smart she is."

"Are you smart, Collier?"

"Not as smart as I'd like to be."

"How smart would you like to be?"

He laughed. "Smart enough to answer your question."

Graceanne came out behind us. The wind was blowing her hair all around and she was wearing the Notre Dame sweater. She had the sleeves rolled up over her strong little wrists.

Collier stood up and whistled. "It looks cute on you, Grace."

"How come you call her Grace instead of Graceanne?" I said.

Graceanne gave me a little Mexican Hanky and said, "Mind your beeswax, Charlie."

But Collier said, "Because of the way she moves. You should watch your sister move sometime, Charlie. It's a lesson, the way she moves. She sure got the right name."

They started down the stairs. I watched Graceanne moving, but she just moved like she always did. I went down the stairs, too. Graceanne stopped.

"Get back up there, Charlie Farrand."

"Why?"

"Because two's company, three's a crowd, and four in the backseat is not allowed."

I sat down on the steps, and they walked away toward the river. The wind kept blowing around the leaves and I could hear Mike the dog's chain. I went around the side and old O.U.B. was out there bringing some water and a hot dog to the pit. The dog was wagging his tail and whining and jumping up at the end of his chain, yanking his own neck around.

O.U.B. put the water down and gave him some rough pats and held the hot dog up in the air. Mike the dog jumped and got it and ate it in one bite. The dust in the pit was blowing into the water dish.

I walked to the edge of the pit and O.U.B. opened his empty mouth and gave me a grin. "Hello, boy. I guess you like this old nigger's dog, huh?" He laughed and some of the dust blew into his mouth. He smelled like something old and broken in a basement. He walked back to his door and went inside.

Mike the dog kept standing up on his hind legs and dancing around the pit, the long hairs on his legs waving like flags. I wished I knew how to worm him. I walked through the back yard and swung on the clothesline pole and I saw Wanda come out to the fence and look at me. I kept swinging and she kept watching and I looked at her dark hair and how the wind didn't make it move at all. I dropped off of the pole and went upstairs to Fort McBain and made myself some tomato soup and an orange. Kentucky still wasn't home, so I made up her bed for her and went back to my room and saw the radio on the window and thought how I ought to go and put it back in Mike the dog's house where it belonged. Through the front window I saw Wanda had come around to stand on the sidewalk. That was public property, so she could stand there no matter what Edie's New Rules said. She had a little box in her hand wrapped in Christmas paper. I took off out the front door and ran to the sidewalk.

"Wanda. If you stay on the public property, you can tell me how to worm the dog."

"I said I'd worm that dog for you, Charlie, and I will. You just stop your worriting."

"Is that box for Graceanne's birthday?"

"That's right."

"You gonna give it to her on public property?"

"Charlie, I don't think you understand. We're not supposed to associate on *any* property."

"How you gonna give it to her then?"

"You just wait and see."

I looked down the street toward the river. The sidewalks on both sides of McBain Avenue were covered with leaves, and the branches overhead were almost bare and were dark and looked as tough and heavy as iron, meeting and tangling over the street. The sky was grey through them and I wondered why I hadn't noticed any bare branches over on Lewis and Clark Hill but only piles of red and gold leaves on the ground, the long, slick track of grass between that was supposed to be the Northwest Passage, and the kids on their cardboards, the white explorers headed for the Pacific.

Raindrops, one or two at a time, plopped through the iron branches and fell to the street. I could smell the rain and the sky was darker now up beyond the iron trees. Lights were going on in the Development houses and in the tiny white clapboard houses that had been on McBain Avenue long enough to be ready to fall down. I wondered how old Nigger Town was, if those tiny houses had always been colored houses, where the colored people had all come from, and what O.U.B. did to earn his rent and liquor money and money for hot dogs he gave to the dog.

Graceanne and Collier appeared at the end of the street from the direction of the river and their two Notre Dame sweaters came along under the dark branches. I could see Graceanne was talking and Collier was listening and I wished I could hear them and that she was telling him about the New Rules because I thought her sweater came under the one about permission for the opposite sex.

Wanda stood there until Graceanne and Collier were about ten feet away. Graceanne wasn't talking anymore. She was looking at Wanda.

Graceanne stopped and said. "There's a girl standing there, Collier, that looks like she'd be so smart she'd know how to worm a dog and how to fight with a knife and how to stay out of trouble that comes from white trash."

Wanda turned aside and Started talking to a tree. "There's a girl on the sidewalk that looks like she'd be so nice she'd be best friends with a colored girl and never put anything in her hand for a fight and let trouble come on her without making enough noise to bother the neighbors."

Wanda put the box in Christmas paper down on the sidewalk, stepped into the street, walked around Graceanne and Collier, and went to her house. She opened the door and went inside without looking back.

Graceanne was slow coming to get the box and when she picked it up, she put it in the pocket of the sweater and didn't open it.

"Grace," Collier said, "don't you want to open it?"

"I know what it is."

"What is it?"

"Private property. It's between me and her."

Collier stayed a few minutes, but the rain was setting in hard and he left. We went inside and Graceanne went to the kitchen to get a glass of milk and we opened the back door and sat on the sill with our feet on the porch and watched the rain. Mike the dog was in his house looking out at us.

"Graceanne, did Collier kiss you again?"

"No."

"Why not?"

"He just didn't. Mind your business."

"But why not?"

"We were skipping rocks."

"Did you like it when he kissed you on the porch?"

"Not much."

"Why not?"

"Mind your business."

"But why not?"

"Charlie, I don't know. It just felt strange to have somebody touching me that wasn't family and wasn't fighting me. Now leave it be."

The rain smelled good as it fell and made the dust in the pit lay down.

Kentucky finally came home, but she didn't say where she'd been all day. She read the New Rules and laughed. She tore up her library card and put the pieces in the household kitty. I got my card and did the same. I asked Graceanne where her card was and she said Edie'd already got it.

Kentucky got supper, which was fried hamburgers and succotash. I set the table. Edie came home and we ate. Then Edie went into the Garden Room and brought out an envelope with a bow taped on it and put it on the table in front of Graceanne.

"Open it, Graceanne," Edie said, and she put her thumb on one end of her mouth and her ring finger on the other end and started pulling them together toward the middle.

"I know what's in it."

"Well, open it so we can all see."

Graceanne used her butter knife to slit the envelope and she took out a blue check made out to the Cranepool's Landing Library System for $59.16.

"Thank you, Mama."

"Happy birthday, Graceanne. Let's hope this is a good lesson."

"Let's hope, Mama."

"Who cut your hair? You look quite nice, Graceanne, although I expect those curls won't last. They're just wrinkles from your braids."

"I cut it myself."

"Well, you did a good job. When you've finished cleaning

the table, you can leave that sweater on my bed."

Graceanne scraped the plates into the Gallon of Goodies tub from the freezer, and everybody settled down to listen to the rain and read their books and put on an extra pair of socks. I kept wondering why Kentucky hadn't given Graceanne a present.

We were getting ready for bed when Edie came into our room. "You better stay home from church tomorrow, Graceanne. It looks like you might be getting an infection on your mouth. Face the light and let me have a look."

Graceanne turned her head and Edie checked her.

We got in bed and Edie shut off the light.

I could hear Mike the dog's chain moving, and I looked at the window. It was covered with drops of water that sparkled from the streetlight. There was Graceanne's planet radio, all covered with reflections from the raindrops.

"I wish I'd gotten you something nicer, Graceanne."

"Stop that talk. I'll whale you good if you make any more cracks about my radio. Why don't you turn it on so we can listen to Saturn?"

I got out of bed and touched the piece of yellow clay that had the ring I had rolled thin between my palms and got back in bed.

"That's nice," Graceanne said. "Goodnight, Charlie."

I listened to the rain and the music from Saturn and fell asleep.

December 1960

The Ice Baby

Eighteen

$\mathcal{W}$inter brought some early snow and a couple of ice storms bad enough to bring down power lines, but McBain Avenue shimmered under its glaze of ice, and diamond dust coated our windows. The trees that overhung the street dipped heavily and swayed in the icy blasts from the river, and they produced a cracking and wheezing that, combined with the whistling from across the water, brought a strange music to the Developments. The newer stucco unit buildings, standing as they did in fields of white gravel and contructed without any gables or front porches or interesting angles or any sign at all of imagination, took the coating of ice as though it had been painted on with a roller, the only variation in texture being the icicles that hung from the gutters surrounding the flat roofs. The smaller, older houses, however, interspersed among the development homes, were weirdly beautiful and sometimes satisfyingly creepy in the twisted, mangled shapes the ice wrapped around them. At night, when the streetlights were working, the neighborhood looked like a town made out of sugar by a pair of rival confectioners competing for the house trade: one who spread his creations with even strokes of the spatula, one who worked with mad, spastic drama and an egg whisk.

The river shouldered against its banks, pushing cracked and jagged plates of ice up under the roots of shore oaks that teetered and then settled back into their loose soil. The water looked black and fast out in the middle, straight and smooth without the churning, boiling currents of spring.

That December, we were waiting to see how our new president would behave. Missouri had given its electoral votes to John Kennedy, but Cranepool's Landing had voted almost solidly for Richard Nixon, and Graceanne's stickers were still up on the light poles, visible under the ice as reminders of her underhanded campaign on behalf of the losing candidate and the eventual choice of Cranepool's Landing. Edie would never tell us who she voted for—"a vote is a sacred and private matter"—but I always felt it must have been Kennedy. Whatever had angered her enough to include Graceanne's campaigning in the New Rules, I did not believe that Edie had actually figured out Graceanne's twisted strategy.

By winter that year I had celebrated a birthday, too. Mine was marked with more pomp than Graceanne's, thanks mainly to her efforts. She made a disaster of a cake—a spongy, thick, glutinous mass of coconut and chocolate and balls of flour, and she iced it with caramels melted in a pan over a burner. Edie was going to throw the pan away, with a cheerful remark about its "being retired after a strenuous tour of duty," but I salvaged it from the trash and sneaked it out to Mike. He licked the burned caramel for about a minute before he gave it up and spent the next twenty minutes or so at his water dish, chewing through the layer of ice on the top. There was snow in his pit, and icicles hanging from the roof of his house, which had been treated by the conservative confectioner's smooth spatula, and Mike's breath floated around his long tongue like fog around a streetlight.

My best gift was clandestine and known only to two people. On the morning of my birthday, I was in the kitchen early and I happened to glance at the window on the door where I saw a dark shape moving in the yard. The window was covered with ice crystals, and I had to scrape it with the sleeve of my pajamas, but through the circle I made on the glass I saw Wanda carrying a bowl toward Mike's pit. Whatever she had in that bowl shook like Jell-O and appeared to have the consistency of mashed potatoes when she dumped it into Mike's pan. He lapped it up and then went running in circles around his doghouse, dragging his chain through the snow and ice. Wanda sat on her haunches and watched him with her head to one side as though she were judging a dog-in-the-snow contest of some sort, then she shook herself, took her bowl and walked away, shuffling her boots to sweep away her footprints and leaving a wide line in the snow. Mike spent the greater part of that day scratching himself on the icy pit, relieving himself all over the snow, and lying in his doghouse on his side. Old O.U.B. went out with a shovel and cleaned the pit and Mike had two home-cooked meals in one day and was wormed.

Graceanne gave me a bag of quarters totaling seven dollars and a piece of paper she had drawn to look like a gift certif-icate from Parks Department Store, and I submitted them both to Edie with a request for new shoes. She took me down to the store that day, contributed money to the gift certificate, and I had my first pair of normal shoes. They were a rather horrifying and thick representative of the saddle oxford line of cruel and unusual fashion, practical and cheap, the kind of shoes only jerks wore, but they were *normal* and they fit and I was pleased. Graceanne wrote her name in blue ink on the white toe of the right shoe and suddenly they were not so jerky. Kentucky added her name, Edie signed her initials, and I wrote "Thumper" on the heel of the right shoe and went out to stroll in the snow, also wearing the red mittens Kentucky had crocheted for me. There were green giraffes embroidered on them with tiny, intricate stitches. Edie asked her where she had learned to embroider, but Kentucky smiled and said, "Ask me no questions, Mama." I knew only one person who could embroider like that.

Since Graceanne's dark and miserable rainy birthday, Kentucky had developed more and more of a secret existence, staying away from home whenever she could and giving careful, evasive answers when we asked her what she did with all her time. She didn't get on the bus with Graceanne and me after school, and the only days we knew for sure where she was were those days when the choir practiced over in the church. She would arrive home in time to get supper on the table, or, if she didn't, she would have made a quiet arrangement with Graceanne to cover her lateness by offering to do the dishes or iron Graceanne's uniform blouse.

Getting supper on the table was not much of production because we ate a great deal of Gallon of Goodies that winter, and that, once made, only had to be ladled into a pan and heated up. Graceanne apparently felt so inundated by the wretched stuff that she memorialized it in her book:

THE JUPITER COOKING HOUR
brought to you by Eden's Bellyache Dogbiscuits

Good evening and welcome again to the Jupiter Cooking Hour. Tonight's featured menu comes to us all the way from the Great Red Spot. Here's how to make Gallon of Goodies.
Ingredients: everything you can scrape off plates, including everything but bread, even the ketchup, kept frozen for months
one FRESH can tomatoes, cut up

macaroni
water and salt to taste

Procedure: Thaw it and warm it and stir in the noodles.

Caution: It has no taste of its own and looks like glue, but it will STICK TO YOUR RIBS and PUT HAIR ON YOUR CHEST and LIFT YOUR SPIRITS and PUT A ZING IN YOUR STEP and KEEP BODY AND SOUL TOGETHER.

And that's how the Vomit People of Jupiter came to look the way they do. Tune in next time for our show on 1,001 things you can do with Gallon of Goodies in the privacy of your own home.

When I saw something as close to home as Gallon of Goodies on the planet Jupiter, I began to understand that Graceanne's book was not about a fictional girl, and I felt I had two great keys to unlock the vault of imagination where both memory and imagination are stored and write a book of my own: I knew that the Mackerel Catechism was a coded record of the times Edie beat Graceanne to shape her up right, and I knew that Gloria Rosina Festitootitoo was the girl who shared my room. I tried again to set down my own thoughts in a pristine notebook, but once again I found myself writing a story about a boy who had a sister, a girl who found a radio that . . . and so on. I came to believe that the secret to the whole process lay somehow in coming to terms with the Martian astronomers who were so central to Graceanne's book.

Tonight on Mars, we are sad to report, there has been an outbreak of the Phobosian plague. The scientific community has been especially beset by this ailment which was thought to be under control by shots. The observatories are being manned by Channel Monkeys trained to push buttons, but they cannot do the job of the sick astronomers, and we appeal to your generosity to give money so a cure can be found or new astronomers hired so that once again the work of knowing everything can be done so people can be happy.

Graceanne certainly was not happy that winter. The ban on "the Negro element" had deformed her impulses and was stifling the part of her fierceness that was all bound up in her friendship with Wanda. She had other friends, but none who could match her in tough games, or share "serious" books with her, or who were interested in going along when she went to the river with her ice pick. Graceanne wanted to learn how to carve ice, and Wanda not only knew how, she had spectacular examples of her work all over her front yard. Everyone on McBain Avenue was using the ice for something. There were ice castles in the yards where there were kids, and some colored people were hanging their clothes out to dry on a web of ice because their clothesline was frozen to the ground, and older kids were carving their initials in the ice and scratching out what Edie called "vulgarities-there-ought-to-be-a-law." Even old O.U.B. was breaking off the icicles from over his door and taking them into his unit, but I never could figure out what he was using them for.

I went with Graceanne to the river and helped her haul out slabs of the grey and brown river ice, because Fort McBain, with its tightly fitting coat of ice stuck to the building as slick as paint, could not provide Graceanne with the materials she needed. She needed wilder ice than we had on our house. Down by the cracked and heaving shoreline, I would hand her the ice pick and the knife Wanda had given her in the box with the Christmas paper, but nothing she tried to make came out looking like what she said it was going to be. She'd try and try and end up kicking the chipped and slashed slab of ice back over the bank and into the black water of the Mississippi.

"It's just like when I try to draw people, Charlie. They all come out like stick men. I'll never be an artist like Wanda."

"That's what you want to be? An artist?"

"No. I just want to be able."

"Why?"

"Charlie, didn't you ever want to do something just because it made you ache to see other people doing it? You know, like when you were still a dead kid and watched us going down the slide at the lake."

"I guess. But I reckon Wanda has the hands, like her Mama, and Graceanne, you can't even draw good on paper."

"I know that! Charlie, you just don't understand."

But I did understand. I was aching to have my own book like Graceanne's only I couldn't tell her that for some reason and I couldn't tell her I was unable.

But Wanda was able, and she had used the fantastic ice from her house, and her yard was full of little people and animals—a little Graceanne, a little Charlie, a little O.U.B., two little Mike the dogs, little bees, and a beautiful tall statue of her mother, sewing with a needle of ice. Graceanne used to go to the fence and stare over at Wanda's ice and shake her head. Wanda'd come out and stare back and go to whittling on a slab of ice and suddenly there'd be someone in her cold dark hands that I'd recognize.

It was tearing Graceanne apart to see all that ice turn into people she couldn't make, and I could tell she wanted to knock Wanda on the shoulder and get her to show her how to do it with her own pieces so they wouldn't come out looking like something the cat dragged in.

The sun was out real low and the light was slanting yellow

across Wanda's front yard when she started on Edie. Wanda had a big piece of ice that she'd pulled off where it was hanging from the roof and it was a thick, wavy piece that looked like a bathroom window, only much thicker, about like a wall. We watched her throw it on the sidewalk to break it and then she took the thickest middle piece and dipped it in a can of hot water. It was dripping all over her bare dark hands and she went after it with an ice pick and the side of her thumb. She'd lean her thumb into it and hold it there until the ice melted a little from her own warmth. She'd get up and go in the house and come back with her hands smoking from steam and she'd start to work again. Soon, under those steaming hands, there was Edie's face, with her little nose and her wide forehead and her square jaw that looked like Graceanne's and her mouth that looked like it was too small.

Wanda put Edie down on the ground and got one of the broken pieces from the sidewalk and put it on top of Edie where the chest should be and poured the can of water over it and went back inside. We waited and watched while the ice-Edie lay there sparkling in the sun on the sidewalk. When Wanda came out, the two pieces were one piece and she started whittling. It took her a couple of hours, and we had to go in to eat, and I fed Mike the dog some fried baloney, and when all that was done, Wanda had a two-foot Edie standing on her sidewalk and the sun was shining on it like a lamp on a soap bubble.

Graceanne and I stood at the fence with our hands poked through the chain links, and Wanda stood back and looked at what she had made. She got her blue wool gloves off the porch rail and put them on. She took the snow shovel from the side of the porch and came and gave the sparkling woman a whack across the neck. The head went flying into the street, bouncing and chipping.

"White trash," Wanda said, and put the shovel back against the porch.

Nineteen

$\mathcal{W}$e stood around the fence, looking at the ice head in the street for a while and then Graceanne went and picked it up and carried it back to Wanda's yard and stood there holding it.

"There's an ice contest over at our church for the Blossoms in the Snow Festival," she told Wanda, and I thought her first words to her friend in more than a month should have been something more important, something like "this was their finest hour," or something Juliet had said, or something that Collier had written in a letter. But Graceanne just went on like all that time that had passed hadn't passed at all. "You oughta make an entry."

"Wanda's a Baptist," I yelled through the fence.

Graceanne gave me a look. "So? The rules don't say you have to be a goddamn Catholic. There's only rules for **execution, originality,** and **appropriateness** of *theme*—not for your persuasion."

"What's the theme?" Wanda asked, looking Graceanne over like she had a new coat on, which she didn't.

"Christmas. Funny how they want us to be original and they come up with that."

"I could make something, I guess."

"I could help."

"Graceanne, you can't carve ice worth a squat."

"You can show me."

"What'll we make?"

Graceanne looked at the ice head in her hands. "A person. You make them better than anybody."

"What person?"

I put the toes of my saddle oxfords through the holes in the fence and stood up higher. "Make Santa Claus," I said.

Graceanne snorted like a horse. "He's too easy. Everybody will make him. All's he is, is a bunch of circles. Besides, Wanda oughta make a real person."

"Make John Kennedy," I said through the fence.

"What the hell's he got to do with Christmas?"

"He's the president."

"What's that got to do with Christmas?"

"He's probably gonna give his kids a pony or something like a nice dog for Christmas."

"Charlie, shut up or go in the house."

I closed my mouth and watched through the fence. Graceanne was turning the ice head around in her hands. "Why don't you make the Baby Jesus and all that Bethlehem **melodrama?**"

Wanda sat down on her porch steps. "I don't know. I never made a baby before. And I don't have one around to look at."

"You could chop off pieces of this head to make it smaller. Babies are just smaller than real people. And you could go down and look at the new baby at the Walters' house."

"I could. But what's so original about making the Baby Jesus?"

Graceanne frowned and looked at the head she was holding. "Yeah. Nothing, I guess. I'll think of something else."

I started shaking the fence back and forth and the icy links made a racket like Mike moving his chain. Graceanne and Wanda turned and looked at me.

"You wish to speak, child?" Graceanne said.

I rattled the fence.

"Okay, Charlemagne, you *may* speak, but it better not be something stupid again like John Kennedy or I'm gonna march you into the house and whale you good."

"Make the Baby Jesus," I said, shaking and shaking the fence I was so excited.

"Charlie, we already decided that's not original."

"Make him a NIGGER," I yelled.

The sun was shining on their heads and they looked at each other and they looked at me and Graceanne started pawing her feet on the ice.

"Jesus was white," Graceanne said.

"Maybe he was colored," I said.

"No, he was definitely white."

"Does it say in the Bible?"

"I never heard it, but I would've heard if he'd been a colored baby." Graceanne put her hands on her hips like Edie sometimes did. "You think half the whole goddamn world would be worshipping a Negro, Charlie, and still going around and making Whites Only? What the hell you got in your head? Gallon of Goodies?"

"The Bible's too hard to understand," I said, rattling the fence. "Maybe it says he was colored and nobody can tell that's what it says. He got hung like a nigger and they smote him on the head. And they wouldn't let him stay in any of the inns. And he got the sacrament from John the *Baptist*."

Graceanne and Wanda looked at me like I'd grown a bald head.

Wanda pulled on Graceanne's red coat. "Wouldn't it be a kick in the ass if Jesus was colored?"

Graceanne smiled so wide I thought her jaw would crack.

"Charlie, where'd you get the brown paint for my radio?"

"I made it!"

"Can you make some more?"

I took off for the house and fell when I was going up the steps and scraped a hole in my brown corduroy pants and went into our room and got out my pot paints. They were all dried up, but I went into the bathroom and ran hot water in the pots and soon it was paint again. I poured some red into the green and put the lid on again and shook it. And there was radio brown, my new Negro paint. I went running outside and stood by the fence with the pot in my hand. Graceanne and Wanda were down on their knees and Graceanne had her knife out drawing pictures. She had scraped and broken through the ice so she could draw in the snow underneath. "This'll be the manger, which I will make out of river ice. The baby will fit in right here. We need some real straw."

"We can get packing straw from Cronin's Grocery," Wanda said.

I rattled the fence and Graceanne came and got the pot from me. She poured a little bit on the broken Edie ice head but it ran off and the ice was just as white as it always was. "This ain't gonna work."

"What you need is to make holes in the head so the paint will go in 'thout running off like that," Wanda said.

"You can't have a Baby Jesus with holes in his head, you moron." Graceanne hauled off and gave Wanda a good shove.

Wanda shoved her back onto her butt. "I can use my mama's needles. The holes'll be so small nobody can see 'em, but they'll let the paint come into the ice."

"That might work."

"It'll work. I know ice and I know needles."

Graceanne gave Wanda a look. "What'd you shove me for?"

"You ast for it."

They fought for a while and then Wanda settled down to whittle on Edie's head to make it a baby size and Graceanne went off to the river to drag out some ice for the manger. Without even being asked, I went down to Cronin's and got the packing straw that pork came in.

When I got back with it, I rattled the fence and said, "He had to be colored. The prophet said, 'Out of Egypt I have called my son.' Egypt's in Africa and Jesus was called out of there. He was born in Egypt."

Graceanne came around the fence and cuffed me on the shoulder. "He was not. Jesus was born in Bethlehem. Everybody knows that. Everybody except you."

"Where's Bethlehem?"

"It ain't in Africa."

"Well, he went to Africa."

"He did not."

"He did so, Graceanne. To Egypt."

"So?"

"So Egypt's in Africa."

She gave me another cuff. "I know that."

"Well, I bet Wanda hasn't been to Africa."

Wanda gave me a look. "Charlie, if you think that means there's a chance I ain't a Negro, you can go think again."

When it was getting on for dark-thirty, they took all the parts and put them under Wanda's porch and we went home and acted like we hadn't been associating with a Negro.

At dinner I asked Edie if Jesus was white.

"Of course he was, Charlie. Why would you ask such a question?"

"I was just wondering."

"Well, of all the things to wonder about, that takes the cake." Edie did that thing she did with her fingers pulling on her mouth and I looked at her to see if she looked like the icehead Wanda'd made.

"What was his religion?" I asked.

"Catholic," Edie said. "You sure are full of strangeness tonight."

Graceanne looked up from her plate of Gallon of Goodies that Kentucky had warmed up. "Jesus was a Jew, Mama."

"Don't you say such a thing at this table, Graceanne."

"He was, Mama. It says in the Gospel that he was circumcised. Circumcised was one of the things Hitler made his soldiers look for when they were rounding up the Jews." Graceanne looked like she wanted to say something else but was thinking about it. "Hitler was an Austrian Catholic, Mama."

"Graceanne Farrand, I'll wash your mouth out with soap."

"Well, he was. He was raised Catholic."

"If you're so all-fired smart, how come you can't remember that we don't talk about religion at this table?"

"I didn't start it! Charlie did."

I looked around the table. Nobody was eating except me so I put my fork down.

Edie said, "Charlie started this by asking about what race Jesus was. That's race, not religion."

"Well, I guess you can't talk about Jesus without talking about religion," Graceanne said.

"Never mind that now," Edie said. "Let's just eat our supper like civilized people."

"I don't think civilized people eat Gallon of Goodies."

"That's enough smart remarks out of you, Graceanne."

I picked up my fork when I saw everybody else did. I ate for a while. "Mama, what's circumcised?"

"You don't need to know about that, Charlie. We don't have any Jews in Cranepool's Landing."

Suddenly Kentucky looked up from her plate. "Oh yes there is. Greg Novak is a Jew."

Graceanne's eyes got big behind her cracked glasses. "Greg Novak? How do you . . ." She stopped whatever she was going to say and turned red and looked down at her plate and put a big forkful of Gallon of Goodies in her mouth. Edie looked like she was going to choke. Kentucky just sat there and looked like she was thinking about the weather. I looked around and made a list in my mind.

1. Greg Novak was a Jew.
2. Jesus was a Catholic or a Jew.
3. Hitler was a Catholic.
4. Jesus was white.
5. Tucka had a secret way of telling if people were Jews.
6. I was white and Catholic.
7. It was a big surprise about Greg Novak because he went to our church.

"Mama," I said, "are we circumcised?"

Graceanne spit her Gallon of Goodies all over the kitchen table and Kentucky started laughing.

"Well, are we?"

Edie took her fingers and pulled them on her mouth. "No, Charlie, we're not."

"Why not?"

"Because only Jews can be circumcised."

"Oh."

8. I was not a Jew.

Everybody ate for a while except Graceanne who was cleaning her spitout Gallon of Goodies from the table with her knife and trying not to laugh. I thought awhile. "Is Mike circumcised?"

Graceanne slipped under the table and started laughing out loud and pounding the seat of her chair.

"No, Charlie," Edie said. "Only Jew boys, human Jew boys, can get circumcised."

I had one more question. "What race is the dog? He's brown and white. Is he white or a nigger?"

From under the table Graceanne's laughing voice yelled, "He's a whigger!"

"That'll be enough now," Edie said, but she was trying not to laugh. "Charlemagne will think we're making fun of him."

Graceanne's head appeared over the table. "Now I got a question." The laughing was all gone from Graceanne. "I just all of a sudden realized. How come we can't make fun of Charlie? How come he doesn't get KP? How come he doesn't get belted? How come you laugh when he breaks the dinner table rules? I'll bet you even gave him his library card back. He's adopted, isn't he? I'll bet he's adopted. Charlie's adopted!"

Edie pushed her chair back and stood up. "How can you say such a cruel thing in front of your brother? Of course he's not adopted. I would never do such a thing to a child! You shame me, Graceanne."

"I didn't mean it to shame, Mama." Graceanne's face was all serious and soft. "I wish I was adopted."

"What on earth for?"

"Then someday I could go find my real mother."

"I suppose you think you could find a better mother than me?" Edie was starting to turn red.

"No. No, ma'am."

"I should say not! How many other mothers do you think would slave twenty hours a day just to keep a roof over your heads and food in your mouths and clothes on your backs? And pay for a good Catholic education? And give up her whole life so you wouldn't have to see wanton drunkenness and carrying on? And never wear a pretty new dress or go anywhere or even see a movie because you kids take every nickel I'm made of?" Edie was breathing real hard and her hands were twitching.

"I didn't mean anything by it, Mama," Graceanne said, looking at the edge of her plate from where she was still kneeling by the table.

"Jesus was adopted," I said.

Edie turned and gave me a look over her nose. "Shame on you, Charlie. He was not."

"Joseph wasn't his real father. He adopted Jesus and didn't mind that Mary wouldn't let him get any on the honeymoon in Egypt."

Kentucky burst out laughing. "Next thing you know, Charlie'll be asking if *our* Daddy was God like Jesus' Daddy."

"He *is*," I said. "Father, Son, and Holy Ghost. He said so himself."

Edie slapped her hand down on the table and the forks rattled on the plates. "That's enough. I won't have sacrilege at this table. Graceanne, go to your room."

"Me?" Her eyes opened real big. "What'd I do?"

"You've been teaching Charlie un-Christian lies and slanders. Oh, I know, all the Baptists preach that free-living nonsense about Mary. Well, she was the Mother of God, and you got those lies and slanders from your little nigger Baptist friend."

"Well," Graceanne said and she stood all the way up. "All I can say is, one, I didn't. Two, it's my turn to do dishes and I'll be glad to go to my room. Three, this is the most unfair thing that ever happened. And, four, you said you'd never say 'nigger.' " She squeezed her wrinkled napkin down on my Gallon of Goodies and said, "There, Charlie, you little brat. Put that on your angel wings and give 'em a good polish."

"Don't you say 'brat,' " Edie yelled. "It's a bad word."

"Okay, then, he's a little Mama's boy. Mama. Boy. Not a bad word in sight."

My throat hurt when Graceanne said that. "I'm not a Mama's Boy. I'm not anybody's boy!"

Edie made a noise in the back of her mouth and her hand came shooting out and she grabbed Graceanne's hair so hard I could hear it squeak. "I'll beat you silly for that!" She dragged Graceanne to the kitchen door and pulled it open and threw her onto the porch so hard she hit the rail. I could hear the ice cracking under Graceanne's tennis shoes. Edie went onto the porch and lost her balance and grabbed the rail and gave Graceanne a shove and I could hear the ice groaning and cracking and Mike the dog's chain dragging across his pit and he was whining and yipping and Edie gave Graceanne a smack on her cheek and then I heard a loud crack and a crunching sound like hard cookies being thrown all over the icy yard and a smooth swishing sound and I knew that Mike the dog had got loose. The ice must've cracked his chain, and the cookie sounds were his feet going through the glaze on the snow around the yard and his chain was dragging behind. Edie grabbed the handle of the door and put her foot in the kitchen and she got in and closed the door with Graceanne on the outside.

She went through the kitchen holding her mouth with her two fingers and slammed the door of her room. Kentucky got up and threw her fork on the table so hard it bounced off onto the floor and she went and opened the back door. Mike the dog had come up the stairs and was jumping all over Graceanne and licking her. She was squatted down with her arms covering her curly head. Kentucky took the dog by the collar and pulled him off Graceanne and dragged him sliding and yipping down the stairs and she picked up a piece of ice and broke it on old O.U.B.'s door. When he opened it, she yelled at him. "Tend to your goddamn dog, you mean old nigger. You don't deserve to have such a fine, friendly, decent animal. You oughta know enough to keep a dog inside on a night like this."

She stomped back up the stairs, putting her feet just right so she didn't slip and put her arms around Graceanne and brought her inside. She saw me standing next to the refrigerator and said, "Told you she was afraid of that dog."

Out the door I could see the snow looking blue in the moonlight, and the dog's cookie prints running all over, and the track where Wanda had come to worm the dog, and the ice hanging from the clothesline pole like a bunch of rags, and each star in the black sky was a hole that needed patching so all the shame in our yard wouldn't run out into the universe.

Twenty

*W*hen I got up the sun was yellow on the ice glued over my window. Graceanne was gone, Kentucky was gone, and Edie was gone. I got dressed and put on my coat and went to see Mike the dog. His chain was hammered into the ground by a new spike through one of the links and he was running in a circle that was smaller than the old one that had dug his pit. I sat down so he could come over and get on my knees. I pulled some of the ice balls from his fur and broke through the glaze on his water so he could get a drink.

I went back inside and had some Cheerios from the box and went on into the Garden Room. I saw the letter box on Edie's dresser and sat down on her bed and wrote a letter:

> Dear Mama:
> I know I'm not adopted because I can tell by my jaw that I'm the same as you and Graceanne. Please don't be so mad.
> Charlemagne

I stuffed it in the box and went outside. The schools were closed early for the winter recess on account of the ice and lots of colored kids and some white trash were standing in front of Wanda's yard watching her and Graceanne make our entry in the Our Lady of Lourdes Blossoms in the Snow Festival Ice Contest. I had to put my hand up to block the sun because it was slanting off the ice like there were steel swords planted in the ground and they were all on fire. I saw Graceanne get up on Wanda's porch and start talking, the way she had wagged her tongue for the Nixon work, so I ran over to the fence.

"This is going to **establish** once and for all what color the Baby Jesus was. We're asking God for a sign to open our eyes and let us have a miracle. Most all of the miracles have kids in them, so you all say a prayer and be quiet."

She got down off of the porch and she crawled under and got the paint pot. She shook it, but there was a loud clunk like there was a brick inside it. She took it inside and brought it back out with a white bowl that had hot water in it. She dumped the chunk of brown paint in the bowl and stirred it around until the water turned brown, but I thought it was too loose for paint.

Wanda was sitting there with matches and a needle. She'd light a match and stick the needle in the flame to get it hot and then stick the needle into the face of the ice baby lying there on the sidewalk. I came closer and watched her. There were tiny holes all over the baby's face and it looked like she was putting a spell on him like the Red Indians did.

Graceanne went back up on the porch and started talking again. "We're just about ready. We're going to call this the Our Lady of McBain Miracle, because that's her baby on the sidewalk, and now let's all bow our heads for a moment of silence." All the kids bowed their heads but most of them kept their eyes rolled up all the time they did the bowing. Then Graceanne brought the bowl of water and asked Wanda if she was ready and Wanda said, "Ready." Graceanne poured the brown water slowly over the baby's head.

The ice baby's face looked like a real baby's face with its eyes open, and all the traces of Edie were gone. It was a new face. The sun was shining on its forehead and green and orange sparkles were inside the eyes. The brown water went over the eyes and I could see some of it hold and run inside through the tiny holes but some of it ran off onto the sidewalk. The kids all came closer and their shadows covered the baby. Graceanne kept pouring the water over the baby and its nose got a little smaller from the warm water, but the water was holding in the holes Wanda had made and we could see the baby getting darker and darker as Graceanne kept pouring.

When the water was gone, some of the dried chunks of paint fell out and hit the baby on the face. Wanda brushed them off with the pink underpart of her hand. Graceanne had to push a couple of the kids so she could stand up. "Stand back," she said, "and let's see God's answer."

The kids all took a few steps back and the shadow rolled away and the sun came back on the baby. Wanda stood up and turned her head this way and that and stared at the baby. Everybody stared at the baby.

Graceanne had a funny look on her face, but she went back up on the porch. "God has spoken and there's his answer on the sidewalk. That is the Miracle of Our Lady of McBain right there on the sidewalk. That's what color Jesus really was. I don't know of anything more original than a miracle, so you kids should all come to the Blossoms in the Snow Festival over across town and see that baby win the prize. Go home now and be sure to come to the Catholic church at four o'clock to see the Miracle Baby."

The kids stood around the baby for a while and then they all started going off to their houses because it was getting windy out. Graceanne put the packing straw into the manger she had made, which looked like a big scooped-out potato boat between two squares. Wanda put the baby in.

"What color would you say that baby is?" Wanda said.

"I don't know if that even *is* a color," Graceanne said. "I'd say he's dirty."

Baby Jesus looked dirty. His face was streaked and he had brown pin-size dots all over his whitish-grey face.

"Well," Graceanne said. "I guess that's the best we can do."

"Is it a real miracle, Graceanne?" I asked.

"A miracle is as a miracle does, Charlie. We'll see if it's a miracle when they give out the prizes." She put her wet mitten on my forehead. "Listen, I don't really think you're a Mama's boy. I was just beating my gums last night."

"I know. But I couldn't be a Mama's boy anyway. I'm more of a dog's boy."

"You sure are."

"Graceanne, why are you afraid of the dog?"

Wanda gave me a look. "Graceanne ain't afraid of no dog. She just *chooses* not to associate with that dog. Your sister ain't afraid of nothing."

"She's afraid of Mama."

"I ain't either," Graceanne said.

"My mama says Edie is a sick woman, Charlie," Wanda said. "She says it's a thing about power. She ain't got no power, no money, no time for herself. So she feels it all slipping away and to feel her some power, she takes it out on Graceanne and that makes her feel better because she takes away some of Graceanne's power and has it for herself. Graceanne's got a lot of power, as I knew right away when I met her."

"I don't want to talk about Mama," Graceanne said.

I did want to talk about Mama because nobody ever really did much. "Tucka says Mama's got a tiger inside her."

Wanda put her hand on my shoulder. "Everybody has a tiger. Even Mike's got a tiger. I got a tiger. My mama got a tiger. But my mama lets her tiger out through her fingers when she's sewing. Mike lets his out when he's licking off your face or digging his pit, but it don't get out all the way because of his chain, so you got to watch out for his tiger. That's why Graceanne chooses not to associate with that dog."

"Where's my tiger?" I asked, looking as hard as I could at Wanda's eyes that looked like glass in the bright sun shooting off the ice all around.

"Charlie, I reckon you're too young to be properly acquainted with your tiger just yet, as it is."

"Well, I know where Graceanne's is."

"Where?"

"It's in her book."

"What book?"

So Wanda didn't know about Graceanne's book. I thought Wanda knew everything about us. I couldn't make up a lie because I couldn't lie to the person who had wormed Mike the dog, but I couldn't tell her the truth because it was up to Graceanne to tell about that.

Finally, Graceanne said, "I got a book that I write, but it's dumb and I would've told you but it's just about stupid stuff."

"It is not," I said. "It's about the planets."

"See what I told you?" Graceanne said. "It's not even about Earth. That's how dumb it is."

It was sort of about Earth. It was about Jupiter, and Saturn, and mostly about Mars. About the astronomers on Mars. And I thought about how I had seen the sky out the door over the backyard when the dog's prints got on the yard. And I didn't know where Mars was. Now I could see the sun all around on the ice, and the baby was lying in his manger that Grace-

anne had made, and there was the straw from Cronin's Grocery, and I wished it was night so I could find Mars because
if it was up there over our yard then I'd know what the
astronomers were looking at.

We put the baby in a cardboard box.

"Graceanne," Wanda said, "this is the worst baby I ever
saw."

"Yeah, I know. Think we should heave it in the river?"

"You can't throw Jesus in the river. That would put a curse
on you or something or mess with the spring planting. We're
stuck with the baby. Maybe that's why we had the bad floods
last spring—some dumb stupid morons like us threw Jesus
in the Mississippi."

"Think they made a jinx?" Graceanne said.

"Might be."

We went into Wanda's house to eat peanut butter and margarine on saltines and have some apple juice. Wanda had some
fish heads in her room and we looked at those for a while and
played some records on her record player. Mama wouldn't let
us have Elvis records, so we listened to Wanda's and they
practiced dancing on the bed until it was time to go to the
church.

We pulled the cardboard box down McBain Avenue and I
told all the kids who came outside that we were taking it to
the church no matter how bad it looked because we didn't
want the Mississippi to flood in the spring. We hauled the
baby across town in the box because the heat on the bus
would melt the baby and it took us a long time to get over
the ice and the snow that was everywhere. We dragged it
through Sulphur Springs Park and down past Parks Department Store and the Crown Drugstore. Graceanne looked
down the street at the Lewis and Clark Hotel as we went by
to see if there was anybody there she could get a quick quarter
from by carrying some bags but there wasn't.

When we got to Our Lady of Lourdes parking lot, there were a lot of cars and and a few colored people from the Developments standing in a group by themselves and the whites were in a different group and we dragged the box over the cinders to the church. Wanda and Graceanne got in line to get their number and then went over in front of the school and set up our entry with the others on long green cloths laid out on the ground over the ice and snow. There had been a barbecue earlier and a paper flower show and booths with Christmas decorations for sale and people were cleaning tables out of the icy parking lot and carrying them into the church basement.

The contest judges came and talked to all the people about their statues. There was a table with Christmas cookies and popcorn balls made by the Ladies' Sodality, and the ladies gave the colored people some stares with their cookies.

Graceanne had been right about Santa Claus. There were three of him, and some ice houses all decorated for Christmas, and some Christmas trees with packages underneath, and an ice table all set with ice plates and an ice turkey that I thought would win the first prize, and a herald angel with a long trumpet, and a big ice candy cane that looked like it was real, but ours was the only Baby Jesus. The colored people came and looked at our entry and shook their heads like they were expecting something else.

"Holy Moses," Graceanne whispered. "Do they ever hate our baby. We should've heaved it in the river and taken our chances."

"You see?" Wanda said. "God's punishing us for asking for a miracle. It's a jinx like you said."

The choir came out of the church and walked across the parking lot together singing "Adeste Fideles" in Latin, with their candles not lit and boughs of evergreens and holly in their arms. Kentucky was walking in front, and she had on a shirt under her silver-and-white drape because it was so cold, and there was a little bee embroidered on the shoulder of her drape. The choir gathered up on the school steps and it was getting dark. The judges came by and looked at all the ice entries again and went over by a table and did some talking to each other and came and put the third prize yellow ribbon on the herald angel. And they put the second prize red ribbon on the candy cane. And they put the first prize blue ribbon on the ice table with the ice turkey.

A taxi pulled into the lot about then and parked at the end of the cars and Edie got out in her hospital whites and her brown carcoat. She came over and gave Graceanne a look and saw she was standing with Wanda behind the baby. Edie waved to Kentucky over on the steps and she came and stood by me, her face all lit up like she was happy. "I got a bonus, Charlie." She looked at the people again. "What are all the colored people doing here? I even see that Wanda Gladwill over there."

Sister Clothilda saw Mama and she moved over the parking lot like she didn't have feet under her. I looked at her long habit and saw she had on a new pair of black boots. "Mrs. Farrand, I just want to tell you how proud I am of the children. To see them getting along so well with their colored brethren has touched my heart and they'll be in my prayers tonight. I know the Christ Child has filled their hearts with love. My goodness." She took out an old hanky from her sleeve and gave her red nose a wipe, and I could hear her old rosary rattling. "They get away from you so fast, don't they?"

Edie looked surprised like she didn't know what Sister was talking about, but she put her fingers on her mouth and smiled at Sister and put her hand on my head. "I've got good kids, that's for sure. They cook and clean and take care of Charlie like he was their own."

I heard the pitch pipe sound its one note, and the choir

started humming. Everybody in the parking lot got quiet. The choir sang "Silent Night," "Joy to the World," and "Little Town of Bethlehem," and then they started passing around the flame to light their candles. I had the gooseflesh on my arms inside my coat because that meant "O Holy Night" was next.

The altos sang the harmony so soft I had to stand on my toes to hear it:

> O holy night, the stars are brightly shining.
> It is the night of our dear Savior's birth.

The second sopranos joined in, and the people in the parking lot around me moved a little so I could hear their coats against their clothes, and the music went out over the cars:

> Long lay the earth, in sin and error pining
> Till He appeared, and the soul felt its worth.

The high voices of the first sopranos flowed in like a river on top of the voices already singing:

> A thrill of hope, the weary world rejoices
> For yonder breaks, a new and glorious morn.

Then there was the hush for about two seconds and Kentucky stepped out from the chorus on the school steps. She put her hand in front of her candle's flame because the wind was dragging it like a leaf on the ground. Her silver-and-white drape was pulling softly in the wind and everybody watched her face when she opened her mouth:

> Faaaall on your knees. O, *hear* the angels' *voi*-ces.
> O ni-ight, di-i-vine, O-oh night, when Christ was
>   born.

The rest of the choir stepped up to stand where Kentucky was singing near the cinder lot:

O night divine, O night, O night divine.

A tremendous silence hung over us all. The stars were coming out looking like silver ice in the sky and nobody moved to get in their cars. The only sound was the wind in the icy branches of the elm trees and the memory of those silver notes still floating over the choir. Then, all of a sudden, the singing started again, but none of the Catholics were doing it. It was only the Baptists:

Truly He taught us to love one another;
His law is love and His gospel is peace;
Chains shall He break, for the slave is our
    brother,
And in His name all oppression shall cease.
Sweet hymns of joy in grateful chorus raise we,
Let all within us praise his holy name;

And all together the Baptists sang Kentucky's solo music, but the words were different:

Christ is the Lord, O praise his name forever!
His pow'r and glory evermore proclaim!

Then they finished the song:

His pow'r and glory evermore proclaim.

The Catholics were all looking around at each other because it seemed like the Baptists had sneaked in a secret part of the song that nobody else had ever heard. It was quiet again, but

the quiet was filled with people stirring and putting their
hands in their pockets and wondering what was going on.

Father Weiss stepped out from the crowd in the front and
went up on the steps with the choir. He was old and rickety
and Kentucky reached over to hold his elbow. His voice was
deep and didn't sound old.

"I can never hear this song without the feeling that I have
gone back two thousand years and am fortunate enough to
stand in the fields with the shepherds chosen to hear the
angels' voices announcing the birth of Our Savior. Forgive an
old man his fantasy, but it's never really Christmas for me
until the choir harmonizes that song and our very own angel,
Kentucky Farrand, steps out to sing her solo. Merry Christmas, everyone." He blessed us with his hand and I could see
he had tears in his old baggy eyes. "We have a number of
Baptists here with us this evening, and we all heard your
voices raised at our church. Welcome to you all and merry
Christmas. There's an ice statue of Baby Jesus over there that
I'm told was made by two children of different faiths. I'm
also told," Father grinned so wide I could see his gums, "that
it's the ugliest baby the world has ever known." Everybody
laughed, and the colored voices were all in one group and the
white voices in a different group, but I couldn't hear Edie at
all, and Father Weiss started talking again. "We're going to
put that ugly statue out in front of the church in our crèche
before midnight mass and ask God to bless our children and
give us harmony in the coming year. Now, I wonder if the
choir would sing one more song before we all freeze to the
ground."

Everybody started clapping and the sound was strange with
everyone's gloves.

I saw it was Kentucky who had the little red pitch pipe.
She turned and said something to the choir and blew on the
pipe. She turned back around and all together, without one

note lagging behind, they began "The First Noel," and everybody who knew the words joined in and the rest just hummed.

Edie was looking at Graceanne and Wanda and the ugly baby whose skin looked like it was dirty. I looked around at the colored people singing "The First Noël," and I wondered if they knew more secret verses that the Catholics didn't know and I thought the Baptists were only there because Graceanne and Wanda were too chicken to heave the ugly baby into the Mississippi on account of bringing on the floods.

Twenty-One

*F*ather Weiss went over the cinder-and-ice parking lot with the choir and they carried the ugly baby to the front of the church that looked south toward the big bend in the river, facing St. Bernadette's over on the Illinois side. The choir took the regular baby and its manger inside to be next to the altar. The ugly baby was left in the center of the outdoor display, with his mother in her blue robe and the three Wise Men and lonely old Joseph and the sheep. The sky was dark and there never was starlight that could have given a good look at that baby's color, but Edie followed along behind the choir and came to stare at the baby to see what Father Weiss had been talking about. She touched its cold head and put her hand in the straw and said, "I don't see what's so terrible about this baby that everybody laughed, Charlie. It's quite attractive, and the eyes look so sad."

I looked again to make sure nobody had put a different baby there, but it was our baby, with its streaked face and its too-small nose that Graceanne had melted with the warm paint-water. "Maybe they meant the manger, Mama. That's the part Graceanne made."

"Explain this to me, Charlie. Your sister made the manger, and Wanda Gladwill made the baby?"

"Not exactly. I mean, Graceanne made the manger, all right, but the baby was kind of my idea and we all talked about it on account of Africa, but Wanda did the hard part and I made the paint, except that Graceanne added too much water." I was going to add the part about asking for a miracle, but Edie looked like she still didn't understand how that baby came to be standing out in front of Our Lady of Lourdes with the other ice things.

"And you made it here, at the church?"

"No, ma'am. At Wanda's."

"Oh."

Her voice sounded like a radio voice or like it was coming through a dead log, but her face still looked happy from her bonus and she didn't put her fingers on her mouth and I knew she didn't understand that Graceanne and Wanda had been associating and the baby had come from that. What Edie thought was that the baby was a church project, and that somehow the baby had forced the girls together and that it all had something to do with Father Weiss because he had made a joke and moved it to the front of the church and the Baptists were there.

"Charlie, I'm gonna give you bus money to get you and your sisters home. You go find them and tell them to get supper on. I'm going to stop and buy a surprise." She put her fingers on my chin and smiled. "And you tell Kentucky there will be no Gallon of Goodies. Tell her to make something fresh."

"Can we have tuna?"

"She can make anything that doesn't need to be thawed." She bent over and put some coins on my mitten.

"How's Wanda gonna get home?"

Edie stood up straight. "That's none of my concern, or yours. Father Weiss will see that she gets home. It's all I can do to get my own children home without making a business of worrying about the whole neighborhood. You get now." She touched my shoulder and I couldn't see the freckles in the starlight.

Kentucky got a ride from Dennis Lister, who had the deepest voice in the choir, so Wanda got to take the bus with Graceanne and me, only I didn't tell her she was riding on Kentucky's fare when I put the money in the box. We all sat on the backseat and horsed around because Wanda couldn't ride in the front and we liked the back better anyway because we could act up without getting yelled at by the bus driver and made to sit down so our heels touched the floor at all times. An old white woman shouted back at us, asking were we nigger-lovers, and Graceanne said, "No, we're all just plain niggers, you old coot. Ain't nobody can tell because I dye my hair. Lawsy, lawsy."

We got off at McBain Avenue and walked to Wanda's in the dark, and I looked for Mars but I forgot to ask Graceanne to find it for me.

"What's going to happen to our baby after Christmas?" I asked.

"It'll melt, you jackass," Graceanne said. "What the hell's the matter with you?"

"It won't melt right away. You think Father Weiss will just leave it in front of the church until the thaw?"

"Oh, well, I guess not. I'm sorry I snapped your head off, Charlie, but you gotta admit you say some **uncommon** stupid things. Maybe Father Weiss'll heave it into the river himself. God. That's the most amazing question. I hope he doesn't make us come and get it. Then we'll be right back where we started from."

"I 'spect," Wanda said, hitching up her blue jeans and

kicking the ice from her shoes, "they'll have to perform a ceremony to burn it, the way the soldiers do with the flag."

Graceanne's face was solemn and her mouth was open and she poked Wanda's arm with her finger. "I don't know why you hang around with a moron like me, Wanda. I would never've thought of burning it."

Wanda laughed. "I'm just doing my good deed by the white folks this year, taking you in and helping you with your Catholic contests so you don't bring on a flood in the spring."

"I wish I could come in your house and look at your fish heads."

"Yeah, but it's about that time."

Graceanne and I went around the fence and up to Fort McBain. We scraped some ice off the door to make faces and went inside. I asked Graceanne how they burn ice, but she just gave me a look. Kentucky was sitting on Graceanne's bed with a package on her lap all wrapped in green Christmas paper, and I was taking off my coat when Graceanne started yelling and dancing around like a scarecrow, with her arms and legs and neck all loose. "Tucka's got a hickey! Tucka's got a hickey! Look at her neck!"

"Shut up, Graceanne, or I won't give you this present."

"Lemme see that **hematoma** up close." Graceanne stuck her face up to Kentucky's neck until her glasses touched Kentucky's skin and when she stood back I could see a purple mark the size and shape of a silver tap from the heel of a penny loafer. "Dennis give you that for Christmas?"

"Shut up, Graceanne." She held out the package. I thought it was clothes because it flopped over like there was a shirt inside. "This is your birthday present and your Christmas present combined. I only just finished it yesterday. Hurry up and open it before Mama gets home."

Graceanne sat on the bed and tore off the wrapping paper. When she got it open, she stared for a minute, and then she put it down on the bed still in its wrappings and left the room. When she came back, her hands were red. "I had to wash my hands first," she said. "I never got anything this **pristine**."

She pulled the wrapping paper away again and there was a piece of white cloth embroidered all over with flowers, and bees, and green leaves. She held it up so the folds would open. It was a rectangle with flaps sewn on both ends and I knew it was a cover for Graceanne's book. She put it down next to Kentucky and slid under the bed to get her book. She brought it out and dusted it off with the hem of her faded pink blanket and slipped the cover on over the notebooks that were tied together. It fit snug, and along the spine there were three white buttons that looked like they came from an old uniform blouse. "That's so you can add another notebook when these are filled up," Kentucky said, running her long red fingernail down the buttons. "You just open these up, and there's extra cloth inside."

Graceanne lifted the book and looked at it for a long time and then she turned it around so I could see. On the front, embroidered in tiny gold stitches, it said, *By Graceanne*. The words were just as shiny and yellow as goldenrod in the meadows up below the river bluffs, and the bees were so real they could almost be alive, and their black stingers were sewn to such a point that they looked painful.

"I'm going to write a poem about this cover right away," she said. She looked somewhere over at the wall and seemed to be thinking, and her tongue was licking her lips. "It'll say:

> "There's books about Juliet and her lover,
>   and about Hitler and wars and greed.
> Those old tales you'll just have to read.
> But you can judge this book by its cover."

Kentucky grabbed Graceanne's arm and I thought she was fixing to shake some sense into her.

"You peeked, Graceanne!" Kentucky said. "You already knew about this."

"I did not! Get your goddamn hand off of me before I bust you one."

"Then how'd you have a poem all ready?"

"I didn't. I just made it up now this very minute."

Kentucky looked like she didn't believe her. "How'd you get it to rhyme and all so fast?"

"It just came to me, that's all. God, you'd think I set the house on fire or told about your **hematoma**, the way you're carrying on."

"You tell about my hickey and I'll brain you."

Graceanne snorted. "Since when have I ever told on you?" She put her glasses up close to Kentucky's neck again. "You better put some makeup on that. Jeez, it looks like he tried to suck your lungs out through your neck."

"Shut up. You better hide that book before Mama gets home."

"She said for you to make something for dinner that's not Gallon of Goodies."

I felt so lonely. I didn't have a hickey or a book or anything at all to hide from Mama. I was afraid to look at the mirror, afraid there would be a blank space where I should be.

"Charlie, I've got a secret present for you, too," Kentucky said. "Close your eyes and hold out your hand."

I did and I felt something rough in my hand. I opened my eyes. It was a big pot roast bone, and I grabbed my coat, and as I passed the mirror I saw the pot roast bone in my own hand. I went out to see Mike the dog. And because I had something of my own to hide, the loneliness was gone, and before I gave it to Mike the dog and broke the ice on his water bowl for him, I waved the bone at the sky, hoping the astronomers were watching our yard.

When Edie came home she had a little tree, some ornaments, and a red stand. She left it all out on the front steps while we ate dinner. Graceanne said she'd start the conversation, and she asked how old Father Weiss was.

"He must be at least seventy," Edie said. "He's had our parish since I was your age."

"Were you a Catholic then?"

"No. I became a Catholic after your father and I were married."

"Why?"

Edie moved her fingers on her mouth. "It was the Lord's will to call me then, Graceanne."

"What were you before?"

"I wasn't really anything."

"What? Everybody's *some*thing."

"This is one of those rare times, my dear, when you don't know everything there is to know about religion. When I was growing up, I did not have the benefit of any religion at all. So, put that in your pipe and smoke it." Edie smiled across the table.

"Maybe you were something without knowing it."

"Graceanne, give it up. I ought to know about my own upbringing."

"Then you were a pagan, Mama."

"I most certainly was not."

"That's someone who has no religion, Mama."

"It is not. A pagan worships golden idols and runs around wearing leaves and drinking wine. Hah! Think you're so smart."

"Well, it's almost Christmas, so I'm gonna let that one pass, Mama, and you can have your own way over it." Graceanne sat there looking like butter wouldn't melt in her mouth.

Edie put down her fork. "It's not having *my* way. It's what's correct. I happen to be right about this, smarty pants."

"Whatever you say, Mama."

"Go get the dictionary."

Graceanne jumped off her chair like she couldn't wait and when she got back she had the big blue book open and a sad look on her face. "I wish you hadn't **insisted**." She put the open book next to Edie and went and sat down to eat.

Edie put her finger on the page and held it there while she read. She slammed the book shut.

We put up the little tree in the Garden Room on top of Mama's dresser. She had to move the letter box, and my letter about being adopted fell out. "What's this?" she said. She read it and laughed a little, and said, "I knew you were too smart to be taken in by Graceanne's craziness, Charlie." The way she said it, like it didn't matter, made me change my mind and think maybe I was adopted after all.

We popped some corn that Kentucky sewed into strings, and she shook some cinnamon into a pan of water and boiled it on the stove so it would smell like Christmas with the sap from the tree. Edie put some little presents under the tree that I could tell were clothes, and I went and got my presents. They were just junk I'd made, and I wished I could sew like Kentucky or work at the hotel like Graceanne, instead of making potholders and tack boards.

Kentucky put some little things under and we all stared hard at Graceanne because she was the only one who hadn't put anything under the tree.

"Boy, that tree sure needs something," she said, looking so smart I thought Kentucky would reach over and give her a Chinese Massage. "It looks kind of empty. Oh, well, I guess I'll go take a nap and maybe Santa Claus will come."

"There isn't any Santa Claus," I said. "You sure say some uncommon stupid things, Graceanne."

"Don't tempt me to tie your eyeballs behind your head, Charlie Smartmouth," she said and traipsed off into our room, flopping like a scarecrow again. She got on her bed and started snoring real loud.

We waited. Graceane kept snoring.

"I better put out the lights," Kentucky said. "Maybe that's what she's waiting for." Kentucky switched off all the lights except for the Christmas tree and we sat around listening to Graceanne snore.

Just when I thought I'd really fall asleep, sitting on Mama's throw rug and leaning my head against the mattress, there was this swishing sound and in came Graceanne dragging a cardboard box which she shoved over next to the dresser.

"What's in it?" I asked.

"Let Mama open it," Graceanne said. "She's the only one will know what to do with it."

Edie's surprise was all over her face. "Why, Graceanne, you never think I know anything. You contradict everything I say."

"That's not true, Mama. You knew how to pay my library fines when I was in flat despair."

"Well, let's not talk about that."

Edie opened the flaps of the box and reached in and took out a store turkey. Without the lights on it looked like it was the ice turkey from the blue ribbon entry at Our Lady of Lourdes, and at first I thought it was a joke. But one of the legs had a tag around it and the weight and price, so it was a real turkey from the market.

"How could you afford this, Graceanne? I can't remember the last time we had such fine food."

"I just kept hauling suitcases and beating my gums at the hotel, Mama."

Edie laughed. "Well, nobody can beat their gums like you. I never knew anyone so bold. You've got the gift of gab, Graceanne, I'll say that for you. *That's* something that doesn't run in the family."

"Graceanne," I said, "what's it called if you tie somebody's eyeballs behind their head?"

"You can't really do it, Charlie, so it hasn't got a name." She scratched her head and worked her glasses up on her nose by making frowns. "But if you could really do it, I expect you'd call it a Red Communist Bonnet."

Edie put the turkey in the refrigerator and we kept the lights off to get ready for mass because the tree made Fort McBain look so different, like somebody else's house. Kentucky had on her white turtleneck to hide her hickey. Edie had her good black dress on and she pinned a shiny red ornament from the tree on the side of her black hat, "just like Jackie's pillbox," she said.

Graceanne was brushing her hair and told me to stop staring at her if I didn't want a Red Communist Bonnet, so I went back to the kitchen to sneak a look at the dog. The sheer blue curtain over the window was pulled shut and it looked different, I thought because of the lights from the tree and it being dark in the house. It looked like someone's head was floating on the other side of the door, but I hadn't heard anyone come up the stairs on the cracked ice. I couldn't make myself lift the curtain aside. I knew there was nobody out there, but that shape outside behind the curtain made me stop, and the dog was yipping and whining and yanking on the end of his chain. I could hear the chain pulling at the new spike and I heard the dog step in his water dish. I thought if I peeked under the curtain I'd see my Daddy's face and his bald head and his eyes staring at me under the curtain.

"What are you doing, Charlie?" Edie said. She was behind me and her voice made me jump.

"I think someone's out there, Mama. The dog's making a racket."

She touched the curtain to pull it aside. The dog barked, and it sounded mean and deep. Edie jerked her hand away like the curtain was hot. "It's probably just the wind."

But we stood there together, neither one of us touching the curtain, neither one of us moving away from the door, like we were tied there by invisible strings, both of us thinking we saw a head on the other side of the curtain. The door moved a little and I could feel the wind on my ankles. Edie reached out her hand like a flash and pushed the button lock, and the door stayed put.

She took my hand and whispered, "Come along," and we went into the Garden Room. She tiptoed over to the closet and took Kentucky's county softball bat. Kentucky stood up right away from where she was sitting on the bed as soon as she saw that and went with Edie into the kitchen. They whispered together, and then Edie faced the door with the bat put up over her shoulder. The door handle turned on its own and we all watched it. I could feel Graceanne breathing over my shoulder.

The door was locked tight, and the knob just spun back to where it was supposed to be. Edie twitched her hand and made Kentucky get behind her. It was quiet for a minute, and I could see Edie choking up on the bat, standing there in her good black dress, and then all of a sudden the window glass burst into the kitchen all over Edie's dress and the wind blew her hem and it was icy cold and the dog was howling so deep it raised my hair. Edie stood like she was made out of stone, but her fingers kept twitching on the tape of the bat. A dark hand came snaking in under the curtain through the hole in the window, and still Edie waited. The hand twisted the button on the knob and turned it, and the door pulled away from the sill out over the back porch. Standing there with snow and ice behind him and framing him all in brightness, was the biggest colored man I'd ever seen in my life and he had a sack in his hand and Edie swung the bat so hard it cracked his face and he fell backward over the rail onto the ground and the red Christmas ornament on Edie's hat fell and smashed on the porch. The dog was whining and barking and Edie went down the icy stairs, slipping all over in her black suede shoes and stood over the man in the snow on his back with his blood running onto the ground from his cracked face and turning the snow pink. She yelled for Kentucky to call the police. Kentucky took off through the kitchen and Edie stood over the colored man with that bat held over her shoulder and the wind was whipping her good black dress and her bare arms looked blue and her suede shoes were sunk into the snow so deep I couldn't see her ankles.

Mama yelled, "Charlie, put on your coat and come get the dog off his chain and hold him." I got my coat and ran down the stairs and pulled and pulled the chain but I couldn't get it out of the ground and the dog wasn't acting like I was there at all but his whole attention was on the colored man. "Grace-anne, help your brother." But Graceanne was standing in the door and she wasn't moving, and I could tell she was so scared of the dog she'd never move, so I gave a yank and went down on my butt. The chain came loose and the dog lunged over with his fangs showing and I had to come and grab the collar to hold the dog back.

"That's a good boy, Charlie." Edie's teeth were chattering so hard she could hardly make words, but I understood what she was saying. "Now you just hold that dog, and when this man wakes up, we'll be glad to have the dog here with us." The man wasn't moving and I didn't think he ever would wake up. His sack had spilled when he went over the railing, and all over our snow there was jewelry sparkling and some folding money blowing and a soft white sweater with its arms flapping and a Fabian record that looked like a black plate on the snow. Shortly I heard a siren and heavy boots crunching over the snowy gravel, and then a policeman lifted the bat gently out of Edie's hands. She turned around like she had no idea what he was there for.

Edie was shaking all over when they got her upstairs. She kept counting us kids. One, two. Kentucky was standing in the door at the front. One, two, three. The policeman who had the bat made Edie sit down on the bed. One, two, three. Old O.U.B. was standing at the kitchen door with the dog and looking like he'd been asleep. One, two, three. Every time she'd count us, she'd nod her head with each count. One, two, three. Finally she started wailing, "I could of lost one of my babies!" Kentucky sat down on the bed with her and I could tell Kentucky was saying baby words to her, and Edie just kept shaking, and twitching, and crying, and breathing with long sighs that seemed to come out like venetian blinds going down all of a sudden when you let the cord loose too quick.

The ambulance came and the red lights flashed on and off into the Garden Room through the window. Wanda's mama was standing in the room and I couldn't think where she'd sprung from. "I come to see if the children was all right," she said. She looked around the Garden Room, and then *she* counted us.

Old O.U.B. brought some boards and the police helped him board up the window, but the cold air slipped in some anyway. Kentucky swept the glass off the floor and the broken ornament off the porch as best she could, but some of the red slivers were stuck in the ice. I guessed old O.U.B. had brought the dog in his house because there wasn't any whining or barking or crunching through the snow like somebody throwing cookies.

The police told Kentucky they'd give her a ride to midnight mass, because everybody, even the cops, knew she was the one that sang the solo. Edie said she wasn't up to going, so Kentucky went alone. I looked around and Graceanne wasn't anywhere to be seen. I looked under her bed and in her closet and outside at the snow. Edie was still sitting on her bed with her hat on and the bathroom door was open and no one was in there. I sneaked out the front and went over to Wanda's, but she said Graceanne wasn't at her house and was the man dead. I came back home and got under my covers and wondered where Graceanne could be. Pretty soon Edie came in and asked where she was.

"I reckon she went to church with Tucka and forgot to say," I said.

"I bet that's it. Maybe she said, and I didn't catch it."

I stayed in bed because I could see Graceanne's coat in her closet and I didn't think she'd gone to church without it.

Kentucky didn't get home until it was after two o'clock on the alarm clock, and I thought Dennis Lister with the deep voice probably gave her a ride home. I was still awake, sitting there under my covers.

"Where's Graceanne?" Kentucky said, looking around the room.

"She isn't in here."

"I can see that."

Kentucky went into the Garden Room on tiptoe. She came back in my room. "Get your coat on. We gotta find her."

"Is Mama asleep?"

"I think so."

When we got outside, I said, "I already looked at Wanda's."

"That goddamn Graceanne. What the hell is she up to?"

"She hasn't got her coat on."

"Uh oh."

We walked around on McBain Avenue whispering her name as loud as we could. It was so late all the Christmas lights were out. I made Kentucky hold my hand because all the shadows looked like they had colored men in them with sacks.

We came back to our house and Kentucky said I should

go inside and get in bed and if Mama woke up to tell her that she hadn't come back from mass yet. But I didn't want to go in alone so I followed Kentucky toward the river until she realized I was behind her and she took my hand again. "You're a curse and an affliction, Charlie." But she held my hand hard and I could see she was glad I was there.

We went to the place where Graceanne was always dragging out ice and there she was, sitting against a tree in her Christmas blouse and she looked half frozen in the dark. The river was more silent and still than a place could be, and the water was black and rushing along with stars on it. Graceanne's eyes were open but it looked like she couldn't see anything. Kentucky put her hand in front of Graceanne's glasses and waved it back and forth, but she didn't blink. "Gimme your coat, Charlie."

I gave her my coat and she put it on Graceanne. Then she took off her own coat and wrapped that around Graceanne, too. The wind had died down and nothing was moving but the river, but the air was so cold it felt like bugs biting me. Kentucky made Graceanne stand up and me get on her other side. We made her walk. "Get her moving," Kentucky said. "Let's get her blood moving." After a while Graceanne was walking on her own but Kentucky didn't let go so I didn't either. From in front of Wanda's I could see Edie waiting for us at the door with the lights on behind her and she was wearing her nightgown and had the bloody baseball bat in her hand. Kentucky saw it, too. "You help Graceanne, Charlie." She went up the stairs quickly and took the baseball bat. "It's only us, Mama."

Kentucky took Graceanne into the bathroom and I could hear the bath running and they were gone a long time. I got under my covers when I remembered how cold I was. Edie sat on Graceanne's bed.

"Where were you kids?" Edie finally said.

My head felt empty and I couldn't think what I should tell her.

"Where were you kids?"

"We went for a walk."

"Don't you lie to me, young man."

That was all right with me, about not lying, because I didn't want to say anything at all, lies or not. So I sat there with my lips buttoned and Edie kept asking me where we were but I didn't answer.

"Well, whatever the story is, it certainly wasn't the fault of the youngest," Edie said, "so you can just go to sleep."

Kentucky and Graceanne were standing at the door and Kentucky said, "Graceanne better get in bed."

"Where were you?"

Graceanne wiggled in behind Edie, got in bed, and put her head under her pillow with her glasses still on.

Kentucky said she wanted to talk to Edie in the Garden Room. They went in there, but I could still hear.

"Mama, we found her down at the river, without her coat on, and I reckon she was so scared she just went into a state."

"What did she have to be scared of? I'm the one that had to hit that darky."

"She told me in the bathroom that the sight of his face all bloody was the scariest thing in her life."

"I'll teach her to be scared of something. What the hell's the matter with her? Is she some kind of hothouse plant that she wilts at what others face up to?"

"Mama, I only know what she told me and I'm passing it along if you want it. If you don't want it, then forget what I said."

"Graceanne's just trying to get attention. What did she have to be scared of? I'm the one who should be scared."

Everything was quiet then. Kentucky turned out all the lights and the house was dark. I couldn't sleep or get warm.

It seemed like the hours were passing like slugs through the room, going so slow the only way I could tell they were moving at all was the trail they left on my eyes that kept getting more and more scratchy and sore.

April 1961

Muddy River, Mackerel Kids

Twenty-Two

7he green budding spread swiftly, radiating out in waves from the banks of the rolling river to colonize the bare branches in both states we could see from Cranepool's Landing. Cottonwoods and sycamores and oaks and maples and ash—they were all in tender bud at once, and only the willows were ahead of them in lush, dense promise. Local wisdom accounted for this richness by citing the previous spring's floods and the consequent freshening of the earth, well beyond its usual cycle of renewal. Trees, the local sages said, were like people; they needed new soil occasionally so they could grow strong and straight.

The thief my mother had hit with the baseball bat lived and stood his trial. He was sentenced to six years at the work farm at Algoa Correctional Facility in Jefferson City, on charges of petit larceny, breaking and entering, and armed robbery. He had been carrying a switchblade—in our town that was more solid evidence of sheer wickedness than a gun—as he foraged through the Developments taking advantage of the attendance of the neighbors at Christmas services to rob their homes of holiday loot. He had almost certainly included Fort McBain because we had kept our unit dark to

savor the newness of our single string of tree lights. His name
was Lawrence Griffin, but he came to be known as Black
Santa in Cranepool's Landing, and children there still invoke
his shade to scare each other silly once a year. He died in a
car accident in 1967.

My mother acquired new names, too, for a time, as the
legends grew up around Black Santa. Elevated and alliterative
epithets with quasi-Christmas themes such as Avenging Angel, and Noël Nemesis, and Shivering Shepherdess of the
Sharp End of Town—such names had a brief run in the
newspapers and in local parlance, but the lowly title that stuck
was Beatin' Eden, which was transmuted on our tongues to
Beaden Eden, and that's what she was called behind her back
in the Developments until the whole episode was closed into
the book of memory and we went on to the creation or em-
bellishment of other chimeras to populate our epic outlooks
on growing up along the mighty river. Heroes, it seemed, did
not have the enduring appeal of villains in the lore of Cranepool's Landing, and Beaden Eden was forgotten quickly even
as Black Santa took on a creepy stature and a permanent place
in river mythologizing.

There were uncomfortable feelings in the Developments
after the episode, when some talk of lynching came up among
the older white men, and talk of protecting poor defenseless
"grass widows" came up among the older white women. The
town briefly acknowledged that it had what it called a "color
problem," but it did so with polite surprise and the quietly
expressed sentiment that such a thing would go away as
quickly as it had come, as a soldier returning from overseas
might acknowledge a case of the clap. It was understood—
very privately—among the religious whites in Cranepool's
Landing that God did indeed work in mysterious ways, and
that Eden Farrand—"God, that woman has spunk"—had
been sent with her brats to "put the fear of God into the

darkies," only the "uppity few" of whom, it was also understood, carried switchblades and committed burglaries. In reaction to those "private" expressions of racial superiority and
natural respect for social order, it was understood—somewhat
less privately—among the outraged Negroes of the Developments that Beaden Eden had been sent by the same mysterious forces that had always shaped their lives, and her
mission was to add to their humiliation, to the rigidity of the
color barrier, to the general hidebound disposition of Cranepool's Landing, and make their lives worse, if possible. And
there was minor-key rumbling about the East St. Louis riots
of the thirties, but that talk receded with the ice as the thaw
set in, and race relations quickly and quietly went back to
what was normal for us then: separate, where possible; equal,
nowhere; mutually respectful only among high school athletes, who wouldn't have dated each other's sisters; and, above
all else, unspoken.

Graceanne and Wanda helped the town move on to other
topics by supplying fresh stuff for its history. The girls felt
they had insufficiently let loose their talents on the town with
their ugly baby, and Father Weiss ministered to their vanity
by encouraging their artistic partnership, showing them his
library of Italian Renaissance prints and pandering shamelessly to their hungry intellects and inflated egos. Their odd
coalition resulted in the fashioning of a life-size ice statue of
JFK as the town's contribution to the new president's inau-
gural celebration.

"We should have listened to Charlie in the first place,"
Graceanne said. "We could have skipped the baby and gone
ahead with political art." The statue was an uncanny likeness,
mainly because Graceanne's role was strictly supervisory, and
Father Weiss allowed them to erect it in front of the church,
overlooking the bluffs and facing both the river and our sister
parish of St. Bernadette's across the Big Muddy Crud in Il-

linois. Newspapers from river towns in both states sent photographers, the girls declared they were famous, and the Kennedy statue was ultimately trundled onto a pickup truck and taken across Big Neighbors Bridge for a tour of duty in New Cranepool, Illinois. We could see the statue through Father Weiss's field glasses, and Graceanne called it "a **secular** triumph, because JFK isn't a virgin or a martyr," and she longed to start on a representation of Dwight David Eisenhower "because he isn't even Catholic," but Wanda and Father Weiss had become obsessed with producing copies of Giovanni Bellini's "St. Francis in Ecstasy," and before they could come to blows with Graceanne, the thaw had set in and they were out of raw material, just when they were rich in ideas.

"I wonder what would have happened if we had made Kennedy a nigger," Graceanne said.

"Why would you make him *colored*?" Father Weiss asked, shaking his head as though he had a flea in his ear.

"Well, that's what we tried to do to Baby Jesus."

"Why?"

Graceanne glanced at Wanda, clearly unsure about this point. "I guess just to see. Anyway, it was Charlie's idea."

Father settled the question of the color of Jesus for all time. "He was a Semite, girls."

"What color is that?" Wanda wanted to know.

"White."

Graceanne had made a fitful peace with the heroine of the only other color story of that winter. The morning after the incident that made Edie a passing byword in Cranepool's Landing and sent Graceanne on her lonely, cold vigil at the river, we heard our mother get up to go to the bathroom so we jumped back in our beds and straightened out our covers. It was just about dawn, neither one of us had slept, and we had been out of bed seeing if we could bend the back of the flimsy full-length mirror to change the way we looked. Edie came in and sat on Graceanne's bed and pulled the cover back.

"Sit up, Graceanne."

Graceanne dragged her covers as well as she could with Edie sitting on them and got up on her elbows.

"You had no right to go running off like that to the river and making your sister and brother frantic with worry. I don't know who you think you are."

"Mama, is that colored man dead?"

"I've seen worse injuries than that in the emergency room at Saint Audrain's. He'll live. And then I hope he goes to jail."

Graceanne looked so happy I thought she'd go dancing around like a scarecrow again, but she stayed put. "I hope he gets to serve a long jail sentence, Mama. I up and forgot you knew about medical things. You'd have known right off if he was dead."

"Well, I hope you don't think I'd kill a man? My goodness."

"I just thought you might have made a mistake."

"I wouldn't make a mistake that big."

Graceanne shivered under her blanket. "Mama, let's not have fights anymore. I won't contradict you and answer back and sass and be disrespectful and think I know everything and talk just to hear myself and be a thorn in your side and act like a Red Indian and make a nuisance of myself and try the patience of a saint and be too big for my britches and make you wonder what you ever did to deserve such a devil as me."

Edie put her fingers on her mouth. "If you mean it, Graceanne, I won't punish you for last night like you deserve. We'll have a fresh start, you and I. Won't that be nice? All I ever wanted was peace anyway. Peace is one of the finer things of life, as fine as good china and good families."

Edie went back to the Garden Room. Graceanne listened for a few minutes to see if Edie got back in bed. With her pink blanket around her, Graceanne dropped off her mattress and rolled under her bed for a while and when she came out she had her book in its embroidered cover.

"That sure is beautiful, that Tucka made," I whispered.

"And what I write from now on has to be beautiful to be worthy of the cover."

"Did you just write something under the bed?"

She scooted over and showed me the new poem she'd written:

RIVER SMART

River shouldn't fight its banks
River shouldn't flood
River should just flow on by
And save its poison blood.

"That's a nice poem, Graceanne, the way it rhymes and all. Is the river poison?"

She opened her mouth and a big yawn came out like she was a hippo. "I'm gonna go to sleep, Charlie." She put her book away and got up on her mattress. "The river's not poison. The river is full of life and it's going new places every day carrying its life with it."

"Is your blood really poison?"

"What do you think? I went and took a pill to cure it? Go to sleep." She turned over and while I was listening to her breathe, I fell asleep, too.

Graceanne's poison blood entered many of our conversations after Christmas because Edie started practicing taking our blood again. She was applying for a job with Dr. Lodenson, and, she said, "Healthy patients are a far cry from the trauma victims I see on call." Edie was exhausted from taking call, rarely sleeping through the night, and her fingers were rough from washing them so often, and from the acetone she used to clean pipettes. Now that she was a practicing medical technologist, we were her only models for improving her technique, because she no longer had her classroom practice in the morgue or with fellow students. My mother was very gentle with the needles, and talked to us so we wouldn't think about the procedure; sometimes she even made us laugh with jokes about labs where drunken monkeys handled the instruments, and I think she was proud of her skill. Sometimes, when our fingers and arms were too sore, she would practice drawing juice from oranges, and she often let us try so we could see what a delicate process it was, but I did not know whether I should envy the oranges their thick skins or pity them the greater depth the needle had to travel and I didn't like sticking them. I asked Edie if oranges had blood types, and she laughed and said, "A-sweet, B-sour, and O how I hate to get up in the morning."

"If one orange got sick and needed blood, could it take blood from another orange?"

"Certainly. It just couldn't take apple juice."

I knew when Edie was teasing, but I had a far less exact feel for the things my sister came up with.

"I have to be very careful," Graceanne said, "when Mama takes my blood, because if any gets on her, she'll die from the **toxins**. I'm the universal poisoner. I don't know what I did to deserve such blood."

Edie apologized to us for the need to improve her skill so she could get the new job, and she was never kinder to us than when she had a needle in her hand. We were taught not to fear the needles, and to be dignified about pain. We were good students, but, in the book under Graceanne's bed, the rhetoric concerning the Martian astronomers increased in its intense call for knowledge, and her poetry became more brooding, more serious, sadder, more personal, more tormented, and it touched my heart while it tortured my vanity and my ambition:

MUDDY RIVER, MACKEREL KIDS

Muddy river, vein of life,
lies in bed a virgin wife.
Beneath her skirt, in fathoms deep,
are three fish children fast asleep.

Their scales are thin, their guts are cold,
their fishy eyes are made of gold.
Boyfish wears a twisted fin, Girlfish silver throat,
Crosseye sleeps upon an embroidered, private note.

Their mama swims in freckled skin,
her needle nose as sharp as sin.
She pokes her face through ooze & reeds
& threads her nose with slimy weeds.

She pricks her kids & pulls the thread
& sews their skin until they're dead.
The lame fish wakes & shakes his head
& sees his mama on his bed.

His sister wakes & sings a song
to tell the river what is wrong.
The water rages, its currents weep:
"Who dares disturb the children's sleep?"

The third fish rises in her bed
& feels the needle in her head.

She breaks the thread, & swims on top:
"Who can make the needle stop?"

She sees the stars, their spangled lights
that sleep the days & rouse the nights.
"Who is watching? Who can see
Mackerel Mama's sewing spree?"

The stars all wink their silver eyes.
She hears their answer, faint and wise:
"Mackerel Kid, go back to bed.
Your poison blood will make her dead."

I admired the rhymes and the way the lines sounded to my ear as I whispered them aloud under Graceanne's bed, her flashlight casting a pale glow on the ugly handwriting, and I memorized every syllable, and I thought my tiger must be a snarling, cowardly thing, filled with covetousness and a sneaking rage, and I wondered why God had given Graceanne so much talent when I was the one who wanted it.

I didn't envy Graceanne all of her talents. She had what Edie called "good veins," and she was stuck frequently and never uttered a squeak of protest when called to duty. In fact, Graceanne was behaving with a rare restraint in all her dealings with our mother. She seemed to have an unusual sympathy for Edie then, deriving from my mother's profound loss at the hands of her church.

Edie had been denied access to communion at the beginning of January because her divorce proceeding was on the court calendar, and divorce was a mortal sin. In the eyes of the church, Edie might as well have been a murderer. She was so disgusted, so outraged, that she, the "innocent party," should be denied the sacrament, that she was threatening to withdraw her children from the parochial school she supported with her prayers and threatening to stop going to church at all if Father Weiss did not change his mind. When he proved impervious to her use of pressure tactics, she changed her strategy and started fasting and doing strange penances (going without milk was one of them), convinced that she and she alone, through her own efforts, could change "that old man's petrified mind."

When she learned that it wasn't one old man, but rather the cold, solid will of the Vatican that she be denied communion, Edie raged that it was "unfair and un-Christian and anti-American," and she "didn't know what she had done to deserve it," but when she issued her challenge and approached the communion rail, wearing her good black dress and in the full gaze of the interested congregation one Sunday in February, Father Weiss passed her by with a sad shake of his head and left her kneeling there grinding her teeth.

Graceanne was stunned and she quietly stopped taking Communion, too. "It's wicked and unfair to deny Mama what gives her strength just when she needs it most, and all because she couldn't live with a man who beat up on her. And so I tell Father Weiss when we talk."

The discussions with Father Weiss, when they were not about Italian Renaissance art, were characterized by passionate utterance, frank airing of opinion, and militant posturing on all sides. The old priest seemed to have recaptured a corner of his youth, and his face glowed pink with renewed vigor. We sat with him out in front of the church, looking at the river, and he seemed to take pleasure from honing his sermons on two girls who were both ready to insult his logic, quarrel with his reason, and ridicule his sources. One ongoing argument had to do with the gift of faith. "If the one true faith is a gift, straight from the Holy Ghost," Graceanne argued and argued, "and Wanda is a Baptist, does that mean the Holy Ghost didn't give her any true faith? And why not? Doesn't he like colored people?" Graceanne never seemed satisfied with Father's answers, but she kept after him on that one question about faith and the Baptists. Her other burning issue was Edie—"Making a business about not letting Edie go to communion—what kind of Divine Love is that?" They argued long and hard, but Father and the girls were at least of one mind and one heart on the only other religious question Graceanne thought worthy of discussion—racial equality, and that gave them the trust in each other that fostered other debates and, in the end, enduring respect.

"That old eunuch is getting himself looked at in this town," Edie said. "Strange goings on when a man of the cloth takes to associating with wild girls. What can he possibly find to talk about with you?"

"We are not wild girls," Graceanne said. "And we are talking about the nature of God's love." She looked down at her plate and shook her head. "Faith is the hardest thing there is because almost everything about God is unbelievable."

"How dare you talk like that about God? Go to your room."

Graceanne also got Collier involved in her search for answers about God.

Collier's letters had tapered off and he had not visited over Christmas, although Graceanne knew from his brother Tyler that he'd been in town. She was waiting for the summer for Collier to get home from school so they could work together again, and she thought the bad feelings about Black Santa had something to do with Collier's curious change toward her, but she was confident that whatever the trouble was, it would go away when they were together. She continued to write to him with prolific insistence and her deteriorating handwriting. His infrequent responses touched on his college perspective on God:

Dear Grace:

My mother told me how sad it was when your mother tried to get communion and was denied at the altar. I haven't been going to church because I feel God is a cosmic order that exists in all things, wherever I happen to be, so why go to one particular place over others?

Yes, I heard they were remodeling the lobby, but without a swimming pool, they're going to lose a lot of business to the new Howard Johnson's over by the highway. Also, the Lewis and Clark needs its own restaurant, but I don't think they'll go that far.

I don't know exactly where I'll be working come summer, but hotels are all I know so far, although I hope that will change when I get my degree. I sure as hell am not going into the service when I graduate in '63. The army was all right for my dad, but that was a different world, with different needs, and I'll never make a soldier boy.

I'm glad you finally read *Romeo and Juliet*. A girl with your ability as a writer should read as much of Shakespeare as she can. The poem you sent me about the fish was sad, but a little heavy on the metaphors.

Kick the registration desk at the hotel for me.

Love,
Collier.

Graceanne had not only read *Romeo and Juliet*, she had talked Wanda into borrowing a copy of Shakespeare's complete works from the library for her. Wanda was reluctant to let Graceanne have the book for the long periods of time it took to read the tragedies, because, she said, Graceanne was "a known offender," but she buckled under Graceanne's persistence, and together they read and relished all the bloodiest tragedies, including even the abominable *Timon of Athens*, which they loved. The romances and histories, they declared, "weren't gory enough."

After they read *Hamlet*, everything was some form of "to be or not to be" ("to smoke cigarettes or not to smoke cigarettes, Wanda, that is the question"—they decided "not to smoke" because their only attempt made Graceanne turn green) or some form of "get thee to a nunnery" ("get thee out of our business, Charlie") and once, when Edie told us to clean up the mess in our room, Graceanne said, "there's something rotten in the state of Fort McBain." She and Wanda turned their turtlenecks black with packages of Rit Dye from Cronin's Grocery. They spent a couple of afternoons in Wanda's kitchen, making her mother nervous about her embroidery while they boiled the dye in a big pot on the stove and slopped their shirts around until they got the right color.

I wondered what Edie had done with the Notre Dame sweater that Collier had given Graceanne for her birthday. I never saw it after Graceanne left it on Edie's bed. I never saw it on anyone in town, which meant Edie had not put it in the box for the poor children. I knew all the poor people in Cranepool's Landing by sight, because the pockets of poverty were neatly contained on the two ends of town I knew best— Lewis and Clark Hill and the Developments.

By the time the buds were on the trees, Edie had her divorce. Kentucky was the only one of us who had to go in to court and testify, and she was only asked if it hurt when Edie practiced medical technology on us. Edie said Daddy had put his lawyer up to that to prove that she was unfit to have custody, but everyone knew Daddy was a drunk, she said, and she'd stack her reputation up against his any day, and she got us kids officially along with her divorce. What was surprising about all of that was the absolutely stupefying thought that Daddy had countersued for custody and apparently wanted us, and that there'd ever been a question about living with Edie.

On the last day of the proceeding, we were all dressed up in case the judge called us to testify. He didn't, and we waited outside on the steps of the courthouse. Edie came out wearing her good black dress. She walked down the steps toward us, the ruffles on her sleeves flipping over in the breeze. Daddy came around behind her in full dress uniform and passed her on his way down the stairs. He put his hat on his bald head and squatted on the steps where we were sitting.

"How are my little army brats?" he said.

"We're doing okay," Kentucky said, and it didn't seem like Graceanne and I had to say anything.

"You all have decent shoes?"

"Our shoes are okay," Kentucky said.

"You miss your Daddy?"

"We miss you, Daddy," Kentucky said.

"What's the matter with you younger ones? Eden cut out your tongues already?"

Graceanne spoke up then. "How come you put your lawyer up to that countersuit? Don't you think Mama's fit to have custody of us, Daddy?"

He stood up and the sun sparkled on all his medals and his ribbons had every color in the rainbow and his chest seemed to be covered with glory and his brass belt buckle seemed to catch fire. The visor on his hat was shining, too, and he put a pair of dark glasses on over his eyes, and I could see us kids on the stairs in his glasses.

Edie came to stand behind us and Daddy saluted her.

"Your mother's a goddamn wolf," he said, and walked away down the street, shining and sparkling.

Twenty-Three

Child support checks were supposed to start arriving once the divorce decree was issued. Edie said that Daddy had not paid before because he was waiting to see her "fall flat on her face." The extra thirty-eight dollars a month, plus Edie's new job at Dr. Lodenson's, meant that Graceanne could finally get new glasses, and she went and picked out some frames at Making Eyes Optical the very afternoon we saw Daddy on the steps of the courthouse.

She picked out her new frames, a pair of black (for Hamlet) winged things that made her look like whatever we thought Fu Manchu looked like, for that's what we called her without ever having seen the villain, or heard him described. When Graceanne challenged our ignorance, saying "You don't even know what Fu Manchu looks like," Kentucky simply said, "Fu Manchu looks like you."

After Graceanne piddled around with just about all the frames in Making Eyes, she had to have her pupils dilated. This was a process so fraught with mystery, so charged with chemical significance, that we suffered agonies of jealousy because Graceanne got to be blind for the rest of the day, and her eyes looked like a cat's.

Edie left us downtown and went to her new job on Little Lewis and Clark Street to unbox pipettes and an autoclave ordered especially for her, so we got to lead Graceanne around and make her step over things that weren't there and watch her trip. Kentucky finally got bored because Graceanne started falling down on purpose, and she took off with Dennis Lister, who we ran into outside the Crown Drugstore.

"Is that Dennis Lister playing hickey from school—I mean *hookey*?" Graceanne asked, moving her hand around in empty space like she was feeling for him. "You better spit out Kentucky's lungs before you bring her home, you hear?"

Kentucky gave Graceanne a smack, and I was left to pull Graceanne along and help her up when she fell in front of people on the sidewalk. She made me lead her to the Woolworth's, and she gave me a few quarters to go in and buy a plastic cup and two pencils. She carried the cup around in front of her with the pencils in it and looked at people with her cat's eyes, one of them wandering around, but she didn't get any money because everybody knew her in town, even in her good clothes, and guessed it was a joke. We went over to the school so we could rub it in on the other kids that they had to be there and we had the day off for the divorce.

We went inside and she bumped into doors, and finally she fell into her own classroom in her good clothes and her cat's eyes without her glasses and one eye wandering. At first Sister Clothilda didn't seem to know who she was.

"Can I help you, child?"

Graceanne felt around with her hand in the air. "I'm looking for the confessional. Bless me, Father, for I have sinned, it's been six days since my last confession. Since that time I have . . ."

Sister grabbed her and pulled her off the floor and marched her out into the hall. "Graceanne Farrand, you little monster. Why aren't you down at the courthouse?"

Graceanne knew that the mere removal of her carcass would not inhibit public interest in her confession, so she kept talking all the way. ". . . told forty-six lies and disrespected my elders and led my brother into a **near occasion** of sin seventeen times and I'm the Black Santa."

Sister hustled her out of the building, told her she'd make her copy out a page from the dictionary when she got back to school, and we decided to go to Wanda's school. Wanda went to Cranepool Junior High, and we went in through the north gate to the big room where the band was practicing, and Graceanne right then and there decided she could play drums blind. I stayed out in the hall as lookout, and she sneaked into the back of the room and found the sticks by feeling around and started playing drums until they made her leave when they found out she was a parochial kid. "But if you ever enroll in this school," the man who was getting rid of her said, "you can take band and play the drums for us anytime. Do you have a set of your own at home?"

"No, I learned to play by watching my Daddy at night."

"Oh, does he play the drums?"

"No sir, he beats my mother."

We never found Wanda, so we left and went over to the river.

I knew Graceanne couldn't see much more than shapes with her pupils open that big, but her eyes were so strange it seemed to me that she had some sort of hypervision, some gift that would make her eyes look that alien.

"Charlie, the river looks really funny when you can't see any of the waves and currents, but only the shape and size. This must be what the river looks like from Mars. But I'd know it anywhere by the smell. Nothing in the world smells like the Big Muddy Cruddy. What would you call that smell?"

"I don't know. Maybe water?"

"No, Charlie. That's earth. The river smells like earth. The biggest water around, and it smells like dirt. That's a kick in the ass, isn't it?"

"I guess."

"The biggest water around. Charlie, with a real good telescope, you could see this river from Mars. Forty-nine million miles away, and they can see the Big Muddy Crud, and they don't know it smells like dirt."

"What else can they see?"

"Probably the Grand Canyon, and that probably smells like dirt, too."

"Can they see us?"

"Not with their current telescopes, but they're working on new ones. They'll be ready soon."

"How do you know?"

She gave me a Japanese Band-Aid and said, "I listened to that radio you gave me, dummy."

I rubbed my wrist to get rid of the sting. "Show me how to do that."

So she showed me how to make Japanese Band-Aids and when our arms were good and red we decided to walk up to Big Neighbors Bridge. It was farther than I thought, and the land was rising into the bluffs north of town when we could see the shadow of the bridge on the water. I looked up at the underside of the bridge and saw birds' nests and rusted girders. At the highest part of the curve of the span, it must have been fifty feet off the water.

"Why'd they have to make it so tall, Graceanne?" I asked, craning my neck to see the bridge and see if bending my neck would change my voice.

"So the boats can get under."

We had to go under the highway to get up on the bridge, but when we got there we weren't tired, and Graceanne said, "Charlie, let's go to Illinois."

"Mama'll skin us alive."

"She won't if she doesn't know about it. Don't you want to be able to tell the kids you've been in another state?"

"Lots of kids have been to Illinois."

"Well, *we* haven't."

From the Missouri end of the bridge, Illinois looked like it was only a few yards away. We started walking across on the side with the pavement. There wasn't any traffic but a couple of pickup trucks going the other way over to Missouri. We stopped halfway across and looked down. The water looked like the brown polish Edie used to put on my corrective shoes. It was moving fast, changing color where the currents were dragging the top water down, and every now and then we'd see birds that Graceanne said must be crested kingfishers diving at the water and coming out with silver dangling from their beaks.

"Graceanne, do you reckon they're catching mackerels?"

"I can't see what they're doing, but there ain't no mackerels in this river."

"But there are in your poem."

"The only mackerels are in the ocean. I just made that up because of the way a mackerel's back looks all striped like me."

"You don't have stripes."

"Sometimes I do."

"Did you make up the kingfishers?"

"How the hell could I be telling the truth when I can't see my hand in front of my face?" She dropped her blind cup and the pencils in the river. "Charlie, does it look like the river's just been stirred and somebody yanked out the spoon too fast?"

I looked at the water. "Yeah, about. Graceanne, how come nobody lets us swim in the river? It looks like fun."

"It looks like fun all right, but you can't see any but the

easiest currents. The bad ones are underneath."

"What if somebody fell in and got taken by one of the currents?"

"They'd probably drown, because most folks fight back at the currents. You do that, you got no chance. You want to respect the current and let it have its way, because it's going to have its way no matter what you do. You just let it take you and swim the way it wants to go."

"Did you ever go in the river?"

"I'm not that dumb."

"Then how do you know about the currents?"

"Kentucky told me what it was like when she went in for that crud Bobby Stochmal."

We went on over to Illinois and touched the dirt with our hands and came back. It was just under a mile across, and I lost count of how many of my footsteps would get me across the bridge, but when I stopped counting, about halfway back to Missouri, it was 1,004.

"I can say I've been to Illinois, but I can't say I've seen it," Graceanne said.

"Why don't you just make it up like you did with the mackerels?"

We went back under the highway and walked along the river toward Cranepool's Landing. There was early spinach growing in fields on the bottom land, and we walked the rows, looking for waterbugs under the leaves. "They like spinach because it's made of iron," Graceanne said. "That's what makes waterbug shells so hard."

I didn't know if that was a kingfisher story, but I didn't want to show my ignorance, so I kept my mouth shut, especially when Graceanne tried to make me eat some of the leaves.

"Come on. What're you afraid of?"

I shook my head and kept my lips buttoned.

"Come on, Charlie. Popeye eats it, and look at him."

"You eat it."

"I will." She put some leaves in her mouth and chewed them up and then pretended she was swallowing. With her mouth full, she said, "Now feel my muscles. Just like water-bug shells." She flexed her arms and I felt and they felt hard all right. "Now I wish there were some carrots, because then I'd be able to see again." Everybody knew carrots were good for your eyes, so, figuring the kingfisher stories were over, I tried some spinach. "Tastes like grass, doesn't it, Charlie?" So I swallowed and she spit hers out.

We walked past a little bend in the river where an old willow was, and we went under the tree's hanging branches into what she called "the weeping room" where it was dark around the tree. "You know why this is called a weeping willow, Charlie?"

"Because it looks like it's crying, with its branches hanging down like tears."

"No, it's because if you happen to make a wish while you're standing under it, the wish will never come true. So be careful what you're thinking. Don't think about candy or money or things like that."

Once she mentioned wishes, that was all I could think of, so I bolted out from under the tree. We kept walking and reached the place where the long path started, at about the Cranepool's Landing city limits, and then we headed down for McBain Avenue.

"Graceanne, remember the New Rules?"

"Yeah. So?"

"You think Mama forgot about the one that says you can't associate with Wanda?"

"No, but now that Father Weiss likes Wanda and Mama wants to take communion, I bet she's afraid to put a jinx on herself."

"What's a jinx?"

"That's a spell you get when you go against nature."

"What happens if you get a jinx?"

"You lose what makes you happy."

"Did you ever go against nature, Graceanne?"

She stopped and looked out over the river with her cat's eyes. "Everybody does. I did last year when I took the glands from the little dead muskrats. I should've left them alone with proper respect. I'm pretty sure that's why Mama got me with the coat hanger. What you got to worry about is the size of the jinx. There's mortal and venial jinxes, Charlie. Better leave dead creatures alone so they can go where they're supposed to go."

I wondered where Ugly Blue Man had been going when I sent him to the quarry lake, and if I had a jinx on me. I tried to think what I could lose that made me happy to have, and I couldn't think of anything but Graceanne and Kentucky. So I started crying.

"What the hell's the matter with you?"

"Must be that spinach."

"You're getting to be an awful liar, Charlie Farrand."

We walked up McBain Avenue in the dark, and Graceanne said she could see and the blackness in her eyes was getting smaller. I could see the stars through branches covered with the soft buds that gave them a little coat that looked like fur in the dark. The lights were on in our house.

"Things'll be different with Mama not taking call anymore," Graceanne said. "Maybe she'll fix dinner now."

We left our shoes on the steps because of the mud from the spinach fields. Graceanne opened the door and the light came out at us and I saw Edie fixing to sit down on Grace-anne's bed and she had the book in her hands that were touching its embroidered cover.

"Hello. I put a pot of Dutch spaghetti on, and we'll have

real home cooking tonight. Where've you been?"

I saw her freckled hand smoothing over the embroidery on the cover of Graceanne's book, touching the bees and the leaves and the flowers and the little gold letters. I wanted to look at Graceanne's eyes to see if they still looked like a cat's and if she could see what Edie was doing, but I couldn't make my eyes move off of Edie's hand stroking those stitches of the things sewn all over the beautiful cover.

"We went to get the stink blown off," Graceanne said. "I took Charlie for a walk along the river and explained about nature."

I was still looking at the freckled hand touching the bees like they were made of something warm and soft.

"That was sweet of you, Graceanne, to show an interest in your brother like that. What is this? I found it under your bed when I was cleaning."

"That's my private, personal diary, Mama. It doesn't have any interest to anyone but me."

"It's awfully big for a diary."

"Well, you know how I run on and on."

"I'd like to see it. It must be very special to rate a cover like this."

"It's only a diary, Mama."

"Where'd you get this cover?" Her freckled hand kept touching the bees and flowers and leaves.

"Tucka made it for me."

"Do you let your sister read your diary?"

"No."

"How long've you been keeping it?"

"Couple years."

I thought about the poem that said, "I hate her, I hate her, I hate her," and I started praying in my head that Edie wouldn't open the book. And then I thought about my one sentence about Ugly Blue Man and I was too scared to pray.

I was scared for me and scared for Graceanne and scared for that pregnant woman on the house in Hard Labor Creek with her triangle shovel that she'd probably killed a man with.

"Did you write anything about your Daddy and me?"

"No, ma'am. Not a word. It's only about me."

"I think a mother ought to know what's on her daughter's mind. Maybe I should read this."

I shut my eyes and squeezed them with my lids and couldn't swallow.

"Mama, I think a daughter ought to be able to have a little privacy. I have to share a room with my brother, and that book's the only private thing I have."

"So you just put girl stuff in it?"

"I don't like to talk about what I put in it. That's why I write it down instead."

"Oh." Mama turned over the cover and the book was open on her lap and I could see it was the poem about the mackerels in the river.

"Mama, I'll do anything you say. I'll make dinner the rest of my life, and scrub the floors, and bring home straight A's, and *anything*, if you will leave my book alone."

"It must be pretty important for you to make all those promises."

"It's the most important thing in my life."

I squeezed my eyes again. I knew Graceanne had said the wrong thing.

Edie's freckled hand moved on the page of ugly handwriting, moving like a waterbug under a spinach leaf. "More important than your own mother?"

"More important than anything."

"You must think you're quite a little prima donna if you think this book is so important in the scheme of things. It looks to me like it's just a cheap notebook with handwriting a white person wouldn't own to."

I could hear Graceanne grinding her teeth. Edie heard it, too. She looked at Graceanne's jaw and her eyes.

"Mama, my book is sacred to me."

"You better bite your tongue and I better have a look, then. It seems unhealthy to have a girl's thoughts all locked up in a *sacred* notebook when she could talk to her parish priest or her mother about what's on her mind."

"I can't talk to you, and I won't talk to you, and if you read my book I'll never forgive you." Graceanne stumbled a little but she made it to the bed and grabbed the book. She got it away from Edie and ran out the front door. Edie went chasing after her, but there was no way she could ever catch Graceanne even without the head start.

"Graceanne, you come back here with that book!" She stood on the steps and kept hollering but Graceanne was out of sight and on her way to the river. I ran around Edie and ran as fast as I could. "Charlie Farrand, you get back here! I'll whip you both!"

I was all out of breath when I caught up with Graceanne. She was on her knees in the mud right at the river's edge, tearing out the pages and throwing them in the water. They were floating and swirling and turning muddy and sinking, and there were the crinkly edges from the spiral all over the ground. I tried to grab the book away from her, but she pushed me down with one hand and kept tearing out the pages and throwing them in. Her teeth were grinding so hard she didn't sound human, and her face was dark, and she looked like somebody else without her glasses on.

The sound of the tearing was so mournful, and the river was slapping up on the mud, and her teeth were grinding, and all around was the smell of earth. I could see the little drawing of the mackerel spinning around on the skin of the river, and some of the story about the Martian astronomers. The cover was the last thing Graceanne threw in. The beautiful white cloth all covered with bees and flowers and green leaves floated only for a moment before the muddy water swallowed it and took it under the starry, muddy surface.

Graceanne and I walked back to Fort McBain. Our socks were all muddy because our shoes were on the steps the whole time with the spinach mud on them that we didn't want to track into the house. We didn't say anything to each other and I kept thinking Graceanne ought to cry because I couldn't if she didn't because it wasn't even my book. When we went in, Edie sent me to the backyard. I sat out there with Mike the dog, letting him lick my face and get on my knees. I knew Edie was giving Graceanne her medicine to cure her of her disrespect, but I understood that Graceanne had chosen the medicine over having Edie's freckled hands on her book.

The dog got quiet in my arms and we sat there on his pit that had a new, lower circle he'd dug because of dragging around his shorter chain.

And I thought how rich and blessed Graceanne was because I had nothing that could be taken from me that would have meant half as much as that book.

July 1961

Big Neighbors Bridge

Twenty-Four

$\mathcal{A}$ creosote factory upriver on the Illinois side burned to the ground late in June, and the sharp but not disagreeable smell lingered in the trees. Their leaves stirred up memories of the two-day arson blaze whenever the wind was in the right direction and the heavy, humid air swayed over the bottom land like an overfed animal, fat and ungainly, cantankerous, close to the ground and full of territorial humors.

Silk was thick on the cornstalks. All the farmers around Cranepool's Landing were cautiously jubilant, crossing their fingers and smirking at the same time, the way farmers do in those rare times of good fortune when the earth and the sky and their own hard efforts unite to produce a succulent green tenderness so full the air seems to ache with throbbing anticipation of its plenty and trembling fear that at the last minute the boon will be snatched away. Extra scarecrows were put up in the fields, and some of the taller kids found work keeping the circling birds off by swinging burlap bags. The movement of their feet through the rows of corn also kept air circulating around the roots of the vigorous plants, and everyone's hopes were high that this crop would more than make up for the disaster of the previous summer when the corn was stunted and had to be harvested early for feed.

I was too small to get hired for this primitive form of pest control. The reach of the burlap swingers had to exceed the cornsilk, and I would have been a destructive nuisance in the fields, worse than the birds, but I badly wanted a job because everyone else in the Farrand family had one, and burlap swinging looked like a dance and a celebration, and hardly like work at all.

Kentucky was hostessing at the Pancake House up on the highway, and Graceanne was still a bellboy at the Lewis and Clark Hotel. The three-year difference in age between me and Graceanne seemed an insurmountable barrier for such a short span of time—like the Egyptian dynasties that managed to put up pyramids and enslave Hebrews and suffer plagues all in the space of a few pages in my history textbook—and nobody would hire a ten year old. I had been trying since the spring to earn money, and I had fallen back on the only economy in Cranepool's Landing whose superstructure had a niche for me: bottle trading. The sidewalks and trash cans along McBain Avenue and the river were fertile fields of glass, and by the end of school I had earned almost five dollars in deposit money from Cronin's Grocery for my harvest. I bought embroidery silk at Parks Department Store with some of my earnings, acting on the instructions and suggestions of Wanda's mother, but when I turned them over to Kentucky and asked her to make a new book cover for me, she sat me down and said, "You don't want to start on learning how to get in trouble, Charlie. That book is over and done with. Leave it be and don't provoke Mama. You can't win, and there's no help against her."

Kentucky had met an itinerant folksinger named Shannon Mann at the Pancake House, where he was working as a cook. He was tall, as good-looking as she was, and his hair was wild and long and the color of cornsilk. She brought him home a few times to Fort McBain, and we all sat out on the front steps while he played his guitar. She sang folk songs he had taught her and church songs she was teaching him, and we harmonized on songs we all knew, and even Edie joined in sometimes with a pretty soprano that surprised me.

Kentucky and Shannon quietly left Cranepool's Landing together in late June and headed for Florida where Kentucky said she'd get work singing in clubs. She packed her bags and told Edie she was going, and they said goodbye politely like a couple of strangers in a bus station. Kentucky hugged Graceanne and kissed me, and told us both to be good, and they drove across Big Neighbors Bridge in Shannon's Chevrolet, and they were gone. Their route to Florida brought Kentucky no singing jobs, and they ended up eventually in Northern California, were married, and started working as house parents in a halfway house for runaways, as we learned from their few letters addressed to Graceanne and read by Edie, but I never saw Kentucky again.

Graceanne had finished the school year with straight A's, so she was spared another sentence in the Enrichment Penitentiary and her softball career was resumed. When she wasn't at the hotel, she was out on the field, "whaling hell out of the opposition," as the coach said. She always played with rigid fairness, but within the rules she was ruthless and fierce and the best and meanest player in the northern part of the state.

Her stance at the plate underwent a slight change that June, and, as small as she was, there weren't many infielders that could face her without either abject fear or the heart of a lion to match hers. She'd get up to the slab of rubber, give it a little kick, and dig in the toes of her shoes; her hips would rotate slowly, she'd grind her teeth and spit, and she'd choke up on the wood and squint at the pitcher through her new black glasses, and then the end of her bat would sketch a tiny circle in the air as though she were issuing a silent dare and she'd wait for the ball.

She could hit anything that came at her, and she'd slice the ball belt-high through the infield, so close to the player she was aiming at that most players couldn't possibly catch it. A couple of parents complained that Graceanne was trying to peel the skin off their kids; the ball would come so fast and so hard and so tight that the only sensible thing to do was to hit the dirt when they saw it coming and hope the ball would snag up on the grass and she'd be held to a triple. None of our jaded umpires, laboring too many bored years in the unproductive and sleepy field of girls' softball, could see anything illegal in clean, mathematical, killer line drives that turned the game into epic material, and the parents were told to let the kids play ball or take them home if they were so lily-livered. A couple of parents complained that Graceanne was really a boy and it wasn't fair to let her play with their girls though Graceanne didn't look like a boy at all, even with her hair cut short and with the Brylcreme she put in it to keep it out of her eyes—the kind of grease tough boys in leather jackets were using to keep their ducktails in place. The umpires told the parents the team doctor had certified Graceanne to play and they should let the kids play ball or take them home if they were such panty waists.

Graceanne was just as fearsome in the field as she was with a bat in her hands. Her arm was dead accurate and fast, she covered the shortstop position like she was a demon octopus with extra eyes, and nobody went into second base smiling when she was waiting to tag them out. Players who ran into force plays at second were unfailingly polite to the point of groveling and grinning, because nobody wanted to be anywhere in the line of fire when she threw to first. She was the first player named to the county team.

Wanda was the second player named, and the first Negro

girl to play on one of our county teams. At first, Wanda's mother was stunned by the wild sport her daughter had been talked into by Graceanne, and Graceanne knew all the most ruthless subtleties of the game she had taught Wanda, including some she made up herself. There was nothing demure, gentle, or second-class about the theoretical basis of county-level play, because in the northern river counties, Little League hadn't taken yet with the girls, so they still played with the boys' rules.

Wanda didn't have Graceanne's dead-eye swing, but she had everything else Graceanne could teach her, including the whole range of intelligent psychology designed to fake out an opponent: things like sliding into the plate with a foot aimed at the catcher's mask, like spitting on first base when the pitcher tossed the ball over to hold them on the bag and tease them out of a steal. There were still some county fields that were supposedly Whites Only, but that was never enforced because Graceanne and Wanda were the only show other than the burlap swingers that was worth watching in Northern Missouri that summer.

People lined up two or three deep around the fence when there was no more room on the bleachers to see this sensational pair of cutthroat players blister the competition with the best—and most terrifying—softball anyone in those parts had ever seen. And the fierce refusal in Graceanne even to imagine *losing* drove her to such heights of performance that she really did become famous, not with the kind of fame she had briefly shared with Wanda over the John F. Kennedy ice statue—that brief flicker of notoriety was merely local and a fame she had borrowed in part from the new president, from a copy of his body—but with a fame that depended on the precise, magnificent control she exerted over her own fearless body and on her courageous, stubborn heart. And her fame was statewide.

It was such a pleasure to watch her make her little body do things that bigger and stronger kids couldn't do, wouldn't ever be able to do, could only dream they'd have the opportunity of seeing her do. She'd risk her neck diving for line drives in blurring somersaults and bring up the ball with a stern face and a kick of her foot before she threw it back into play; she'd leap for long balls like she was playing on a trampoline, and once she leapt up so high her shirt came out of the waistband of her pants and even from the bleachers we could see her skinny ribs as she snagged the ball as if she were a cloud floating over left field. She came down and scraped her back on the top of the fence, but she never complained and we all saw the blood on the back of her uniform with the famous number twenty-two. She'd steal bases by sliding under tags aimed by girls who thought they'd finally get to bean her, but she was so much like a greased snake that she was caught stealing only once before July. Everybody knew she'd be the first player named to the State All-Stars, and all the newspapers came to her games—she was photographed so many times she grew to be a natural with cameras, and Daddy even started mailing her stories and pictures he had clipped.

But he never came to see us. He had once-a-week visiting rights, Graceanne found out from Father Weiss, but he never exercised them. "With your Daddy," Father Weiss explained, "it's all or nothing. He won't be a part-time Daddy."

"Then I hope he goes to hell," Graceanne said. "Looks like he's pretty happy having a choice in the matter. I wish I had a choice."

"It won't do you any good to curse your father."

"Well, what will do me some good?"

Father Weiss put his gentle old hand on her deadly left throwing arm. "You can stop worrying about whether his soul's going to hell, and start worrying about your own destination. Someday, Graceanne, you'll really be on your own."

"I'll worry about my destination then."

She was practically on her own at work. She wasn't making as much money at the hotel as she had, because the army shifted their basic training program to Fort Leonard Wood in the middle of the state and that cut down on casual family visits to Jefferson Barracks. Graceanne would still horse around, or kid people, and try to talk them out of their money, but traffic at the hotel was sluggish and she was looking around her for other things to do. Collier was working days while she worked nights, and she looked like a little statue standing out under the neon sign on the steps waiting for people with luggage who never came. Edie'd send me after dinner to sit on the steps until Graceanne was finished doing her waiting so we could walk home together. Collier wanted to drive her home in his car but Edie said, "That would lead to behavior unbecoming in a lady. It's all I need to have Graceanne run off to Florida thinking she can sing." It was okay for Collier to drive her if I was along, and Graceanne started calling me "Mike" because, she said, I was her watchdog.

"I don't care about riding in the car, **per se**," she'd said. "What I care about is fairness. I **loathe** being treated like a child just because Tucka went and put out for every boy in Cranepool's Landing who wanted a piece, not that I blame her for what got her out of the house."

Collier had given Graceanne a gold necklace with a heart, and she wore it even with her county softball uniform. I longed for the days when she was writing her book because I wanted to know why Collier had given it to her, and why he had stopped writing so many letters for a while and why, now that he was home again, he was treating her the way he used to. She said there had been an argument over a matter of faith, but that explanation lacked the clarity for me of seeing the history of the argument myself in their handwriting. Wanda told me there had been another girl in South Bend, but that explanation, too, was inadequate for me. The absence of Graceanne's book opened up gaps in my ability to see my sister's life the way I was accustomed to, and the consequent lonely feeling urged me on in my effort to replace the book.

Wanda's mother did not have time to teach me to embroider, but she showed me how to thread the needle she gave me, taught me a cross stitch and a satin stitch, and let me borrow an embroidery hoop when Wanda told her what it was for. I could see that my stitches were awkward, and knotted sometimes, and that the white cloth was getting dirty—that was the most difficult thing about embroidery, I discovered: keeping the cloth clean—but the bees looked like bees to me, and the flowers were the same colors as the ones Kentucky had sewn. When I stitched on the words *By Grace- anne*, they were readable, and I folded the cloth and put it away inside my winter coat, which I took out to the dog's house to hide. I told old O.U.B. it was mine so he wouldn't throw it out by mistake.

During the long hot June days when Edie was at work and Graceanne was playing ball, I spent many hours under her bed in our room, reconstructing the words and drawings I had seen in her book, and trying to reconstruct the conditions under which they had been entered into the book. I always wrote under the bed, and always with Graceanne's flashlight stuck up in the bedsprings and shining on the pages. On the rare occasions when my memory let me down, I thought that my superior handwriting would make up the difference, because there was no question that my script was much prettier than hers. I was as faithful as I could be to the original, and by the middle of June I had nearly filled two of the notebooks I had bought with the money from the soda bottles. My hand- writing was smaller and neater than Graceanne's, so I hadn't

needed all three notebooks as she had. Everything was there—
the drawings, the poems, the catechism, the story of the Martian astronomers.

I started adding new material when I had copied everything
from my memory. I thought it would be all right to add more
if I just used my eyes and ears, and made it as close to what
Graceanne would write as possible, and I started recording
the parts of her life that I was commanded to witness in my
role as watchdog. For me the new paragraphs did not have
the intensity and pith of Graceanne's Martian tales, but I was
filling pages as I followed my famous sister's career off the
field and on.

I stopped writing as much when Graceanne and Collier
quit their jobs and went to work in the cornfields. My arm
was tired, it was hot and dark under the bed, and the cornfields were full of drama and color that summer.

Collier and Graceanne said it was the slow trade at the
hotel that made them quit, but the kids in the cornfields were
organizing hayrides and picnics, and Graceanne certainly
didn't want to be left out of those. It never occurred to me
for one minute that Collier had helped with the decision to
leave the hotel or did anything but ride the tide of whatever
enthusiasm was created by Graceanne's ideas. She could only
work at the burlap swinging early in the morning because of
her softball schedule, and the farmers were glad to get her
because most kids wanted to sleep late in the summer, and
even though she wasn't really tall enough for the work she
had a fantastic way of swinging the rough cloth that made up
for her lack of height. They were glad to get Collier because
of his long arms. I went along because, Edie said, "that way
Charlie'll know how to do it next year when he's taller."

"Not if I kill him first," Graceanne said. "Which I will do
if he doesn't stop following us around. You don't make him
come to all my softball games."

"You won't get in any trouble at the games. That's good healthy exercise."

"I can get in trouble anywhere if I work at it."

"Are you looking for a slap, young lady?"

"If I was, I guess I came to the right place."

Edie picked up her hairbrush from the dresser and slapped Graceanne hard on the front of her neck with the flat side. Graceanne couldn't eat for two days, not solids anyway, and it was quiet around Fort McBain.

Her appetite that summer in general was bad. She ate candy bars at the hotel, drank soda at the games, and, later, when they worked on the farm, she and Collier and the other kids had permission to raid the tomato stakes and eat the fruit like apples, but at the dinner table she was twitchy and she played with her fork and didn't eat much. Edie said Graceanne missed Kentucky, "as we all do," and that accounted for her lack of interest in food, but sometimes after a meal Graceanne would go down in push-up position beside her bed and slide under for a while. And I knew that it was her book that was bothering her.

"Aren't you ever going to write again, Graceanne?"

"What for? Throwing my book into the river was like tearing my face off and feeding it to the fish. I'll never do that again."

"What if you had your book back?"

"I'll never have it, Charlie. It's gone forever."

"But you could start over."

"I've lost the beginning of my story, Charlie, and all that hard work."

"Maybe I could write a book."

"Maybe you're worse stupid than you look."

I thought about that for a while and we went out in the backyard. I went to see that the dog was chained up good and tight so he wouldn't spook Graceanne, and Wanda came over, and we caught fireflies for a while. Graceanne wouldn't let us pull their lights off to make rings and bracelets, because "you don't want to interfere with Nature that way. Jewelry you give yourself is only for giant cruds, anyway."

We always accepted Graceanne's judgments about cruds, so we let the fireflies go after we caught them, without stealing their lights. Her Crud Laws probably would have been written down in her book that summer, if she was still keeping it, but Wanda and I heard them often enough to give them a certain codified aura, and they ended up in my version of *By Graceanne*.

1. Only cruds had to go to Summer Enrichment.
2. Cruds made the rule that divorced women cannot take communion.
3. Animals couldn't be cruds.
4. You didn't have to be white to be a crud.
5. Daddy was a crud.
6. Hitler was a crud.
7. Cruds tried to work out a walk when it was their turn to bat.
8. Cruds ate Jell-O.
9. Whites Only was cruddy.
10. Italian painters could not be cruds.
11. *King Lear* was a cruddy play, except the part where Gloucester's eyes get poked out.
12. It took a real crud to say that colored kids couldn't work as burlap swingers because the crows didn't fear them.

That's what Mr. and Mrs. Pinnell had told Wanda when she wanted to get a job on the farm they owned. "It's not that we're prejudiced, my dear. It's just that the black birds aren't afraid of your people."

So, since the girls had to pay for their own softball uniforms, Wanda spent the early part of the summer babysitting. "Slavery isn't over," she said. "It's the ownership that's been changed. Now my master is a goddamn baseball uniform." But when she wasn't slaving with "squalling brats and barking dogs," Wanda came out to the Pinnell farm anyway and worked with Graceanne or Collier without being paid. The mystique she shared with Graceanne as the most accomplished and meanest athletes in the state, and perhaps the entire Midwest, as well as their very real fame, gave Wanda an entry into the otherwise closed world of the kids who were swinging burlap and doing "assorted chores," which, Graceanne said, was "a **euphemism** for nigger jobs, no offense."

Burlap swinging had come to be the glamour job for a kid in Cranepool's Landing that summer, especially after Graceanne brought Collier into the fields to add to the considerable glory the job had gained by engaging the interest of the town's most famous girl. The job was, in itself, an **art form**, Graceanne and Wanda said, playing down their roles in making it popular. And somehow having a Notre Dame boy there added to the elevation the job had already achieved by virtue of its peculiarly flexible interpretation. Individual style was given full rein among the corn rows, dances were spawned and grievances taken out under the guise of chasing crows and grackles, and, because the fields were so vast, supervision was simply unthinkable. The "assorted chores," like cleaning chicken coops and weeding carrot patches and washing the farmhouse windows and babysitting farm brats, were rotated around among the kids, but because Graceanne was one of the few "early birds," she was almost exclusively a burlap swinger, rarely doing anything more lowly than gathering eggs, which she liked doing anyway because, she said, the hens were "so **accommodating** and soft."

It was an interesting blend of young people who worked

the farms that summer because it wasn't just the poor kids who wanted work. Some of the Hulen's Lake kids came out in their cars to work alongside Lewis and Clark Hill army brats and the trash from the Developments who walked to work, and everybody worked for stupidly low wages—for most it was a nickel an hour. I worked it out one morning under Graceanne's bed that a farmer could employ as many as six kids, working various and overlapping six-hour shifts, for as little as $1.80 a day, and get all the cruddy jobs done cheaply, all because the burlap swinging was so popular. There were seven big farms north of Cranepool's Landing that were using the cheap kid labor, and that meant that about forty-two kids were doing the work of seven men at less than 20 percent of what the men would have cost the farmers.

The farmers who were taking advantage of all the willing young labor salved their consciences and astronomically increased the popularity of the work by supplying hay wains once a week for hayrides under the stars, and the only people who got to ride were the ones who had put in a week's work. Sometimes it was possible to sneak in a date who was not employed on the farms, but that didn't happen often because of the close camaraderie that had sprung up among the swingers. Even Wanda, who worked unacknowledged and unpaid, was content on Saturday nights to receive the boon of hayrides and singing and the beer the farmers supplied under the hay. I got to ride, too, although I didn't get any beer, because all the kids knew that if I didn't come, Graceanne and Collier couldn't come, and probably Wanda would have stayed home without them.

It was on one of the Saturday night hayrides late in June, when the wains were stopped under the stars on a private dirt road without a name that wound among the farms, that the idea for the scarecrow contest was born. The idea was passed from wain to wain and back down the line until everyone had heard some version of it and everyone had approved. The criteria that evolved and were passed like magic through the air from wain to wain stated that (1) the scarecrow must be visible from a public road, (2) it had to be assembled in one day, (3) no one could spend money on the materials, and (4) it had to be a working model, one that did a real job and frightened away birds. Everyone agreed to ask the Knights of Columbus to provide judges, set July 4 as the assembly date because they didn't have to work that day and July 5 as the judging date, and collectively expressed pity for the poor cruds that were spending their summers getting all-over tans at the lake or staying fish-belly white in their fathers' stores and offices.

The burlap swinging kids had "farmer tans" from the T-shirts that had become their uniforms when they worked in the fields, meaning their arms (excepting Wanda's) were two-tone: brown as hickory up to about three inches above the elbows, and white as sheets the rest of the way. And farmer tans included permanent sock marks on the hickory-brown legs, because no one was stupid enough to work without thick socks—the lower stalks were dry and could slice through skin invisibly, leaving wounds like paper cuts.

The final criterion for the scarecrow contest was that (5) you had to have a farmer tan to be allowed onto farming property on July 4. Wanda was given a dispensation when Graceanne had a fit and pointed out that she needed Wanda on her team.

"You gonna let your goddamn little brother on your team, too?" Sterling Hofbauer yelled all the way from the back hay wain in his nasal voice. "We don't want any babies out here on the Fourth."

"My goddamn brother's farmer tan is better than yours, Sterling Hofbauer." Graceanne stood up in the hay on our wain and squinted at him. "Charlie's IQ is higher than yours,

Mr. Ninety-eight, and his brains are twice as useful. The only idea you ever had in your thick head was wrong." She gave him a look. "Besides, Charlie's not a baby. He held a dog on Black Santa. I never saw anything so brave in my life."

Everybody laughed, and said it was all right to bring Charlie, and nobody ought to provoke Graceanne because the only idea she ever had was to make horsemeat out of people who stood up to her.

Twenty-Five

I thought we should make a Richard Nixon scarecrow but Graceanne rejected that idea immediately and with disgust when we started talking about the contest on the way home, the four of us walking along beside the river in the dark.

"Don't be such a pest, Charlie. Everyone but you has already forgotten that man." Her hair didn't have Brylcreme in it and it was all curly even though her braids had been gone a long time, which proved the curls hadn't ever been braid wrinkles, as Edie still insisted, but real curls. Graceanne put her hand in her hair and started thinking. "We need something really frightening. I'll bet the K. of C. judges will be looking for something that will scare people as much as birds."

"How 'bout Black Santa?" Wanda said.

"I thought about that already," Graceanne said. "But if I already thought of it, so did some other kids. We need something more original."

Collier was holding the hand that wasn't in Graceanne's hair. "We could do Lady Macbeth. A little Shakespeare in the field wouldn't be a bad idea."

Graceanne looked at him like he was going to try to hit

one past her and she felt sorry for him, but not sorry enough
to let it get by. "That'd be fine for you, and me, and Wanda.
But if anybody else in Cranepool's Landing can tell Lady
Macbeth from Jiminy Cricket, I'll be **electrified** with surprise."

I thought Collier was given to airs about being in college,
so I was glad to see Graceanne take him down a peg.

"And," Graceanne said, "it really ought to be someone
Charlie's heard of, out of fairness, since he's on our team
whether we like it or not."

Then I was wishing Collier would take Graceanne down a
peg.

"Well," Wanda said, her voice coming out real slow like
she was an old woman, "we can always make a Negro scarecrow. That'd scare the Pinnells, at least." She seemed to be
thinking. "I reckon I better move their outhouse back a foot."

"That outhouse is just a *relic*," Graceanne said. "They've
got indoor plumbing."

"Then I'll soap their windows."

"You're not concentrating, Wanda."

We walked along. There was a three-quarter moon floating
in the muddy water, and I kept thinking the currents would
wash over it and get it dirty. The water lapped against the
banks, and I wondered where the pieces of Graceanne's book
had all wound up. Maybe some of the poems were down by
Ste. Genevieve; maybe some of the stories about the Martian
astronomers were down at the bottom of the river, at the foot
of McBain Avenue. I wondered what the bottom of the river
was like.

"What's the bottom of the river like?" I asked.

"We can't make a scarecrow like the river bottom," Graceanne said. "What are you thinking of?"

"I was just wondering."

"Well, don't interrupt your elders, son."

We walked along and the moon kept up with us, moving downstream, looking like part of a greasy paper plate floating just under the skin of the water. We stopped and sat around on the grass. Collier got up and skipped some stones and tried to hit the moon, and he bounced a couple over its surface but he never got a direct hit.

"There's lots of frightening things around," Graceanne said. "Only it's hard to think of them when you want to. Mostly they just sneak up on you when you don't want them."

"Hitler was scary," Wanda said.

"Scary to us," Graceanne said. "But he wouldn't work with crows and grackles."

"Maybe it should be something funny," Collier said. "If it's got loose clothing, it'll scare birds, and if it's funny, it'll amuse the Knights of Columbus."

"Like who?" Graceanne said. "Who'd be funny?"

"What about Sister Clothilda?"

Graceanne put her chin in her hand, looked at Collier, and leaned her elbow on her knee. "This has definite possibilities. And she's a good sport."

"We could make a wimple, and hang a rosary around the neck, and stuff it with pillows, and put black boots on it," Collier said. "Everybody would know who it was supposed to be. We'd win for sure."

Wanda threw a stone and bounced it flat off the face of the moon. "I won't be a party to any sacrilege. Father Weiss would be sure to hear about it, and he might have a heart attack."

Collier tried another stone, but he missed again. "Well, do you have a better idea?"

Wanda and Collier kept talking, and she kept hitting the moon dead center and he kept missing, and Graceanne seemed to melt away into the dark, so I followed her. She walked in the grass and found a place to sit down next to a tree. She put her back against it and just sat there.

"What are you doing, Graceanne?" I asked.

She jumped. "Jesus Christ, Charlie. You scared the living hell out of me. Why do you always ask me what I'm doing? I'm sitting, that's what I'm doing."

I sat down on the ground. She looked at me like she'd never seen me before. I knew better than to say anything stupid, so I just sat there getting sleepy and letting her look at me.

"Charlie, I got an idea."

"What?"

"It's a bad idea."

"You better stop thinking about it."

"Yeah, I better had."

I could hear Collier and Wanda arguing and the rocks hitting the river.

"Charlie, I can't stop thinking about it."

"Try thinking about something else."

"Like what?"

"Like the Martians or something."

"I don't think about them anymore."

That made me sit up and the sleep went away like it was pulled away on the skin of the river like topsoil during a flood. "You don't even think about them? Not even in your head?"

"No, but maybe they're still up there, trying to know everything, I guess. Stop asking stupid questions."

"What's your bad idea?"

"Didn't I tell you to stop asking questions?"

I sat there for a while and put my head on my knees and started pulling up the wet grass.

"My bad idea is to make an Eden Farrand scarecrow."

My mouth must've fallen open because Graceanne took and gave me a New York Bib.

"Mama?" I asked, rubbing my chin. I put my hand on my

chest to see how I was breathing. Graceanne didn't say anything else, and I could hear Collier and Wanda walking around in the grass and bushes, calling our names.

"Don't tell 'em, Charlie. It was a bad idea." Graceanne whispered.

"I think it's a good idea."

"You do?"

"Yeah."

"It's a bad idea, and she'd lay us both out if she knew, but it's a good idea, isn't it, Charlie?"

"Yeah."

When Collier and Wanda found us, we walked down the long path to McBain Avenue, and Collier said he'd keep going because the shortest way to Lewis and Clark Hill was along the river. He gave Graceanne a kiss on the cheek and asked her to walk with him a little ways, but she said, "I gotta get Charlie home before Mama thinks I've taken him to Florida to sing in a bar and dance on the tables like a monkey."

When Collier was out of listening distance, Wanda said, "If you don't put out, that college boy's gonna find somebody who will."

"There's other stuff besides putting out."

"Not for boys there isn't."

"Wanda, you don't put out."

"I also don't have no college boyfriend."

Graceanne told Wanda her idea about the Mama scarecrow.

"You're asking for trouble, girl," Wanda said. "You get in that kind of trouble, there ain't nobody to help you, girl. Nobody can help a kid whose mother's gonna pull her head off her shoulders for her."

"Mama'll never know. She'll never see the scarecrow. She hasn't got a car, and, if she paid for a taxi, she wouldn't ask it to drive her around a bunch of farms. She had enough of taxis when she was taking call, and she says farms are for people who don't care to get on in life."

"That's pretty stupid," Wanda said. "Old Man Pinnell has lots more money than your ma."

"She's says it's not about money. It's about dignity."

"Well, if she thinks it's more dignified to get her hands bloody than to get her hands dirty in God's own earth, then I feel sorry for your ma, Graceanne."

"Don't waste time feeling sorry for her. She thinks she's the Queen of England. Ever since she got this new job, she's been talking about how people roll out the red carpet for her whenever she goes downtown."

"She never."

"That's what she says."

Wanda went into her yard under the maple, and I could tell she was watching us go home because I could see her eyes that looked like glass all the way up to the top step. We went in and Edie was doing her nails in the Garden Room.

"You're very late," she said, waving around her freckled hand to dry the shiny pink nails.

"It was a long walk, and we got tired," Graceanne said.

"You kids have a good time?"

"It was all right."

"What did you do?"

"Just rode the wains and talked."

"Did you sing any songs?"

"Some."

"Did you sing 'Harvest Moon'?"

"We always sing that one, Mama."

"Your Grandma and Grandpa are coming down for the fourth. I guess we'll go to the Lake."

"Me and Charlie gotta be in the Pinnells' field on the Fourth."

"Nobody works on the Fourth of July."

I could see Graceanne trying to find the words that wouldn't be a lie but would get her out of going to the Lake.

"Crows and grackles don't know it's a holiday, Mama."

"I suppose so. Well, we'll see what we'll see."

We went to bed, and when the light was off, I asked Graceanne if she wanted to listen to her radio.

"I guess not, Charlie."

I could hear her moving around in her bed like she had a frog in there with her. "What are you doing, Graceanne?"

"I can't sleep."

I was sitting up in bed. "I could get her Jackie Kennedy black pillbox hat and pin red Christmas ornaments on it like when she hit Black Santa."

"And we could put Tucka's county baseball bat in her hands."

We stopped talking. I could still hear Graceanne moving around. She got out of bed and came over and sat on the floor next to me. "Charlie, don't up and die when I say what I'm gonna say. You promise?"

"Promise."

"Her good black dress has all those ruffles, and if we get a decent breeze, they'd scare the birds out of their minds."

"She'll kill you, Graceanne."

"Not if we don't actually do it. It's only an idea. We've got a couple of days to think of something else."

She crawled over to her bed, but she was still on the floor. The moon was way up in the sky by then, and its white light was so bright I could see each of Graceanne's toes.

"Graceanne, why did you write your book?"

"I guess I just had the story in me, Charlie."

"Don't you have the story in you anymore?"

"I guess not."

I tried to go to sleep, but the moon was so bright I kept seeing shapes moving in the full-length mirror leaning against the wall across from her bed. I could see Graceanne's pink pajamas sitting on the floor, and some of her curls, and the softball uniform hanging over the foot of her bed with the famous number twenty-two, but the numbers were backward and seemed to float away from the uniform and slide up the mirror. There was a darkness deep inside the mirror, behind all of Graceanne's things, and I kept staring, trying to see what was inside the mirror. The pink pajamas rose in the mirror and moved to the side and turned around and lay down. Toes were lined up on the side of the floating numbers, and it looked wrong, because the number was twenty-two backward, and there were ten toes straight up.

"Graceanne?"

There was no answer from under her bed. The pink pajamas were still in the mirror in front of the blackness. I got out of bed and tiptoed to the mirror. Deep in the blackness I could see two points of light. They looked like burning tiger eyes, and I was so scared I couldn't move, and then I realized it was the moon on her glasses sitting on the windowsill behind me.

Twenty·Six

A thick morning mist was lying on the gravel around the house when we got out of bed on the Fourth of July. Fort McBain was so boxlike that the mist couldn't tuck itself into curves and shadows, so it burned off our house quickly, while the older houses like Wanda's were still wrapped up in cotton and wouldn't be free of it until after we left for the farm. When Edie went out to hang the clothes on the line, Graceanne and I went into the Garden Room and took the good black dress from the garment bag in the closet, and the Jackie Kennedy black pillbox, and I took a box of tree ornaments from the cabinet under the bathroom sink. I could hear Mike the dog out there whining at Edie, asking her to let his chain off the spike the way I had done when Black Santa came. Old O.U.B. had his clothes on the line, and I could hear Edie sliding his clothespins down the old dry rope so she could make room to put ours on and she was singing "Harvest Moon" even though it was morning.

Graceanne got a paper bag, and we dumped in Edie's things, grabbed Kentucky's county bat, and took off for the Pinnell Farm. Wanda was waiting outside her house with her own paper bag.

"What's in there?" Graceanne asked.

"Lunch."

"What'd you bring?"

"Tuna fish."

"It'll go bad in the sun."

"It's still in the can."

"Did you bring a can opener?"

"Does a catfish have clean whiskers?"

We went up the long path with our paper bags. There were two riverboats way up under Big Neighbors Bridge in the distance in a ball of mist, big paddlewheels all set for the Fourth of July race down to Herculaneum. The Belle of St. Louis was covered with fresh sky-blue paint, and the Quincy Queen was red, with white crepe banners draped down her sides. The Belle was closer to our side of the river, and the Queen, the Illinois boat, was over at the other side, coming out from the shadow of the bridge and dragging some of the mist with her. Both boats were loaded with people in panama hats that looked like little saucers from where we were watching, and we could hear the banjo and trumpet music and the people laughing.

"There's a good wind," Graceanne said. "We can hear the music already from here."

"Good day for scarecrows, I'll be sworn," Wanda said.

It would have taken a better wind than we had that day to lift the skin of the river up in ruffles and caps, but the leaves were stirring and we could smell the creosote. We walked along beside the river. Graceanne and Wanda had on their thick socks with their tennis shoes, and both pairs of legs looked brown as hickory. They were both wearing their dark blue county softball running shorts, the ones they wore to practice so they wouldn't tear their uniforms or get them dirty. Their T-shirts were outside their shorts, and I thought how Edie always said a lady wouldn't wear her shirt outside the waistband.

"Graceanne," I shouted, "your shirt's tucked out."

"God, Charlie, you gave me a start. For a minute there, I thought the Queen of the Nile herself had come along with us to keep her good black dress company."

Graceanne had her hair up in dog-ears. She had pulled her curls up on each side of her head behind her ears in a rubber band, the way she used to do with her braids, and she had tied white ribbons in them, and it looked like she had doll hair. Her hair was so short that some of it was already falling out of the dog-ears, but it looked better than when she had the Brylcreme in it to keep it out of her softball dead-eyes.

We walked along and the sun was coming up higher off the Illinois banks, its yellow rays just breaking off the hills, and the music from the steamboats was louder. The musicians on the Queen were playing "When the Saints Go Marching In," and on the Belle it was "Meet Me in St. Louis," and the two songs together sounded all right, like they were different choruses of the same song. I thought how nice it would be if Kentucky could come back home and sing on the boats.

Graceanne looked back and asked me if I wanted a turn carrying the bag, and I said I did, so I got to carry it for a while until the road for the farm when Graceanne took it back.

Collier was waiting for us on the Pinnell porch, and Old Man Pinnell had some lumber for us. "You want to make your scarecrow real tall," he said. "That's what the Knights of Columbus will like. Tall scarecrows will frighten birds from miles around."

"Will it scare away hawks?" I asked.

"Nothing scares away hawks, son, but that's okay because they don't eat corn. Hawks clean the mice out of the field, and mice do eat corn."

"Our scarecrow will scare away even the hawks," I said.

"What are you kids doing for yours?"

"Beaden Eden."

"What's that?"

"She's the woman that got Black Santa."

"Well, you kids have a good time. We'll get the wains out around before dark and we'll have some dinner for you. We'll find you when we see the tallest scarecrow in the county. Happy Independence Day to you."

All of us except Wanda said for him to have a happy Independence Day, and we started off for the cornfields.

"Where're we gonna build this thing?" Graceanne said.

"I thought we should go over to the twenty-acre field off of Douglas Lane," Collier said. "There's already lots of cars over there for the start of the steamboat race."

Just then we heard the gun going off from the bridge. The banjos and trumpets were playing "Old Kentucky Home" and "The Battle Hymn of the Republic," and even when the songs mixed like that from the distance, you could still tell that's what they were playing on the boats. The sun was getting hot, and the chickens in Old Man Pinnell's henhouse were settling down quiet. We picked some beefsteak tomatoes from the vines around the gazebo in the back farmyard, and set off south toward Douglas Lane, carrying the lumber. Every now and then, Collier would take the bag from Graceanne and wave it over his head so the rest of our team could find us when they got there.

We went into the cornfields and walked down the long rows. The rows were about three feet apart from each other, and I started counting the ears of corn. For every hundred feet or so that we walked, there were sixty ears on each side, all of the ears fat in the middle and tapered at the end, without a scrawny one to be seen. The heads of the stalks were waving their silk like it was hair, and I started thinking that the field was full of human things—ears, and hair, and heads, and feet.

"Can the corn hear us?" I asked.

"Of course it can," Graceanne said. "Look at all the ears."

If it could hear us, I thought, it was hearing the soft crunch of their tennis shoes and my saddle oxfords on the crumbly dry earth, and the tender swish when we brushed against the dry lower leaves, and the music trailing after us from the boats. It was deep green and hot inside the rows, with sunlight streaking down at a slant in a misty way through the tassels. It was like the narrow side aisles in a church where the stations of the cross were hung, if all the stained glass windows were green and gold and it was a sunny day outside.

Wanda started singing the "Battle Hymn," and I was surprised how she controlled her voice and got it to do more things than Catholics did, except for Kentucky. I guessed Wanda was an alto, but I'd only heard Baptist singing when we had the ugly baby in the parking lot at the church, and Wanda's voice sounded different. All of us knew the "Battle Hymn," and when we all started, Wanda was on the second verse:

> In the beauty of the lilies Christ was born across
>   the sea,
> With a glory in His bosom that transfigures you
>   and me;
> As He died to make men holy, let us die to make
>   men free.
> His truth is marching on.

Graceanne could hardly carry the tune, but she sang loud and swung her arms, and Wanda's alto was sweet and warbly and full of hidden stories and things the Baptists were keeping to themselves, and Collier's baritone was broad and carried over the tops of the stalks, and we were marching along the aisle in time to the music, and suddenly they all turned around and stared at me coming up behind.

"Is that *you*, Charlie?" Graceanne screamed.

"What?" I didn't know why they were staring at me.

"Sing something else."

"What for?"

"Charlie Farrand, for a minute there, it sounded like there was an angel in the field with us," Graceanne said. "Where'd you learn how to sing like that?"

"I just listen, is all."

"Holy Moses, there's one more thing that runs in the goddamn family. Your voice is as pretty as Tucka's."

I didn't like them staring at me, so I looked around at the corn and wished they'd start walking again.

"What else can you sing?"

"I don't know."

"Can you sing 'O Holy Night'?"

"I guess."

"Well, sing it."

"It ain't Christmas. It's the Fourth of July."

"Sing it anyway."

"I don't want to."

"Please, Charlie."

"You all start walking and maybe I'll hum it a little."

They turned back around and walked through the deep green corn rows that didn't seem ever to end in the bright sun, and I started humming, and when they got farther ahead of me, I started singing. They knew I didn't want them to look at me, so they didn't turn around, but I sang the song, even Kentucky's solo part, and it didn't sound at all stupid to sing "O Holy Night" on a hot July Fourth in the fields of rustling corn, and they didn't laugh like I thought they might, and I was surprised I could do it.

We picked our spot in sight of Douglas Lane, dumped the lumber on the ground, and sat down under the cornstalks to wait for the others because they were bringing the ladder and the tools. Collier would get up to swing the paper bag and finally we could hear Marilyn Johansen and Tom Entsminger and Frank Handt who had pulled out the light pole with his bare hands coming along the rows.

It took them all morning to hammer and saw the frame and get it so it would stand up without falling over right away. The crosspiece was true and straight, but the stand was crooked, and they kept sawing at the legs to get it even. Frank took a piece of lumber and dug out a hole with the end in the ground between the rows, and they finally anchored the frame down there and covered the stand with dirt. When the frame was up, it towered over the rows of corn. They let me climb up on the ladder and look around; you couldn't tell when you were down in the corn rows how much you were surrounded by the corn, or where you were, but from the top of the ladder I could see we were at the center of a wide river of bright green and tan and waving white tassels that went all the way to the far hills in the west and almost to the river in the east. I couldn't see the muddy river, but I could see the Illinois bluffs, so I knew where the river was.

We were all hot and sweaty and thirsty, and we sat in the shade of the corn and had tomatoes and tuna and bread, and we had baloney and cookies the others had brought, and some oranges, and water from Tom's thermos. We cleaned up the mess so it wouldn't attract the birds, and Collier picked off a big ear of corn and pretended it was a microphone and sang "Love Me Tender" in his baritone. Everybody laughed and then we all sang the song. It was one of the Elvis songs that Edie said was dirty, but we sang it low and soft and it seemed to fit with the waving corn as much as "O Holy Night" and I didn't see how it could be dirty. It was as mysterious as

Christmas carols; I knew all the words but I didn't understand them much better than "Hark the Herald Angels."

I wondered if I loved anyone tenderly. I knew I loved Mike the dog, who you couldn't sing an Elvis song to because was an animal. And I looked around and saw Graceanne with her doll hair and her glasses and her soft skin and I thought maybe I loved her, who would laugh at me if I sang Elvis to her. It came as a big surprise to me that I loved my sister, as big a surprise as being able to sing. I knew I loved the dog, because he was lonely and loved me, but I didn't know why I loved Graceanne, and I looked over at her again where she was wiping her forehead with the palm of her hand and flapping her gums at Frank.

Wanda got out a burlap bag she had sewn black stitches for eyes onto. There were freckles she had made under the eyes with crayon. We stuffed the sack with dry leaves from the lower stalks and Frank took it up the ladder, put it on the top of the tall two-by-four, and lashed it around with rope so it made a head. I sat on the ground and started pinning the shiny red ornaments onto the pillbox hat. There was more hammering and when I glanced up I had to shade my eyes against the sun to see they had nailed some more burlap to the crosspiece for arms and legs. The burlap dangled and flapped in the light breeze. When they had the burlap up, Graceanne got up on the ladder and lowered Edie's good black dress carefully over the head and threaded the burlap arms through the ruffled sleeves like she was dressing a sleeping baby she didn't want to wake up, she was so gentle. The black ruffles flapped up and down and the skirt blew around a little about the burlap legs and I thought there had never been such a scarecrow.

They had a hard time with the bat. It was so heavy it tore off one of the burlap arms and they had to replace that. It looked for a while like they wouldn't be able to put a bat up there, and that would spoil the whole thing, but Wanda said they could tie rope to both ends of the bat and hang it over the scarecrow's head. It wouldn't be the same as having the bat in her hand, but it was better than no bat, she said, and that's what they did.

The whole time we were building the scarecrow there wasn't one word of disrespect or sass for Edie. I don't know what Graceanne set out to do when she had the idea, but the scarecrow was not my mother, and nobody thought of her— just of getting it up there the right way. It was just a thing made out of caring for the corn they'd been protecting with their burlap bags, and of knowing the ways of the birds, and of the way a nail went into wood. It was the tallest object in the field of corn, and it was a thing we had built together, and it was a problem we had to solve to get the bat up, and I thought it would scare crows.

By the middle of the afternoon, we were done. They made me get up on the ladder with the pillbox and I put it on the head. The little red ornaments tinkled against each other. When the hat was on good and tight, I looked down and saw everybody else looking up.

"It's a good scarecrow," Frank said, wiping sweat off his arms.

"It'll do a fine job," Wanda said.

Everybody clapped and smiled and then Collier got his ear of corn and started singing again, and everybody went and got an ear of corn and Graceanne handed me one and we all joined in and sang "Love Me Tender" to the scarecrow like we were in church.

Wanda gave us a brown crayon and we all took turns getting up on the ladder and signing our initials to one of the burlap legs, and across the other leg Collier wrote, "Pinnell Farm—July 4, 1961."

Graceanne stood and looked at the scarecrow while the rest

of us gathered up our stuff. "It's not as scary as you might have thought it would be," she said. "I mean, don't you ever wonder why scarecrows always work and actually do scare birds away, and farmers have been using them for centuries, and they're still building them and the birds haven't caught on yet, and here it is 1961 and we're going to put a man on the moon by the end of the decade—which is the most **vital** thing—and we're celebrating the greatest democracy on the planet by building a goddamn doll to scare away birds that have as much need to eat as we do?"

Collier came to stand beside Graceanne and he put his arm around her shoulders, which he had to stoop to do, and he said, "We'll be building scarecrows on the moon, Grace."

"I reckon we'll build scaresomethings, anyhow."

We went back along the rows of corn, where the green was now deeper and the shadows of the stalks were lying across the loose dirt in black patterns that looked like the Japanese drawings in my history textbook. The wind had kicked up a little, and the dust blew around, and the black patterns shifted under our feet. Pretty soon we heard the wheels of the hay wain turning on the dirt road.

We rode around and met the other wains and went to all the farms and all seven scarecrows were up tall above the fields. They were all dressed in parents' clothing, one of them in a business suit with a flapping red tie, one of them in an orange waitress's uniform from the Crown Drugstore, one of them in a master sergeant's uniform, one of them in a volunteer fireman's coat and hat, another one in an army uniform but I couldn't tell the rank, and the last one in bib overalls and a tractor hat, because the agreement we had added to the rules was that (6) all the scarecrows had to be some grownup in Cranepool's Landing. That was Collier's idea, to hide the Eden Farrand scarecrow. But the main thing was that all the scarecrows were doing their business, flapping and scaring off

the birds. They were good scarecrows, and I guess after working in the fields in the corn, the kids had all learned to take
care of the sweet, tender corn in the husks. They wanted what
they built to do the job right, and I was glad Graceanne had
had her idea about the Eden Farrand scarecrow because the
good black dress made such a fine, serious scarecrow with just
the right amount of flapping.

We kept passing the other wains and the talk was about
how they got the frames to stand, and how they thought the
scarecrows would keep off the birds until the birds got used
to them and started ignoring them, which was how scarecrows
worked—not scary after a while because the birds got familiar
with how they moved and what they were.

The farmers and their families brought picnic food and
drinks to the Pinnell Farm and fed us at tables set up outside
in the yard. There were thirty-seven of us scarecrow-makers
and a lot of little kids and old people, but there was plenty
of food. There was platter after platter of cold fried chicken,
and bushels of grilled corn on the cob still hot in their foil
wrappers, and potato salad, and green beans, and sliced tomatoes, and peeled carrots, and potato chips, and pickles, and
homemade bread and butter, and fruit salad, and Jell-O molds
(which we kids did not touch because of what Graceanne
called the "crud factor," but she didn't say it so the women
could hear), and gooseberry pies and peach pies and jugs of
milk and coffee. Old Man Pinnell said we could use the hose
to clean ourselves up after dinner, and we hooked it up to
the spigot on the side of the barn and sprayed each other
until it got dark.

We got up on the hay wains and sat on them where they
were all parked in Old Man Pinnell's rutted driveway and
watched the fireworks that were going off on both sides of
the river. On the Missouri side, the Hulen's Lake fireworks
were the closest to us, and it looked like they were spilling

their colors into the cornfields even though they were a good few miles away, but all along the river the sky over both states was exploding with lights, smoke, and noise, and the smell of sulphur and fireworks was all around.

Old Man Pinnell said we could swim in his pond, and everybody got off the wains and ran to the pond and nobody had swimming suits with them so all the old people and their kids went inside the farmhouse and somebody played the piano and we stripped down to our underwear. It was so dark you couldn't see anything anyway except that everyone looked alike with their farmer tans leaving some white skin floating around like ghosts and you couldn't see Wanda at all and when I jumped into the warm water Graceanne somehow knew which one I was and grabbed my arm and yelled, "Hey, I caught a dead fish." And they started throwing me around and catching me and letting me drop in the water.

We let the air dry us when we got out and we got dressed and everyone walked down to the river together and we watched the steamboats coming back. They were all lit up with colored lights, and the people in their panama hats were waving sparklers, and the bands were both playing "My Country 'Tis of Thee" with their banjos and trumpets. The crickets in the grass were loud, and the wakes of the big boats slapped up on the shore and sprayed drops on us, and the United States was 185 years old, and I wondered how long the astronomers on Mars had been watching, and if they could see the river better when it was outlined with fireworks of red, white, and blue, and with the big lighted boats on it, and how long it would take the astronomers to know everything, because I was already happy.

Tom Entsminger had some sparklers and he passed them around. All thirty-seven of us got one and we lit them and waved them at the boats and Collier started "Love Me

Tender" again, and we all sang the song in a chorus with the boys doing the harmony and the girls doing the melody, and over the wide skin of the dark river, we heard both riverboat bands take up the Elvis song and send it back to us.

Twenty-Seven

$\mathcal{G}$randma and Grandpa went back to Chillicothe before Graceanne and I got home, but they left us each a dollar in envelopes on our beds. The light was off in the Garden Room, so we put our own light out quickly and got into bed.

Graceanne sat on her bed and took out her dog-ears and rubbed her head that was still damp from swimming in the pond. "What are you gonna do with your dollar, Charlie?"

"I'll be sure to save it."

"I'm gonna spend mine."

"What on?"

"Maybe I'll buy Mama some nail polish, to thank her for lending us her dress."

"You better hadn't, Graceanne."

"Well, I won't tell her that's what it's for."

"I'll give you my dollar and we'll get her dress cleaned before we give it back."

She slipped off her bed and came over to mine. "Charlie, you're a genius. Collier's gonna get the dress after the judging because I got a game. You give him the money, and he can take it to the cleaners." She put her envelope under my pillow and went back to her bed. "You're the most practical little soul sometimes, Charlie: remembering to give the dog water and making your own paint and counting things and staying out of trouble like you do."

In the morning it looked like rain, and we both worried that the good black dress would get ruined. Graceanne went to work at the farm, and I stayed home and sat out back with the dog. He had rubbed a sore spot on his neck, but I didn't know what to do to cure it for him, so I just gave him a few pats and put fresh water in his dish and let him get on my knees. The clouds were dark and low, and there was thunder over in Illinois, but the rain held off, and I took in the clothes from the line.

Graceanne came home and had some soup and said it hadn't rained yet and the good black dress was all right. She changed into her uniform, but she put her county softball running shorts on under it because the Pike County team had a pitcher with a good move to first base and Graceanne was going to lose some skin off her butt stealing second if she didn't have the extra protection. Wanda came over to our front steps and waited until Graceanne came out. She never came in our house after the Black Santa night. They left together for the game.

In the middle of the afternoon it started raining, just a few drops, enough to make the neighborhood smell like it was wet. The sky was darker and the air was closer and I kept hoping Collier would come, but I didn't know what time the judging was. I sat out on the front steps, got up to walk around the side of the house to look at the dog's neck, and came back along the gravel to the front, and I saw someone coming up the street and I thought it was Collier for a minute, but it was Edie. She had a black look on her face and she was chewing the inside of her cheeks and her uniform was starched so hard it crackled when she came up the steps with a couple of raindrops on the skirt.

"What do you know about this scarecrow contest, Charlemagne Farrand?"

I tried to tell her we were going to get the dress cleaned but I couldn't make words come out of my throat. I kept swallowing and swallowing and nothing happened but my throat got tighter.

She went in and slammed the door so hard I could feel the echo in my spine. I tried to get up off the steps, but I was frozen and a few drops of rain fell on my nose and I couldn't even lift my hand to wipe them off.

When she came back out, she threw the door open so hard it slammed against the side of the house and the doorknob fell off.

"So, you took my hat, too! You weren't content to hold just my dress up to public scorn. You took my hat! I guess you wanted to make sure everybody knew it was me and no mistake."

I just sat there, wondering how she knew, wishing I could move, trying to swallow, picturing Graceanne sliding into second without knowing that Edie was on the warpath.

"Answer me, Charlemagne! Don't sit there like the village idiot. Oh, pardon me, I forgot that you and your sister have *me* all set for that job. I don't know what I ever did to deserve hell-children like you! I thought you, at least, were a good child I could trust in. I feel like you've kicked me in the stomach, Charlie."

She went back inside and I could hear her walking around the house, putting her hand on the furniture, her starched uniform crackling, and I was such a coward I couldn't move. I thought of running off to the softball field to warn Graceanne, and when I looked down at my shoes I was surprised to see they were still there on the steps, not going anywhere.

Finally Graceanne and Wanda came running up the street, laughing and shoving each other, their softball uniforms drenched. When they saw me on the steps, they slowed down but they kept coming.

"What's the matter with you?" Graceanne said.

"Mama's home. She knows."

Graceanne put her hand on Wanda's arm. "You go home now."

"I'm going in with you," Wanda said.

"No, you ain't. I won't have my own Mama killed before my eyes. You go home now."

"I wouldn't kill your Mama, Graceanne."

"I know. That's just something I like to say. But you go home anyway."

Wanda put her hand on my head and I got the two dollars out of my pocket and told her when Collier came to give him the money for the dress.

"What're you going to do, Charlie?"

"I don't know. My legs are paralyzed."

She laughed without her mouth smiling and went to sit on her own porch to wait for Collier.

Graceanne gave me her bat. "I don't want to take this thing in the house." She went inside.

Mama started yelling right away. "How dare you make a mockery of me, you little Jezebel? How dare you steal my dress and put it up in a public place? Who the hell do you think you are?"

"Mama, all the scarecrows are made to be people in Crane-pool's Landing. All the other grownups think it's cute what we did."

"Shut your mouth! I don't care about other people's clothes and other people's ideas about what's cute. I only care about what the world will think of *me*. What do you think people are going to think of me now they've seen my good black dress and my hat on a scarecrow on Douglas Lane?"

"They'll think you're a good sport."

"No they won't. I'll tell you exactly what people will think because I already know. They're laughing at me, Graceanne. They're laughing. They don't show it to my face, but they're laughing. Every patient in the lab today made it a business to tell me all about that scarecrow of yours."

I peeled my legs off the steps at last and went into our room. Edie and Graceanne weren't in there. They were in the Garden Room. I went and stood in the door. I still had Graceanne's bat in my hand and I accidentally dropped it on the floor and I was afraid Edie would pick it up but she didn't even seem to see me.

"This is the worst thing you ever did, Graceanne, and you've done some bad things in your time. You're a sneaking, devious troublemaker. There's something unnatural about you. I swear, I think you sit up all night planning things to make me look like a bad mother. You deliberately kept those books out of the library. You hid for two days in the school and the whole town knew about it. And I bet that stupid book you were writing was all full of lies about me. You just can't do anything without the whole world knowing about it, can you? You can't even play softball like a decent girl. You have to play like there's a devil in you so everyone will take notice and tell you how special you are, like you were God's gift or something. What the hell are you trying to prove? Well, you're going to be sorry. You're grounded for the rest of the summer. That means no more softball, and no more working at that farm, and no more associating with that Wanda, and no more Collier Rodgers. You only let that colored girl play in your shadow so you can call attention to yourself—no other white girl has a colored friend in this town. And it's the same with Collier—a Notre Dame boy helps you get the town's notice, doesn't he? Well, all of that will come to a stop, and you will behave like you've been taught to be a decent lady, and if I think of anything else I'll tell you and if you don't like it you can just move out like your sister did."

Graceanne was breathing through her mouth, and her voice sounded hoarse when Mama stopped for a breath and to wipe her mouth: "Mama, you're wrong about Wanda. I love her almost as much as I love Charlie, and I love him better than anybody. The only thing I do to stand out is play ball better than anybody, and I couldn't do that if I wasn't born for it. Mama, I'm a real champion. Don't make me quit softball, Mama. I'm gonna make the state team. I'll do anything you say."

"You'll do *everything* I say, and you'll do it quick. Get out of that uniform before I tear it off you."

"I won't quit softball. And this is my uniform. I paid for it myself." Graceanne got a look in her eye. "You make me quit softball, everyone will want to know why."

"Shut up! You're quitting softball because you don't deserve to play." Edie grabbed her own mouth with her two fingers and made them come together in the middle of her lips and her hand was shaking. "You will respect my word in this house as long as you live in it. You sass me again and I'll paddle you until you can't sit down."

"I'm too old for you to hit me."

"I'll show you who's too old." Edie grabbed a hanger off the bed and the end caught in her bedspread and she yanked it free and it came whizzing through the air as fast as a ball off the end of a bat. Graceanne almost got out of the way in time but Edie was standing too close for Graceanne to get set and the hanger went across her waist and tore open the uniform shirt and buttons popped off and Graceanne let out a gasp and put her hand inside and held it there and pressed it and I thought she was going to double over but instead she got into her crouch with her knees all flexed and loose and kept her head up and her dead-eye on Edie's freckled hand that had the hanger.

"Come on, Mama," Graceanne said. "Think I'm Black Santa? He never even saw you coming."

"How *dare* you mention that man! I defended my home, like no woman alone should have to do."

"You're not defending your home now. Think about what Charlie's seeing with that hanger in your hand."

"Charlie's my son, and he'll learn what's good for him as I see fit."

Graceanne rocked on her knees once, turned her back, and came through the door and grabbed my arm and said, "Scoot out of the house, Charlie." She got me in front of her and gave me a shove, and I was going but I heard Mama's uniform crackling and I turned around and she grabbed Graceanne with both hands on her shoulders and shoved her so hard she went crashing into the full-length mirror and it splintered into jagged pieces and one of the long ones went into Graceanne's leg and she was sitting on the floor in all the glass. She had her eyes closed and I thought she was knocked out but she was only protecting her eyes from the glass. She reached up her hand and brushed her face and hair off and stood up and the pieces of mirror fell all around her and I could see the number twenty-two backward all over the floor and parts of Graceanne and Edie in the tiny pieces of mirror. Edie swung her hand and I could see hundreds of her arm come through the air and land on Graceanne's cheek and then I couldn't see as well because I was crying and the pieces of mirror were all fuzzy and Edie swung again and Graceanne stepped to one side and the piece of glass was still in her leg and it broke off against the chest of drawers and the doll Peggy's eyeless, wig-less plastic head went rolling onto the floor.

Graceanne was leaning against the chest of drawers and Edie came at her with the hanger and laid it over her legs again and again and I counted twelve times that hanger went slashing onto Graceanne's legs and I looked at her mouth and

I saw that she was screaming but there was no sound coming out at all. I looked down on the floor and there in hundreds of pieces of mirror was Graceanne's blood and her uniform pants were in shreds and her mouth was open in some of the mirror pieces and finally Edie's arm stopped. She was out of breath and she put her hand up on her mouth to wipe it with her two fingers and Graceanne slipped down on the floor on her knees and she still had her baseball cap on and her glasses looked okay and she rolled over onto her back and her mouth looked like it was chewed but I hadn't seen her do that and she said, "Mama, you got a better arm than I do. I guess it runs in the family."

"My family is above reproach, you little snake. Don't you dare to speak of my family in that way."

Graceanne was breathing hard, but slow and regular, and she said, "Where'd I come from, Mama? Did you get me out of a can? How come I'm not above reproach like the rest of your family?"

Edie took the hanger and Graceanne saw it coming and rolled over onto her stomach and she got it again on the legs until Edie wore herself out and stumbled over the pieces of mirror to get back to the Garden Room.

Graceanne got up on her knees. Her blue cap fell off and I stooped and got it off the floor and held it in my hand. Her head was hanging down and her hands were flat on the floor like they were glued there. She tried to stand up but she fell down again and had to start all over. She worked herself up on her knees again and used the chest of drawers to crawl up against and help her stand and when she was standing she held out her hand and I gave her the cap and she put it on her head where not a hair was out of place the Brylcreme was so thick. She pointed to the bat on the floor in the doorway and I stepped over the pieces of broken mirror and almost slipped in some hair grease and picked up the bat and went

to hand it to her. She left the house, leaning on the bat like
an old lady with a cane.

She went down the steps slowly and started for the river.
Soon she started going a little faster like she'd almost forgot
the blood on her legs and her uniform pants in shreds and
whatever was wrong with her ribs where she had put her hand
inside her shirt and pressed. Wanda wasn't outside her house,
and I figured she'd gone with Collier to the cleaners. Pretty
soon Graceanne was out of sight and I was standing there in
the doorway looking out at the rain that was coming down
steadily through the trees. The creosote smell was strong and
I thought about the rows of corn that were getting the rain
and our scarecrow without its ruffled dress.

I went around to the back. The dog was inside his house,
but he came out when he heard me on the gravel and I sat
down in his pit in the rain and wished I had never told Graceanne her idea was a good one. I thought about the Fourth of
July and how we had sung the Elvis song and had sparklers
and how none of that mattered because the next day had come
and the boats had gone back to their home ports of St. Louis
and Quincy. I didn't even know the people who had sung
back to us from the boat or the people who had told Edie
about the scarecrow or why they told her or if they were
laughing at her or why she had to hit Graceanne like that.

I went back inside to our room and sat on my bed. I wondered what Edie was doing, but I didn't go to look. I saw the
mirror all over the floor and went to pick up the biggest pieces
but I saw the one that had been in Graceanne's leg and it
had her blood and I dropped the ones I was holding and they
broke more and I was afraid Edie would hear and come back
to the room in her starched uniform.

I listened to the rain for a while, wishing I could use my
brains to think of how to help Graceanne, and wondering
what I'd ever done that made Graceanne care for me.

The rain was falling on the window and the rainspots were on the stupid radio I had made for Graceanne. I thought what a stupid, useless brother I was, who had the Sacajawea arrowhead and his clubfoot was cured and he couldn't do anything for his sister when bad trouble came on her but could only make a stupid radio that didn't really work and couldn't even write his own book but had to copy hers. I took the arrowhead from my pocket and rubbed it until it felt hot and I thought with her own hands she had destroyed her book and torn it into little pieces and thrown it in the river and I couldn't even stop her from doing that. It was the most important thing to her and I wondered why she went to the river when she was in trouble and why she wrote poems about the river and why she was so sure the astronomers could see the river from Mars and then I knew where she was going and what she was going to do.

For a moment I was frozen again I was so scared, but I dropped to the floor and went under the bed and grabbed the book I had made and looked for a paper bag and found one in the closet and shoved the book inside and took off out the front door and suddenly remembered the embroidered cover was in the dog's house. I ran back there and got in the house and the dog got in with me and wagged his tail and whined and I dragged out the cover and put it in the bag and got out of the house. I ran as fast as I could to the river and I got to the end of the street and I was going so fast I couldn't stop in time and I slid over the muddy bank and let go of the bag when I saw what I had done and I went flying through the skin of the river into the swirling muddy water and tried to start swimming but a current whipped around and caught me and I went under and swallowed muddy water and was turned around with the current pulling my legs out from under me and turning me over and then I remembered and just eased up the way Graceanne said to do if it ever happened and I started swimming the same way the current was going and I made it back to the bank about forty feet from where I went in.

I grabbed the roots of a tree and pulled myself out and shook myself off and went back for the bag and then I didn't know where to go because I thought Graceanne would be there where she had thrown her book away. I didn't know where else to look, but I had to find her because I thought she was going to take herself and tear herself into little pieces like she did her book and throw herself into the river and then I thought of Big Neighbors Bridge and I picked myself up and started running through the rain on the long path up toward the bluffs.

I stopped to look under the weeping willow tree and kept glancing at the river afraid I'd see her floating along on its brown skin and when I got to the bend where you could see the whole bridge, I didn't see her at first and a car was going across with its lights on in the rain and the rain was coming down hard over the river and everything but the river was grey and then I saw her legs dangling from the side of the bridge about halfway across. I ran under the highway and up onto the pavement, and I didn't have a stitch in my side the way I always used to, because I guess I was more used to running.

Once I was on the bridge I walked fast, and I couldn't see her until I was almost past her because she was sitting with her legs stuck out over the river, her arms around one of the wooden crosspieces that made shapes like the letter X all the way across the bridge under the railing. I sat down next to her.

"What are you doing?" I said.

"Charlie, if I died and went to hell and you came and saw me sitting in the fire popping corn with a bunch of other devils, you'd sit yourself down and ask me what I was doing."

I tried to look at her, but the rain was coming down hard and the sky was dark and she was all wrapped around the crosspiece. I could see from the side that her face looked like it did when she went to the river the night of Black Santa and it was so cold.

"I've got something in this bag, Graceanne."

"Why don't you run on home now and leave me be. I'm no good for you, Charlie. All I do is teach you how to be bad."

"Don't you want to know what I've got in the bag?"

"Not especially."

I opened the wet, muddy bag and took out the book and the cover and pulled the ends of the cover over the book and held it out like I was reading it.

She gave it a look. "What the hell is that?"

"It's my book."

"Where'd you get that?" She reached her hand over but I held the book away from her.

"I made it."

"You did not."

"Did so."

"Lemme look at it closer."

I held it so she could see the cover.

"That says it's *By Graceanne*." She gave me a look. "How can it be your book if it says *By Graceanne*?"

"That's the title."

"It sounds like it's the author."

"The title's about the author."

"Read me some of it."

I opened the book to the notebook on top and read out loud, but my throat felt all tight:

The Martian astronomers have all come back to
work and they have polished their telescopes once

again to get on with the work of knowing everything. They report they have seen a big hole on
the planet Earth that they think was made by a
meteor or a comet, and there is a long canal that
makes them think there was once an advanced civ-
ilization on the planet, because the canal appears to
be artificial and very large and is a different color
from the rest of the planet, which is green and blue.
The color of the canal is brown, like the brown of
sunrise on Venus, which the people there call Mudovia. The astronomers have named the canal they
have discovered on Earth the Mudovia River, in
honor of the Venusian contribution to curing the
plague that kept so many astronomers out sick for
so long.

The rain fell on my handwriting and Graceanne was looking out over the river.

"Charlie, what does the river smell like to you?"

I knew the right answer to that question. "It smells like
dirt."

"No, it doesn't. Use your nose."

I gave a good sniff. "It smells like rain."

"Yeah, it smells like rain. The creosote must've washed
away."

I closed the book and held it against my chest and Graceanne looked at me.

"Did you sew all those little flowers and bees yourself?"

"Yes."

"And did you remember all those things I'd written all by
yourself?"

"Yes."

"You had my whole book inside your head all the time?"

"Yes."

"I wonder why you did that."

"I love your book, Graceanne. It's the best thing I ever read."

"That's a nice thing, Charlie." She was shaking her head back and forth and the rain was making the grease in her hair drip onto her face and it looked all shiny in the rain. "You had my book in your head all the time."

"Graceanne, unless someone tears me up and throws me in the river, you'll always have your book."

"I guess I can't throw *you* away, can I, Charlie?"

"No. You can't throw me away."

She hung her head down and the hair was all stringy and over her ears and she said, "Charlie, she took away everything else I care about. She's taken everything. I haven't got anything left and I'm sick of it. Nothing's fair and nothing makes sense and I don't know what to do."

The rain was coming down hard but I was already soaked from the river. Through the grey rain I was looking into a darkness where I couldn't see what was behind the rain until I thought I saw tiger eyes but it was only something on the Illinois side, some lights from a car. And I wished it wasn't true that everything had been taken away from Graceanne, but it was true, and I didn't know what I could do, or any kid could do. I looked down at the skin of the river that could hide the dangerous currents and float over the moon and swallow up the pages of Graceanne's book and hold itself tense and firm against skipped rocks and carry the steamboats and turn into a cradle for an ugly baby and carry whole acres of black soil down to Ste. Genevieve and send the Fourth of July music across to us on the shore with our sparklers and bring Ugly Blue Man into my responsibility and Graceanne said something.

"What are you going to do with that book you got in your hands?"

I looked up, surprised to hear her voice beside me, and I held the book out and looked at it and I loved it because it was Graceanne's book all over again only I had made it and it was mine.

But then I thought that the astronomers could see the river and they might be looking and I knew what I had to do and why Graceanne always came to the river. It was because it was so big that it could be seen from 49 million miles away, and she was so small nobody could see her, but if she came to the river she'd be in the same place the astronomers could see and I suddenly understood everything about the astronomers and why they were in her book and why she threw it all on the river. Coming to the river was what she did to let herself stand out and it was because she wanted the astronomers to see her, and her book was for them.

I took the cover I had sewn and felt it and pulled it off my book and held it out from the bridge and dropped it over the river. It caught on my saddle oxford, but I shook it loose and it floated down and the rain poured on it and it fell faster than I thought it would. I started ripping out the pages and crumpling them up and throwing them into the river as fast as I could and looking up at the sky.

It was a long way down to the water and a barge came under the bridge and one of the crumpled pages fell onto the deck and a man picked it up and opened it and started reading it and then he tossed it over the side but he never looked up and he never knew where it came from. I kept tearing and throwing and Graceanne was watching me the whole time and watching the book go piece by piece into the water. When I had all the pages torn out and in the river, I threw the spirals in, and I had never done anything that hard before, not even swimming at the end of the slide or winning the Sacajawea raking contest or drowning a blue dead man, and I could feel my heart beating like a train was coming at me.

Graceanne pulled her arms away from the crosspiece and scooted back on her butt onto the pavement and stood up like her legs were made out of stone.

"Charlie, you're sure a smart little boy. She can't take it away from me if I don't have it." She held the bat by its narrow end and started twirling it slowly around over her head and it got going faster and faster and whooshing through the air and it made a terrible sound like a thousand birds swooping down at once and she let it go and it went sailing out over the river, spinning end over end in a blur so fast it looked like a helicopter and when it hit the water it slapped so hard I could hear it up on the bridge.

"Graceanne, how are you going to play softball next year without your bat?"

"Maybe you got one of those in your head. I sure hope you've got Wanda in there, too."

She started peeling down her torn, bloody uniform pants. Most of her cuts were scabbing over, but there was one behind her knee that was open and it was puckered up and looked like old O.U.B.'s dark lips in a little smile over his toothless red gums. The place where the piece of mirror had stuck still had a long sliver of glass in it and she pulled it out and a little bright red blood dripped down and she flipped the piece of bloody mirror into the river. She took her pants the way she had done the bat and got them whipping around in the air over her head and she let them go and they went out over the river and went down flapping like a bird with a broken wing. She took her blue cap and tossed it in after the pants. She ripped the gold chain Collier had given her from her neck without undoing the clasp and tossed it over into the water and it fell in a tiny golden splash until it disappeared into the rain and I didn't see it hit the water. She came and put her hands on the rail and bent over and looked at me.

"Charlie, it's a big river, ain't it?"

"Yeah, and it floods so much it gets even bigger sometimes. We should've thrown the ugly baby in so we could have more floods."

Graceanne looked all around at the rain falling.

"We don't need that baby, Charlie. We got plenty of things to throw in the river to make it rise over its banks."

She undid the buttons on her shirt that hadn't popped off when Edie went for her and I could see the sticky blood on her undershirt. She held the uniform shirt out over the bridge and she waved it around in front of her face and the famous number twenty-two was so white it shimmered in the rain. She took a step back and wadded up the shirt and gave it a heave from her killer arm and the shirt went sailing out into the air and it opened up and the number turned around and around on the way into the river.

There were tears falling out of her eyes behind her glasses and she leaned over again and looked down at me where I was sitting with my legs stuck out from the bridge.

"Charlie, I hate those goddamn saddle oxfords."

I looked and saw where we had all signed our names, Kentucky and Graceanne and Edie's initials and Thumper on the heel. I pulled them off and threw them in the river and took off my socks and let them go, too. I stood up and all we had left was the paper bag.

"What should we do with the bag?" I asked.

She looked at the soggy bag like she was going to have to take a test on it.

"Better keep it. A bag like that is useful for carrying books and good black dresses and other stuff. You never know when you'll need a bag."

We stood and looked over the rail at what we could still see of all the stuff we had thrown into the brown river.

I looked over to the west and I could see all of Cranepool's Landing—the top of Lewis and Clark Hill where our old house was and the basin where the hotel and the Crown Drugstore and Parks Department Store were and the other hill where Our Lady of Lourdes was and the bottom land with the Developments on McBain Avenue and the higher land where Maple Heights was with Hulen's Lake on its other side and the cornfields north of town that were full of soaked and tender ears of corn that needed the rain and little things sticking up that must have been the Fourth of July scarecrows.

I looked down at the wide brown river with our stuff on its soft, tough skin that it seemed nothing could ever break.

"Charlie, let's go to Illinois."

"Mama'll tan our hides."

"Not if she doesn't know we did it."

She swung her arms around and started walking across toward Illinois in the rain. She was holding on to the rail, so I got to carry the bag.

I didn't remember ever having a barefoot walk before, except in some swimming hole or other. I thought of telling Graceanne about being half barefoot when I drowned the dead Ugly Blue Man but she already looked so burdened I reckoned that secrets weighed on a person and the best way I could help my sister was to keep my goddamn lip buttoned.